Great Pirate Stories

Joseph Lewis French

Great Pirate Stories

ISBN: 978-1-63637-268-6

CONTENTS

FOREWORD

Piracy embodies the romance of the sea at its highest expression. It is a sad but inevitable commentary on our civilization, that, so far as the sea is concerned, it has developed from its infancy down to a century or so ago, under one phase or another of piracy. If men were savages on land they were doubly so at sea, and all the years of maritime adventure—years that added to the map of the world till there was little left to discover—could not wholly eradicate the piratical germ. It went out gradually with the settlement and ordering of the far-flung British colonies. Great Britain, foremost of sea powers, must be credited with doing more both directly and indirectly for the abolition of crime and disorder on the high seas than any other force. But the conquest was not complete till the advent of steam which chased the sea-rover into the farthest corners of his domain. It is said that he survives even today in certain spots in the Chinese waters,—but he is certainly an innocuous relic. A pirate of any sort would be as great a curiosity today if he could be caught and exhibited as a fabulous monster.

The fact remains and will always persist that in the lore of the sea he is far and away the most picturesque figure,—and the more genuine and gross his career, the higher degree of interest does he inspire.

There may be a certain human perversity in this, for the pirate was unquestionably a bad man—at his best, or worst—considering his surroundings and conditions,—undoubtedly the worst man that ever lived. There is little to soften the dark yet glowing picture of his exploits. But again, it must be remembered, that not only does the note of distance subdue, and even lend a certain enchantment to the scene, but the effect of contrast between our peaceful times and his own contributes much to deepen our interest in him. Perhaps it is this latter, added to that deathless spark in the human breast that glows at the tale of adventure, which makes him the kind of hero of romance that he is today.

He is undeniably a redoubtable historical figure. It is a curious fact that the commerce of the seas was cradled in the lap of buccaneering. The constant danger of the deeps in this form only made hardier mariners out of the merchant-adventurers, actually stimulating and strengthening maritime enterprise.

Buccaneering—which is only a politer term for piracy—thus became the high romance of the seas during the great centuries of maritime adventure. It went hand in hand with discovery,—they were in fact almost inseparable. Most of the mighty mariners from the days of Leif the Discoverer, through those of the redoubtable Sir Francis Drake down to our own Paul Jones, answer to the roll-call.

It was a bold hardy world—this of ours—up to the advent of our giant-servant, Steam,—every foot of which was won by fierce conquest of one sort or another. Out of this past the pirate emerges as a romantic, even at times heroic, figure. This final niche, despite his crimes, cannot altogether be denied him. A hero he is and will remain so long as tales of the sea are told. So, have at him, in these pages!

Joseph Lewis French

THE PICCAROON[1]

Michael Scott

"Ours the wild life in tumult still to range."—The Corsair.

We returned to Carthagena, to be at hand should any opportunity occur for Jamaica, and were lounging about one forenoon on the fortifications, looking with sickening hearts out to seaward, when a voice struck up the following negro ditty close to us:—

"Fader was a Corramantee,
Moder was a Mingo,
Black picaniny buccra wantee,
So dem sell a me, Peter, by jingo.
Jiggery, jiggery, jiggery."

"Well sung, Massa Bungo!" exclaimed Mr. Splinter; "where do you hail from, my hearty?"

"Hillo! Bungo, indeed! free and easy dat, anyhow. Who you yousef, eh?"

"Why, Peter," continued the lieutenant, "don't you know me?"

"Cannot say dat I do," rejoined the negro, very gravely, without lifting his head, as he sat mending his jacket in one of the embrasures near the water-gate of the arsenal—"Hab not de honour of your acquaintance, sir."

He then resumed his scream, for song it could not be called:—

"Mammy Sally's daughter
Lose him shoe in an old canoe
Dat lay half full of water,
And den she knew not what to do. Jiggery, jig——"

"Confound your jiggery, jiggery, sir! But I know you well enough, my man; and you can scarcely have forgotten Lieutenant Splinter of the Torch, one would think?"

However, it was clear that the poor fellow really had not known us; for the name so startled him, that, in his hurry to unlace his legs from under him, as he sat tailor-fashion, he fairly capsized out of his perch, and toppled down on his nose—a feature,

---
[1] From Tom Cringle's Log.

1

fortunately, so flattened by the hand of nature, that I question if it could have been rendered more obtuse had he fallen out of the maintop on a timber-head, or a marine officer's.

"Eh!—no—yes, him sure enough; and who is de picaniny hofficer—Oh! I see, Massa Tom Cringle? Garamighty, gentlemen, where have you drop from? Where is de old Torch? Many a time hab I, Peter Mangrove, pilot to Him Britannic Majesty squadron, taken de old brig in and through amongst de keys at Port Royal!"

"Ay, and how often did you scour her copper against the coral reefs, Peter?"

His Majesty's pilot gave a knowing look, and laid his hand on his breast—"No more of dat if you love me, massa."

"Well, well, it don't signify now, my boy; she will never give you that trouble again—foundered—all hands lost, Peter, but the two you see before you."

"Werry sorry, Massa Plinter, werry sorry—What! de black cook's-mate and all?—But misfortune can't be help. Stop till I put up my needle, and I will take a turn wid you." Here he drew himself up with a great deal of absurd gravity. "Proper dat British hofficer in distress should assist one anoder—we shall consult togeder.—How can I serve you?"

"Why, Peter, if you could help us to a passage to Port Royal, it would be serving us most essentially. When we used to be lying there a week seldom passed without one of the squadron arriving from this; but here have we been for more than a month without a single pennant belonging to the station having looked in: our money is running short, and if we are to hold on in Carthagena for another six weeks, we shall not have a shot left in the locker—not a copper to tinkle on a tombstone."

The negro looked steadfastly at us, then carefully around. There was no one near.

"You see, Massa Plinter, I am desirable to serve you, for one little reason of my own; but, beside dat, it is good for me at present to make some friend wid de hofficer of de squadron, being as how dat I am absent widout leave."

"Oh, I perceive—a large R against your name in the master-attendant's books, eh?"

"You have hit it, sir, werry close; besides, I long mosh to return to my poor wife, Nancy Cator, dat I leave, wagabone dat I is, just about to be confine."

I could not resist putting in my oar.

"I saw Nancy just before we sailed, Peter—fine child that; not quite so black as you, though."

"Oh, massa," said Snowball, grinning, and showing his white

teeth, "you know I am soch a terrible black fellow—But you are a leetle out at present, massa—I meant, about to be confine in de work-house for stealing de admiral's Muscovy ducks;" and he laughed loud and long.—"However, if you will promise dat you will stand my friends, I will put you in de way of getting a shove across to de east end of Jamaica; and I will go wid you too, for company."

"Thank you," rejoined Mr. Splinter; "but how do you mean to manage this? There is no Kingston trader here at present, and you don't mean to make a start of it in an open boat, do you?"

"No, sir, I don't; but in de first place—as you are a gentleman, will you try and get me off when we get to Jamaica? Secondly, will you promise dat you will not seek to know more of de vessel you may go in, nor of her crew, than dey are willing to tell you, provided you are landed safe?"

"Why, Peter, I scarcely think you would deceive us, for you know I saved your bacon in that awkward affair, when through drunkenness you plumped the Torch ashore, so——"

"Forget dat, sir—forget dat! Never shall poor black pilot forget how you saved him from being seized up, when de gratings, boatswain's mates, and all, were ready at de gangway—never shall poor black rascal forget dat."

"Indeed, I do not think you would wittingly betray us into trouble, Peter; and as I guess you mean one of the forced traders, we will venture in her, rather than kick about here any longer, and pay a moderate sum for our passage."

"Den wait here five minute"—and so saying, he slipped down through the embrasure into a canoe that lay beneath, and in a trice we saw him jump on board of a long low nondescript kind of craft that lay moored within pistol-shot of the walls.

She was a large shallow vessel, coppered to the bends, of great breadth of beam, with bright sides, like an American, so painted as to give her a clumsy mercantile sheen externally, but there were many things that belied this to a nautical eye: her copper, for instance, was bright as burnished gold on her very sharp bows and beautiful run; and we could see, from the bastion where we stood, that her decks were flush and level. She had no cannon mounted that were visible; but we distinguished grooves on her well-scrubbed decks, as from the recent traversing of carronade slides, while the bolts and rings in her high and solid bulwarks shone clear and bright in the ardent noontide. There was a tarpaulin stretched over a quantity of rubbish, old sails, old junk, and hencoops, rather ostentatiously piled up forward, which we conjectured might conceal a long gun.

She was a very taught-rigged hermaphrodite, or brig forward

and schooner aft. Her foremast and bowsprit were immensely strong and heavy, and her mainmast was so long and tapering, that the wonder was how the few shrouds and stays about it could support it; it was the handsomest stick we had ever seen. Her upper spars were on the same scale, tapering away through topmast, topgallant-mast, royal and skysail-masts, until they fined away into slender wands. The sails, that were loose to dry, were old, and patched, and evidently displayed to cloak the character of the vessel by an ostentatious show of their unserviceable condition; but her rigging was beautifully fitted, every rope lying in the chafe of another being carefully served with hide. There were several large bushy-whiskered fellows lounging about the deck, with their hair gathered into dirty net-bags, like the fishermen of Barcelona; many had red silk sashes round their waists, through which were stuck their long knives, in shark-skin sheaths. Their numbers were not so great as to excite suspicion: but a certain daring, reckless manner, would at once have distinguished them, independently of anything else, from the quiet, hard-worked, red-shirted, merchant seaman.

"That chap is not much to be trusted," said the lieutenant; "his bunting would make a few jackets for Joseph, I take it." But we had little time to be critical, before our friend Peter came paddling back with another blackamoor in the stern, of as ungainly an exterior as could well be imagined. He was a very large man, whose weight every now and then, as they breasted the short sea, cocked up the snout of the canoe with Peter Mangrove in it, as if he had been a cork, leaving him to flourish his paddle in the air, like the weather-wheel of a steam-boat in a sea-way. The new-comer was strong and broad-shouldered, with long muscular arms, and a chest like Hercules; but his legs and thighs were, for his bulk, remarkably puny and misshapen. A thick fell of black wool, in close tufts, as if his face had been stuck full of cloves, covered his chin and upper-lip; and his hair, if hair it could be called, was twisted into a hundred short plaits, that bristled out, and gave his head, when he took his hat off, the appearance of a porcupine. There was a large saber-cut across his nose and down his cheek, and he wore two immense gold earrings. His dress consisted of short cotton drawers, that did not reach within two inches of his knee, leaving his thin cucumber shanks (on which the small bullet-like calf appeared to have been stuck before, through mistake, in place of abaft) naked to the shoe; a check shirt, and an enormously large Panama hat, made of a sort of cane, split small, and worn shovel-fashion. Notwithstanding, he made his bow by no means ungracefully, and offered his services in choice Spanish, but spoke English as soon as he heard who we were.

4

"Pray, sir, are you the master of that vessel?" said the lieutenant.

"No, sir, I am the mate, and I learn you are desirous of a passage to Jamaica." This was spoken with a broad Scotch accent.

"Yes, we are," said I, in very great astonishment, "but we will not sail with the devil; and who ever saw a negro Scotchman before, the spirit of Nicol Jarvie conjured into a blackamoor's skin!"

The fellow laughed. "I am black, as you see; so were my father and mother before me." And he looked at me, as much as to say, I have read the book you quote from. "But I was born in the good town of Port-Glasgow notwithstanding, and many a voyage I have made as cabin-boy and cook in the good ship the Peggy Bogle, with worthy old Jock Hunter; but that matters not. I was told you wanted to go to Jamaica; I dare-say our captain will take you for a moderate passage-money. But here he comes to speak for himself.—Captain Vanderbosh, here are two shipwrecked British officers, who wish to be put on shore on the east end of Jamaica; will you take them, and what will you charge for their passage?"

The man he spoke to was nearly as tall as himself; he was a sunburnt, angular, raw-boned, iron-visaged veteran, with a nose in shape and color like the bowl of his own pipe, but not at all, according to the received idea, like a Dutchman. His dress was quizzical enough—white-trousers, a long-flapped embroidered waistcoat that might have belonged to a Spanish grandee, with an old-fashioned French-cut coat, showing the frayed marks where the lace had been stripped off, voluminous in the skirts, but very tight in the sleeves, which were so short as to leave his large bony paws, and six inches of his arm above the wrist, exposed; altogether, it fitted him like a purser's shirt on a hand-spike.

"Vy, for von hondred thaler I will land dem safe in Mancheoneal Bay; but how shall ve manage, Villiamson? De cabin vas point yesterday."

The Scotch negro nodded. "Never mind; I dare-say the smell of the paint won't signify to the gentlemen."

The bargain was ratified; we agreed to pay the stipulated sum, and that same evening, having dropped down with the last of the sea-breeze, we set sail from Bocca Chica, and began working up under the lee of the headland of Punto Canoa. When off the San Domingo Gate, we burned a blue-light, which was immediately answered by another in-shore of us. In the glare we could perceive two boats, full of men. Any one who has ever played at snapdragon, can imagine the unearthly appearance of objects when seen by this species of firework. In the present instance it was held aloft on a boat-hook, and cast a strong spectral light on the band of lawless

5

ruffians, who were so crowded together that they entirely filled the boats, no part of which could be seen. It seemed as if two clusters of fiends, suddenly vomited forth from hell, were floating on the surface of the midnight sea, in the midst of brimstone flames. In a few moments our crew was strengthened by about forty as ugly Christians as I ever set eyes on. They were of all ages, countries, complexions, and tongues, and looked as if they had been kidnapped by a pressgang as they had knocked off from the Tower of Babel. From the moment they came on board, Captain Vanderbosh was shorn of all his glory, and sank into the petty officer while, to our amazement, the Scottish negro took the command, evincing great coolness, energy, and skill. He ordered the schooner to be wore as soon as we had shipped the men, and laid her head off the land, then set all hands to shift the old suit of sails, and to bend new ones.

"Why did you not shift your canvas before we started?" said I to the Dutch captain, or mate, or whatever he might be.

"Vy vont you be content to take a quiet passage and hax no question?" was the uncivil rejoinder, which I felt inclined to resent, until I remembered that we were in the hands of the Philistines, where a quarrel would have been worse than useless. I was gulping down the insult as well as I could, when the black captain came aft, and, with the air of an equal, invited us into the cabin to take a glass of grog. We had scarcely sat down before we heard a noise like the swaying up of guns, or some other heavy articles, from the hold.

I caught Mr. Splinter's eye—he nodded, but said nothing. In half an hour afterwards, when we went on deck, we saw by the light of the moon twelve eighteen-pound carronades mounted, six of a side, with their accompaniments of rammers and sponges, water-buckets, boxes of round, grape, and canister, and tubs of wadding, while the coamings of the hatchways were thickly studded with round-shot. The tarpaulin and lumber forward had disappeared, and there lay long Tom, ready levelled, grinning on his pivot.

The ropes were all coiled away, and laid down in regular man-of-war fashion; while an ugly gruff beast of a Spanish mulatto, apparently the officer of the watch, walked the weatherside of the quarterdeck in the true pendulum style. Look-outs were placed aft, and at the gangways and bows, who every now and then passed the word to keep a bright look-out, while the rest of the watch were stretched silent, but evidently broad awake, under the lee of the boat. We noticed that each man had his cutlass buckled round his waist—that the boarding-pikes had been cut loose from the main boom, round which they had been stopped, and that about thirty muskets were ranged along a fixed rack that ran athwart ships near the main hatchway.

By the time we had reconnoitred thus far the night became overcast, and a thick bank of clouds began to rise to windward; some heavy drops of rain fell, and the thunder grumbled at a distance. The black veil crept gradually on, until it shrouded the whole firmament, and left us in as dark a night as ever poor devils were out in. By-and-by a narrow streak of bright moonlight appeared under the lower-edge of the bank, defining the dark outlines of the tumbling multitudinous billows on the horizon as distinctly as if they had been pasteboard waves in a theater.

"Is that a sail to windward in the clear, think you?" said Mr. Splinter to me in a whisper. At this moment it lightened vividly. "I am sure it is," continued he—"I could see her white canvas glance just now."

I looked steadily, and at last caught the small dark speck against the bright background, rising and falling on the swell of the sea like a feather.

As we stood on, she was seen more distinctly, but, to all appearance, nobody was aware of her proximity. We were mistaken in this, however, for the captain suddenly jumped on a gun, and gave his orders with a fiery energy that startled us.

"Leroux!" A small French boy was at his side in a moment. "Forward, and call all hands to shorten sail; but, doucement, you land-crab!—Man the fore clew-garnets.—Hands by the top-gallant clew-lines— jib down-haul—rise tacks and sheets—peak and throat haulyards—let go—clew up—settle away the main-gaff there!"

In almost as short a space as I have taken to write it, every inch of canvas was close furled—every light, except the one in the binnacle, and that was cautiously masked, carefully extinguished—a hundred and twenty men at quarters, and the ship under bare poles. The head-yards were then squared, and we bore up before the wind. The stratagem proved successful; the strange sail could be seen through the night-glasses cracking on close to the wind, evidently under the impression that we had tacked.

"Dere she goes, chasing de Gobel," said the Dutchman.

She now burned a blue-light, by which we saw she was a heavy cutter—without doubt our old fellow-cruiser the Spark. The Dutchman had come to the same conclusion.

"My eye, captain, no use to dodge from her; it is only dat footy little King's cutter on de Jamaica station."

"It is her, true enough," answered Williamson; "and she is from Santa Martha with a freight of specie, I know. I will try a brush with her, by——"

7

Splinter struck in before he could finish his irreverent exclamation. "If your conjecture be true, I know the craft—a heavy vessel of her class, and you may depend on hard knocks, and small profit if you do take her; while if she takes you——"

"I'll be hanged if she does"—and he grinned at the conceit—then setting his teeth hard, "or rather, I will blow the schooner up with my own hand before I strike; better that than have one's bones bleached in chains on a key at Port Royal. But you see you cannot control us, gentlemen; so get down into the cable-tier, and take Peter Mangrove with you. I would not willingly see those come to harm who have trusted me."

However, there was no shot flying as yet, we therefore stayed on deck. All sail was once more made; the carronades were cast loose on both sides, and double-shotted, the long-gun slewed round, the tack of the fore-and-aft foresail hauled up, and we kept by the wind, and stood after the cutter, whose white canvas we could still see through the gloom like a snow-wreath.

As soon as she saw us, she tacked and stood towards us, and came bowling along gallantly, with the water roaring and flashing at her bows. As the vessels neared each other they both shortened sail, and finding that we could not weather her, we steered close under her lee.

As we crossed on opposite tacks, her commander hailed, "Ho, the brigantine, ahoy!"

"Hillo!" sung out Blackie, as he backed his main-top-sail.

"What schooner is that?"

"The Spanish schooner Caridad."

"Whence, and whither bound?"

"Carthagena to Porto Rico."

"Heave-to, and send your boat on board."

"We have none that will swim, sir."

"Very well, bring-to, and I will send mine."

"Call away the boarders," said our captain, in a low stern tone; "let them crouch out of sight behind the boat."

The cutter wore, and hove-to under our lee quarter, within pistol-shot; we heard the rattle of the ropes running through the davit-blocks, and the splash of the jolly-boat touching the water, then the measured stroke of the oars, as they glanced like silver in the sparkling sea, and a voice calling out, "Give way, my lads."

The character of the vessel we were on board of was now evident; and the bitter reflection that we were chained to the stake on board of a pirate, on the eve of a fierce contest with one of our own cruisers, was aggravated by the consideration, that the cutter

8

had fallen into a snare by which a whole boat's crew would be sacrificed before a shot was fired.

I watched my opportunity as she pulled up alongside, and called out, leaning well over the nettings, "Get back to your ship!—treachery! get back to your ship!"

The little French serpent was at my side with the speed of thought, his long clear knife glancing in one hand, while the fingers of the other were laid on his lips. He could not have said more plainly, "Hold your tongue, or I'll cut your throat;" but Sneezer now startled him by rushing between us, and giving a short angry growl.

The officer in the boat had heard me imperfectly; he rose up—"I won't go back, my good man, until I see what you are made of;" and as he spoke he sprang on board, but the instant he got over the bulwarks, he was caught by two strong hands, gagged, and thrown bodily down the main-hatchway.

"Heave," cried a voice, "and with a will!" and four cold 32-pound shot were hove at once into the boat alongside, which, crashing through her bottom, swamped her in a moment, precipitating the miserable crew into the boiling sea. Their shrieks still ring in my ears as they clung to the oars and some loose planks of the boat.

"Bring up the officer, and take out the gag," said Williamson.

Poor Walcolm, who had been an old messmate of mine, was now dragged to the gangway half-naked, his face bleeding, and heavily ironed, when the blackamoor, clapping a pistol to his head, bid him, as he feared instant death, hail "that the boat had swamped under the counter, and to send another." The poor fellow, who appeared stunned and confused, did so, but without seeming to know what he said.

"Good God," said Mr. Splinter, "don't you mean to pick up the boat's crew?"

The blood curdled to my heart, as the black savage answered in a voice of thunder, "Let them drown and be d——d! Fill, and stand on!"

But the clouds by this time broke away, and the mild moon shone clear and bright once more upon this scene of most atrocious villainy. By her light the cutter's people could see that there was no one struggling in the water now, and that the people must either have been saved, or were past all earthly aid; but the infamous deception was not entirely at an end.

The captain of the cutter, seeing we were making sail, did the same, and after having shot ahead of us, hailed once more.

"Mr. Walcolm, why don't you run to leeward, and heave-to, sir?"

9

"Answer him instantly, and hail again for another boat," said the sable fiend, and cocked his pistol.

The click went to my heart. The young midship-man turned his pale mild countenance, laced with his blood, upwards towards the moon and stars, as one who had looked his last look on earth; the large tears were flowing down his cheeks, and mingling with the crimson streaks, and a flood of silver light fell on the fine features of the poor boy, as he said firmly, "Never." The miscreant fired, and he fell dead.

"Up with the helm, and wear across her stern." The order was obeyed. "Fire!" The whole broadside was poured in, and we could hear the shot rattle and tear along the cutter's deck, and the shrieks and groans of the wounded, while the white splinters glanced away in all directions.

We now ranged alongside, and close action commenced, and never do I expect to see such an infernal scene again. Up to this moment there had been neither confusion nor noise on board the pirate—all had been coolness and order; but when the yards locked the crew broke loose from all control—they ceased to be men—they were demons, for they threw their own dead and wounded, as they were mown down like grass by the cutter's grape, indiscriminately down the hatchways to get clear of them. They had stripped themselves almost naked; and although they fought with the most desperate courage, yelling and cursing, each in his own tongue, most hideously, yet their very numbers, pent up in a small vessel, were against them. At length, amidst the fire and smoke and hellish uproar, we could see that the deck had become a very shambles; and unless they soon carried the cutter by boarding, it was clear that the coolness and discipline of my own glorious service must prevail, even against such fearful odds; the superior size of the vessel, greater number of guns, and heavier metal. The pirates seemed aware of this themselves, for they now made a desperate attempt forward to carry their antagonist by boarding, led on by the black captain. Just at this moment the cutter's main-boom fell across the schooner's deck, close to where we were sheltering ourselves from the shot the best way we could; and while the rush forward was being made, by a sudden impulse Splinter and I, followed by Peter and the dog (who with wonderful sagacity, seeing the uselessness of resistance, had cowered quietly by my side during the whole row), scrambled along it as the cutter's people were repelling the attack on her bow, and all four of us, in our haste, jumped down on the poor Irishman at the wheel.

"Murder, fire, rape, and robbery!—it is capsized, stove in,

sunk, burned, and destroyed I am! Captain, captain, we are carried aft here—Och, hubbaboo for Patrick Donnally!"

There was no time to be lost; if any of the crew came aft we were dead men, so we tumbled down through the cabin skylight, men and beast, the hatch having been knocked off by a shot, and stowed ourselves away in the side berths. The noise on deck soon ceased—the cannon were again plied—gradually the fire slackened, and we could hear that the pirate had scraped clear and escaped. Some time after this the lieutenant commanding the cutter came down. Poor Mr. Douglas! both Mr. Splinter and I knew him well. He sat down and covered his face with his hands, while the blood oozed down between his fingers. He had received a cutlass wound on the head in the attack. His right arm was bound up with his neckcloth, and he was very pale.

"Steward, bring me a light.—Ask the doctor how many are killed and wounded; and—do you hear?—tell him to come to me when he is done forward, but not a moment sooner. To have been so mauled and duped by a buccaneer; and my poor boat's crew——"

Splinter groaned. He started—but at this moment the man returned again.

"Thirteen killed, your honor, and fifteen wounded; scarcely one of us untouched." The poor fellow's own skull was bound round with a bloody cloth.

"God help me! Gold help me! but they have died the death of men. Who knows what death the poor fellows in the boat have died!"—Here he was cut short by a tremendous scuffle on the ladder, down which an old quartermaster was trundled neck and crop into the cabin. "How now, Jones?"

"Please your honor," said the man, as soon as he had gathered himself up, and had time to turn his quid and smooth down his hair; but again the uproar was renewed, and Donnally was lugged in, scrambling and struggling between two seamen—"this here Irish chap, your honor, has lost his wits, if so be he ever had any, your honor. He has gone mad through fright."

"Fright be d——d!" roared Donnally; "no man ever frightened me; but as his honor was skewering them bloody thieves forward, I was boarded and carried aft by the devil, your honor—pooped by Beelzebub, by ——," and he rapped his fist on the table until everything on it danced again. "There were four of them, yeer honor—a black one and two blue ones—and a pie-bald one, with four legs and a bushy tail—each with two horns on his head, for all the world like those on Father M'Cleary's red cow—no, she was humbled—it is Father Clannachan's, I mane—no, not his neither, for his was the parish bull; fait, I don't know what I mane, except that

11

they had all horns on their heads, and vomited fire, and had each of them a tail at his stern, twisting and twining like a conger eel, with a blue light at the end on't."

"And dat's a lie, if ever dere was one," exclaimed Peter Mangrove, jumping from the berth. "Look at me, you Irish tief, and tell me if I have a blue light or a conger eel at my stern!"

This was too much for poor Donnally. He yelled out, "You'll believe your own eyes now, yeer honor, when you see one o' dem bodily before you! Let me go—let me go!" and, rushing up the ladder, he would, in all probability, have ended his earthly career in the salt sea, had his bullet-head not encountered the broadest part of the purser, who was in the act of descending, with such violence, that he shot him out of the companion several feet above the deck, as if he had been discharged from a culverin; but the recoil sent poor Donnally, stunned and senseless, to the bottom of the ladder. There was no standing all this; we laughed outright, and made ourselves known to Mr. Douglas, who received us cordially, and in a week we were landed at Port Royal.

THE CAPTURE OF PANAMA, 167[2]

John Esquemeling

Captain Morgan set forth from the castle of Chagre, towards Panama, August 18, 1670. He had with him twelve hundred men, five boats laden with artillery, and thirty-two canoes. The first day they sailed only six leagues, and came to a place called De los Bracos. Here a party of his men went ashore, only to sleep and stretch their limbs, being almost crippled with lying too much crowded in the boats. Having rested awhile, they went abroad to seek victuals in the neighboring plantations; but they could find none, the Spaniards being fled, and carrying with them all they had. This day, being the first of their journey, they had such scarcity of victuals, as the greatest part were forced to pass with only a pipe of tobacco, without any other refreshment.

Next day, about evening, they came to a place called Cruz de Juan Gallego. Here they were compelled to leave their boats and canoes, the river being very dry for want of rain, and many trees having fallen into it.

The guides told them, that, about two leagues farther, the country would be very good to continue the journey by land. Hereupon they left one hundred and sixty men on board the boats, to defend them, that they might serve for a refuge in necessity.

Next morning, being the third day, they all went ashore, except those who were to keep the boats. To these Captain Morgan gave order, under great penalties, that no man, on any pretext whatever, should dare to leave the boats, and go ashore; fearing lest they should be surprised by an ambuscade of Spaniards in the neighboring woods, which appeared so thick as to seem almost impenetrable. This morning beginning their march, the ways proved so bad, that Captain Morgan thought it more convenient to transport some of the men in canoes (though with great labor) to a place farther up the river, called Cedro Bueno. Thus they reëmbarked, and the canoes returned for the rest; so that about night they got altogether at the said place. The pirates much desired to meet some Spaniards or Indians, hoping to fill their bellies with their provisions, being reduced to extremity and hunger.

The fourth day the greatest part of the pirates marched by land, being led by one of the guides; the rest went by water farther up, being conducted by another guide, who always went before

---

[2] From The Buccaneers of America.

13

them, to discover, on both sides of the river, the ambuscades. These had also spies, who were very dextrous to give notice of all accidents, or of the arrival of the pirates, six hours, at least, before they came. This day, about noon, they came near a post called Torna Cavallos: here the guide of the canoes cried out, that he perceived an ambuscade. His voice caused infinite joy to all the pirates, hoping to find some provisions to satiate their extreme hunger. Being come to the place, they found nobody in it, the Spaniards being fled, and leaving nothing behind but a few leathern bags, all empty, and a few crumbs of bread scattered on the ground where they had eaten. Being angry at this, they pulled down a few little huts which the Spaniards had made, and fell to eating the leathern bags, to allay the ferment of their stomachs, which was now so sharp as to gnaw their very bowels. Thus they made a huge banquet upon these bags of leather, divers quarrels arising concerning the greatest shares. By the bigness of the place, they conjectured about five hundred Spaniards had been there, whom, finding no victuals, they were now infinitely desirous to meet, intending to devour some of them rather than perish.

Having feasted themselves with those pieces of leather, they marched on, till they came about night to another post, called Torna Munni. Here they found another ambuscade, but as barren as the former. They searched the neighboring woods, but could not find anything to eat, the Spaniards having been so provident, as not to leave anywhere the least crumb of sustenance, whereby the pirates were now brought to this extremity. Here again he was happy that he had reserved since noon any bit of leather to make his supper of, drinking after it a good draught of water for his comfort. Some, who never were out of their mothers' kitchens, may ask, how these pirates could eat and digest those pieces of leather, so hard and dry? Whom I answer, that, could they once experiment what hunger, or rather famine, is, they would find the way as the pirates did. For these first sliced it in pieces, then they beat it between two stones, and rubbed it, often dipping it in water, to make it supple and tender. Lastly, they scraped off the hair, and broiled it. Being thus cooked, they cut it into small morsels, and ate it, helping it down with frequent gulps of water, which, by good fortune, they had at hand.

The fifth day, about noon, they came to a place called Barbacoa. Here they found traces of another ambuscade, but the place totally as unprovided as the former. At a small distance were several plantations, which they searched very narrowly, but could not find any person, animal, or other thing, to relieve their extreme hunger. Finally, having ranged about, and searched a long time, they found a grot, which seemed to be but lately hewn out of a rock, where were two sacks of meal, wheat, and like things, with two great jars of wine, and certain fruits called platanoes. Captain Morgan, knowing some of his men were now almost dead with hunger, and fearing the same of the rest, caused what was found to be distributed among them who were in greatest necessity. Having refreshed themselves with these victuals, they marched anew with greater courage then ever. Such as were weak were put into the canoes, and those commanded to land that were in them before. Thus they prosecuted their journey till late at night; when coming to a plantation, they took up their rest, but without eating anything; for the Spaniards, as before, had swept away all manner of provisions.

The sixth day they continued their march, part by land and part by water. Howbeit, they were constrained to rest very frequently, both for the ruggedness of the way, and their extreme weakness, which they endeavored to relieve by eating leaves of trees and green herbs, or grass; such was their miserable condition. This day at noon they arrived at a plantation, where was a barn full of maize. Immediately they beat down the doors and ate it dry, as much as they could devour; then they distributed a great quantity, giving every man a good allowance. Thus provided, and prosecuting their journey for about an hour, they came to another ambuscade. This they no sooner discovered, but they threw away their maize, with the sudden hopes of finding all things in abundance. But they were much deceived, meeting neither Indians nor victuals, nor anything else: but they saw, on the other side of the river, about a hundred Indians, who, all fleeing, escaped. Some few pirates leaped into the river to cross it, and try to take any of the Indians, but in vain: for, being much more nimble than the pirates, they not only baffled them, but killed two or three with their arrows; hooting at them, and crying, "Ha, perros! a la savana, a la savana."—"Ha, ye dogs! go to the plain, go to the plain."

This day they could advance no farther, being necessitated to pass the river, to continue their march on the other side. Hereupon they reposed for that night, though their sleep was not profound; for great murmurings were made at Captain Morgan, and his conduct; some being desirous to return home, while others would rather die there than go back a step from their undertaking: others, who had greater courage, laughed and joked at their discourses. Meanwhile, they had a guide who much comforted them, saying, "It would not now be long before they met with people from whom they should reap some considerable advantage."

The seventh day, in the morning, they made clean their arms, and every one discharged his pistol, or musket, without bullet, to try their firelocks. This done, they crossed the river, leaving the post where they had rested, called Santa Cruz, and at noon they arrived at a village called Cruz. Being yet far from the place, they perceived much smoke from the chimneys: the sight hereof gave them great joy, and hopes of finding people and plenty of good cheer. Thus they went on as fast as they could, encouraging one another, saying, "There is smoke comes out of every house: they are making good fires, to roast and boil what we are to eat;" and the like.

At length they arrived there, all sweating and panting, but found no person in the town, nor anything eatable to refresh themselves, except good fires, which they wanted not; for the Spaniards, before their departure, had every one set fire to his own house, except the king's storehouses and stables.

They had not left behind them any beast, alive or dead, which much troubled their pursuers, not finding anything but a few cats and dogs, which they immediately killed and devoured. At last, in the king's stables, they found, by good fortune, fifteen or sixteen jars of Peru wine, and a leathern sack full of bread. No sooner had they drank of this wine, when they fell sick, almost every man: this made them think the wine was poisoned, which caused a new consternation in the whole camp, judging themselves now to be irrecoverably lost. But the true reason was, their want of sustenance, and the manifold sorts of trash they had eaten. Their sickness was so great, as caused them to remain there till the next morning, without being able to prosecute their journey in the afternoon. This village is seated in 9 deg. 2 min. north latitude, distant from the river Chagre twenty-six Spanish leagues, and eight from Panama. This is the last place to which boats or canoes can come; for which reason they built here storehouses for all sorts of merchandise, which to and from Panama are transported on the backs of mules.

Here Captain Morgan was forced to leave his canoes, and land all his men, though never so weak; but lest the canoes should be surprised, or take up too many men for their defense, he sent them all back to the place where the boats were, except one, which he hid, that it might serve to carry intelligence. Many of the Spaniards and Indians of this village having fled to the near plantations, Captain Morgan ordered that none should go out of the village, except companies of one hundred together, fearing lest the enemy should take an advantage upon his men. Notwithstanding, one party contravened these orders, being tempted with the desire of victuals: but they were soon glad to fly into the town again, being assaulted with great fury by some Spaniards and Indians, who carried one of them away prisoner. Thus the vigilancy and care of Captain Morgan was not sufficient to prevent every accident.

The eighth day in the morning Captain Morgan sent two hundred men before the body of his army, to discover the way to Panama, and any ambuscades therein: the path being so narrow, that only ten or twelve persons could march abreast, and often not so many. After ten hours' march they came to a place called Quebrada Obscura: here, all on a sudden, three or four thousand arrows were shot at them, they not perceiving whence they came, or who shot them: though they presumed it was from a high rocky mountain, from one side to the other, whereon was a grot, capable of but one horse or other beast laded. This multitude of arrows much alarmed the pirates, especially because they could not discover whence they were discharged. At last, seeing no more arrows, they marched a little farther, and entered a wood: here they perceived some Indians to fly as fast as they could, to take the advantage of another post, thence to observe their march; yet there remained one troop of Indians on the place, resolved to fight and defend themselves, which they did with great courage till their captain fell down wounded; who, though he despaired of life, yet his valor being greater than his strength, would ask no quarter, but, endeavoring to raise himself, with undaunted mind laid hold of his azagayo, or javelin, and struck at one of the pirates; but before he could second the blow, he was shot to death. This was also the fate of many of his companions, who, like good soldiers, lost their lives with their captain, for the defense of their country.

The pirates endeavored to take some of the Indians prisoners, but they being swifter than the pirates, every one escaped, leaving eight pirates dead, and ten wounded: yea, had the Indians been more dextrous in military affairs, they might have defended the passage, and not let one man pass. A little while after they came to a large champaign, open, and full of fine meadows; hence they could perceive at a distance before them some Indians, on the top of a mountain, near the way by which they were to pass: they sent fifty men, the nimblest they had, to try to catch any of them, and force them to discover their companions: but all in vain; for they escaped by their nimbleness, and presently showed themselves in another place, hallooing to the English and crying, "A la savana, a la savana, perros Ingleses!" that is, "To the plain, to the plain, ye English dogs!" Meanwhile the ten pirates that were wounded were dressed, and plastered up.

Here was a wood, and on each side a mountain. The Indians possessed themselves of one, and the pirates of the other. Captain Morgan was persuaded the Spaniards had placed an ambuscade

17

there, it lying so conveniently; hereupon, he sent two hundred men to search it. The Spaniards and Indians perceiving the pirates descended the mountain, did so too, as if they designed to attack them; but being got into the wood, out of sight of the pirates, they were seen no more, leaving the passage open.

About night fell a great rain, which caused the pirates to march the faster, and seek for houses to preserve their arms from being wet; but the Indians had set fire to every one, and driven away all their cattle, that the pirates, finding neither houses nor victuals, might be constrained to return: but, after diligent search, they found a few shepherds' huts, but in them nothing to eat. These not holding many men, they placed in them, out of every company, a small number, who kept the arms of the rest: those who remained in the open field endured much hardship that night, the rain not ceasing till morning.

Next morning, about the break of day, being the ninth of that tedious journey, Captain Morgan marched on while the fresh air of the morning lasted; for the clouds hanging yet over their heads, were much more favorable than the scorching rays of the sun, the way being now more difficult than before. After two hours' march, they discovered about twenty Spaniards, who observed their motions: they endeavored to catch some of them, but could not, they suddenly disappearing, and absconding themselves in caves among the rocks unknown to the pirates. At last, ascending a high mountain, they discovered the South Sea. This happy sight, as if it were the end of their labors, caused infinite joy among them: hence they could descry also one ship, and six boats, which were set forth from Panama, and sailed towards the islands of Tavoga and Tavogilla: then they came to a vale where they found much cattle, whereof they killed good store: here, while some killed and flayed cows, horses, bulls, and chiefly asses, of which there were most; others kindled fires, and got wood to roast them: then cutting the flesh into convenient pieces, or gobbets, they threw them into the fire, and, half carbonadoed or roasted, they devoured them, with incredible haste and appetite. Such was their hunger, that they more resembled cannibals than Europeans; the blood many times running down from their beards to their waists.

Having satisfied their hunger, Captain Morgan ordered them to continue the march. Here, again, he sent before the main body fifty men to take some prisoners, if they could; for he was much concerned, that in nine days he could not meet one person to inform him of the condition and forces of the Spaniards. About evening they discovered about two hundred Spaniards, who hallooed to the pirates, but they understood not what they said. A little while after they came in sight of the highest steeple of Panama: this they no sooner discovered but they showed signs of extreme joy, casting up their hats into the air, leaping and shouting, just as if they had already obtained the victory, and accomplished their designs. All their trumpets sounded, and drums beat, in token of this alacrity of their minds. Thus they pitched their camp for that night, with general content of the whole army, waiting with impatience for the morning, when they intended to attack the city. This evening appeared fifty horses, who came out of the city, on the noise of the drums and trumpets, to observe, as it was thought, their motions: they came almost within musket-shot of the army, with a trumpet that sounded marvelously well. Those on horseback hallooed aloud to the pirates, and threatened them, saying, "Perros! nos veremos," that is, "Ye dogs! we shall meet ye." Having made this menace, they returned to the city, except only seven or eight horsemen, who hovered thereabouts to watch their motions. Immediately after the city fired, and ceased not to play their biggest guns all night long against the camp, but with little or no harm to the pirates, whom they could not easily reach. Now also the two hundred Spaniards, whom the pirates had seen in the afternoon, appeared again, making a show of blocking up the passages, that no pirates might escape their hands: but the pirates, though in a manner besieged, instead of fearing their blockades, as soon as they had placed sentinels about their camp, opened their satchels, and, without any napkins or plates, fell to eating, very heartily, the pieces of bulls' and horses' flesh which they had reserved since noon. This done, they laid themselves down to sleep on the grass, with great repose and satisfaction, expecting only, with impatience, the dawning of the next day.

The tenth day, betimes in the morning, they put all their men in order, and, with drums and trumpets sounding, marched directly towards the city; but one of the guides desired Captain Morgan not to take the common highway, lest they should find in it many ambuscades. He took his advice, and chose another way through the wood, though very irksome and difficult. The Spaniards perceiving the pirates had taken another way they scarce had thought on, were compelled to leave their stops and batteries, and come out to meet them. The governor of Panama put his forces in order, consisting of two squadrons, four regiments of foot, and a huge number of wild bulls, which were driven by a great number of Indians, with some negroes, and others, to help them.

The pirates, now upon their march, came to the top of a little hill, whence they had a large prospect of the city and champaign country underneath. Here they discovered the forces of the people of Panama, in battle array, to be so numerous, that they were surprised with fear, much doubting the fortune of the day: yea, few or none there were but wished themselves at home, or at least free from obligation of that engagement, it so nearly concerning their lives. Having been some time wavering in their minds, they at last reflected on the straits they had brought themselves into, and that now they must either fight resolutely, or die; for no quarter could be expected from an enemy on whom they had committed so many cruelties. Hereupon they encouraged one another, resolving to conquer, or spend the last drop of blood. Then they divided themselves into three battalions, sending before two hundred buccaneers, who were very dextrous at their guns. Then descending the hill, they marched directly towards the Spaniards, who in a spacious field waited for their coming. As soon as they drew nigh, the Spaniards began to shout and cry, "Viva el rey!" "God save the king!" and immediately their horse moved against the pirates: but the fields being full of quags, and soft under-foot, they could not wheel about as they desired. The two hundred buccaneers, who went before, each putting one knee to the ground, began to battle briskly, with a full volley of shot: the Spaniards defended themselves courageously, doing all they could to disorder the pirates. Their foot endeavored to second the horse, but were forced by the fire of the pirates to retreat. Finding themselves baffled, they attempted to drive the bulls against them behind, to put them into disorder; but the wild cattle ran away, frighted with the noise of the battle. Only some few broke through the English companies, and only tore the colors in pieces, while the buccaneers shot every one of them dead.

The battle having continued two hours, the greatest part of the Spanish horse was ruined, and almost all killed: the rest fled, which the foot seeing, and that they could not possibly prevail, they discharged the shot they had in their muskets, and throwing them down, fled away, every one as he could. The pirates could not follow them, being too much harassed and wearied with their long journey. Many, not being able to fly whither they desired, hid themselves, for that present, among the shrubs of the sea-side, but very unfortunately; for most of them being found by the pirates, were instantly killed, without any quarter. Some religious men were brought prisoners before Captain Morgan; but he, being deaf to their cries, commanded them all to be pistoled, which was done. Soon after they brought a captain to him, whom he examined very strictly; particularly, wherein consisted the forces of those of Panama? He answered, their whole strength consisted in four hundred horse, twenty-four companies of foot, each one hundred men complete; sixty Indians, and some negroes, who were to drive two thousand wild bulls upon the English, and thus, by breaking their files, put them into a total disorder: beside, that in the city they had made trenches, and raised batteries in several places, in all which they had placed many guns; and that at the entry of the highway, leading to the city, they had built a fort mounted with eight great brass guns, defended by fifty men.

Captain Morgan having heard this, gave orders instantly to march another way; but first he made a review of his men, whereof he found both killed and wounded a considerable number, and much greater than had been believed. Of the Spaniards were found six hundred dead on the place, besides the wounded and prisoners. The pirates, nothing discouraged, seeing their number so diminished, but rather filled with greater pride, perceiving what huge advantage they had obtained against their enemies, having rested some time, prepared to march courageously towards the city, plighting their oaths to one another, that they would fight till not a man was left alive. With this courage they recommenced their march, either to conquer or be conquered; carrying with them all the prisoners.

They found much difficulty in their approach to the city, for within the town the Spaniards had placed many great guns, at several quarters, some charged with small pieces of iron, and others with musket bullets. With all these they saluted the pirates at their approaching, and gave them full and frequent broadsides, firing at them incessantly; so that unavoidably they lost at every step great numbers of men. But not these manifest dangers of their lives, nor the sight of so many as dropped continually at their sides, could deter them from advancing, and gaining ground every moment on the enemy; and though the Spaniards never ceased to fire, and act the best they could for their defense, yet they were forced to yield, after three hours' combat. And the pirates having possessed themselves at last of the city, killed all that attempted in the least to oppose them. The inhabitants had transported the best of their goods to more remote and secret places; howbeit, they found in the city several warehouses well stocked with merchandise, as well silks and cloths, as linen and other things of value. As soon as the first fury of their entrance was over, Captain Morgan assembled his men, and commanded them, under great penalties, not to drink or taste any wine; and the reason he gave for it was, because he had intelligence that it was all poisoned by the Spaniards. Howbeit, it was thought he gave these prudent orders to prevent the debauchery of his people, which he foresaw would be very great at the first, after so much hunger sustained by the way; fearing, withal,

21

lest the Spaniards, seeing them in wine, should rally, and, falling on the city, use them as inhumanly as they had used the inhabitants before.

Captain Morgan, as soon as he had placed necessary guards at several quarters within and without the city, commanded twenty-five men to seize a great boat, which had stuck in the mud of the port, for want of water, at a low tide. The same day about noon, he caused fire privately to be set to several great edifices of the city, nobody knowing who were the authors thereof, much less on what motives Captain Morgan did it, which are unknown to this day: the fire increased so, that before night the greatest part of the city was in a flame. Captain Morgan pretended the Spaniards had done it, perceiving that his own people reflected on him for that action. Many of the Spaniards, and some of the pirates, did what they could, either to quench the flames or by blowing up houses with gunpowder, and pulling down others to stop it, but in vain: for in less than half an hour it consumed a whole street. All the houses of the city were built with cedar, very curious and magnificent, and richly adorned, especially with hangings and paintings, whereof part were before removed, but another great part were consumed by fire.

There were in this city (which is the see of a bishop) eight monasteries, seven for men, and one for women; two stately churches, and one hospital. The churches and monasteries were all richly adorned with altar-pieces and paintings, much gold and silver, and other precious things, all which the ecclesiastics had hidden. Besides which, here were two thousand houses of magnificent building, the greatest part inhabited by merchants vastly rich. For the rest of less quality, and tradesmen, this city contained five thousand more. Here were also many stables for the horses and mules that carry the plate of the king of Spain, as well as private men, towards the North Sea. The neighboring fields were full of fertile plantations and pleasant gardens, affording delicious prospects to the inhabitants all the year.

The Genoese had in this city a stately house for their trade of negroes. This likewise was by Captain Morgan burnt to the very ground. Besides which building, there were consumed two hundred warehouses, and many slaves, who had hid themselves therein, with innumerable sacks of meal; the fire of which continued four weeks after it had begun. The greatest part of the pirates still encamped without the city, fearing and expecting the Spaniards would come and fight them anew, it being known they much outnumbered the pirates. This made them keep the field, to preserve their forces united, now much diminished by their losses. Their wounded, which were many, they put into one church, which remained standing, the rest being consumed by the fire. Besides these decreases of his men, Captain Morgan had sent a convoy of one hundred and fifty men to the castle of Chagre, to carry the news of his victory at Panama.

They saw often whole troops of Spaniards run to and fro in the fields, which made them suspect their rallying, which they never had the courage to do. In the afternoon Captain Morgan reëntered the city with his troops, that every one might take up their lodgings, which now they could hardly find, few houses having escaped the fire. Then they sought very carefully among the ruins and ashes, for utensils of plate or gold, that were not quite wasted by the flames: and of such they found no small number, especially in wells and cisterns, where the Spaniards had hid them.

Next day Captain Morgan dispatched away two troops, of one hundred and fifty men each, stout and well armed, to seek for the inhabitants who were escaped. These having made several excursions up and down the fields, woods, and mountains adjacent, returned after two days, bringing above two hundred prisoners, men, women, and slaves. The same day returned also the boat which Captain Morgan had sent to the South Sea, bringing three other boats which they had taken. But all these prizes they could willingly have given, and greater labor into the bargain, for one galleon, which miraculously escaped, richly laden with all the king's plate, jewels, and other precious goods of the best and richest merchants of Panama: on board which were also the religious women of the nunnery, who had embarked with them all the ornaments of their church, consisting in much gold, plate, and other things of great value.

The strength of this galleon was inconsiderable, having only seven guns, and ten or twelve muskets, and very ill provided with victuals, necessaries, and fresh water, having no more sails than the uppermost of the mainmast. This account the pirates received from some one who had spoken with seven mariners belonging to the galleon, who came ashore in the cockboat for fresh water. Hence they concluded they might easily have taken it, had they given her chase, as they should have done; but they were impeded from following this vastly rich prize, by their gluttony and drunkenness, having plentifully debauched themselves with several rich wines they found ready, choosing rather to satiate their appetites than to lay hold on such huge advantage; since this one prize would have been of far greater value than all they got at Panama, and the places thereabout. Next day, repenting of their negligence, being weary of their vices and debaucheries, they set forth another boat, well armed, to pursue with all speed the said galleon; but in vain, the Spaniards who were on board having had intelligence of their own danger one or two days before, while the pirates were cruising so near them; whereupon they fled to places more remote and unknown.

The pirates found, in the ports of the island of Tavoga and Tavogilla, several boats laden with very good merchandise; all which they took, and brought to Panama, where they made an exact relation of all that had passed to Captain Morgan. The prisoners confirmed what the pirates said, adding, that they undoubtedly knew where the galleon might then be, but that it was very probable they had been relieved before now from other places. This stirred up Captain Morgan anew, to send forth all the boats in the port of Panama to seek the said galleon till they could find her. These boats, being in all four, after eight days' cruising to and fro, and searching several ports and creeks, lost all hopes of finding her, whereupon they returned to Tavoga and Tavogilla. Here they found a reasonable good ship newly come from Payta, laden with cloth, soap, sugar, and biscuit, with 20,000 pieces-of-eight. This they instantly seized, without the least resistance; as also a boat which was not far off, on which they laded great part of the merchandises from the ship, with some slaves. With this spoil they returned to Panama, somewhat better satisfied; yet, withal, much discontented that they could not meet with the galleon.

The convoy which Captain Morgan had sent to the castle of Chagre returned much about the same time, bringing with them very good news; for while Captain Morgan was on his journey to Panama, those he had left in the castle of Chagre had sent for two boats to cruise. These met with a Spanish ship, which they chased within sight of the castle. This being perceived by the pirates in the castle, they put forth Spanish colors, to deceive the ship that fled before the boats; and the poor Spaniards, thinking to take refuge under the castle, were caught in a snare, and made prisoners. The cargo on board the said vessel consisted in victuals and provisions, than which nothing could be more opportune for the castle, where they began already to want things of this kind.

This good luck of those of Chagre caused Captain Morgan to stay longer at Panama, ordering several new excursions into the country round about; and while the pirates at Panama were upon these expeditions, those at Chagre were busy in piracies on the North Sea. Captain Morgan sent forth, daily, parties of two hundred men, to make inroads into all the country round about; and when one party came back, another went forth, who soon gathered much riches, and many prisoners. These being brought into the city, were put to the most exquisite tortures, to make them confess both other people's goods and their own. Here it happened that one poor wretch was found in the house of a person of quality, who had put on, amidst the confusion, a pair of taffety breeches of his master's, with a little silver key hanging out; perceiving which, they asked him for the cabinet of the said key. His answer was, he knew not what was become of it, but that finding those breeches in his master's house, he had made bold to wear them. Not being able to get any other answer, they put him on the rack, and inhumanly disjointed his arms; then they twisted a cord about his forehead, which they wrung so hard that his eyes appeared as big as eggs, and were ready to fall out. But with these torments not obtaining any positive answer, they hung him up by the wrists, giving him many blows and stripes under that intolerable pain and posture of body. Afterwards they cut off his nose and ears, and singed his face with burning straw, till he could not speak, nor lament his misery any longer: then, losing all hopes of any confession, they bade a negro to run him through, which put an end to his life, and to their inhuman tortures. Thus did many others of those miserable prisoners finish their days, the common sport and recreation of these pirates being such tragedies.

Captain Morgan having now been at Panama full three weeks, commanded all things to be prepared for his departure. He ordered every company of men to seek so many beasts of carriage as might convey the spoil to the river where his canoes lay. About this time there was a great rumor, that a considerable number of pirates intended to leave Captain Morgan; and that, taking a ship then in port, they determined to go and rob on the South Sea, till they had got as much as they thought fit, and then return homewards, by way of the East Indies. For which purpose they had gathered much provisions, which they had hid in private places, with sufficient powder, bullets, and all other ammunition: likewise some great guns belonging to the town, muskets, and other things, wherewith they designed not only to equip their vessel, but to fortify themselves in some island which might serve them for a place of refuge.

This design had certainly taken effect, had not Captain Morgan had timely advice of it from one of their comrades; hereupon he commanded the mainmast of the said ship to be cut down and burnt, with all the other boats in the port: hereby the intentions of all or most of his companions were totally frustrated. Then Captain Morgan sent many of the Spaniards into the adjoining fields and country to seek for money, to ransom not only themselves, but the rest of the prisoners, as likewise the ecclesiastics. Moreover, he commanded all the artillery of the town to be nailed and stopped up. At the same time he sent out a strong company of men to seek for the governor of Panama, of whom intelligence was brought, that he had laid several ambuscades in the way by which he ought to return: but they returned soon after, saying they had not found any sign of any such ambuscades. For confirmation whereof, they brought some prisoners, who declared that the said governor had had an intention of making some opposition by the way, but that the men designed to effect it were unwilling to undertake it: so that for want of means he could not put his design in execution.

February 24, 1671, Captain Morgan departed from Panama, or rather from the place where the city of Panama stood; of the spoils whereof he carried with him one hundred and seventy-five beasts of carriage, laden with silver, gold, and other precious things, beside about six hundred prisoners, men, women, children and slaves. That day they came to a river that passes through a delicious plain, a league from Panama: here Captain Morgan put all his forces into good order, so as that the prisoners were in the middle, surrounded on all sides with pirates, where nothing else was to be heard but lamentations, cries, shrieks, and doleful sighs of so many women and children, who feared Captain Morgan designed to transport them all into his own country for slaves. Besides, all those miserable prisoners endured extreme hunger and thirst at that time, which misery Captain Morgan designedly caused them to sustain, to excite them to seek for money to ransom themselves, according to the tax he had set upon every one. Many of the women begged Captain Morgan, on their knees, with infinite sighs and tears, to let them return to Panama, there to live with their dear husbands and children in little huts of straw, which they would erect, seeing they had no houses till the rebuilding of the city. But his answer was, "He came not thither to hear lamentations and cries, but to seek money: therefore they ought first to seek out that, wherever it was to be had, and bring it to him; otherwise he would assuredly transport them all to such places whither they cared not to go."

Next day, when the march began, those lamentable cries and shrieks were renewed, so as it would have caused compassion in the hardest heart: but Captain Morgan, as a man little given to mercy, was not moved in the least. They marched in the same order as before, one party of the pirates in the van, the prisoners in the middle, and the rest of the pirates in the rear; by whom the miserable Spaniards were at every step punched and thrust in their backs and sides, with the blunt ends of their arms, to make them march faster.

A beautiful lady, wife to one of the richest merchants of Tavoga, was led prisoner by herself, between two pirates. Her lamentations pierced the skies, seeing herself carried away into captivity often crying to the pirates, and telling them, "That she had given orders to two religious persons, in whom she had relied, to go to a certain place, and fetch so much money as her ransom did amount to; that they had promised faithfully to do it, but having obtained the money, instead of bringing it to her, they had employed it another way, to ransom some of their own, and particular friends." This ill action of theirs was discovered by a slave, who brought a letter to the said lady. Her complaints, and the cause thereof, being brought to Captain Morgan, he thought fit to inquire thereinto. Having found it to be true—especially hearing it confirmed by the confession of the said religious men, though under some frivolous excuses of having diverted the money but for a day or two, in which time they expected more sums to repay it—he gave liberty to the said lady, whom otherwise he designed to transport to Jamaica. But he detained the said religious men as prisoners in her place, using them according to their desserts.

Captain Morgan arriving at the town called Cruz, on the banks of the river Chagre, he published an order among the prisoners, that within three days every one should bring in their ransom, under the penalty of being transported to Jamaica. Meanwhile he gave orders for so much rice and maize to be collected thereabouts, as was necessary for victualing his ships. Here some of the prisoners were ransomed, but many others could not bring in their money. Hereupon he continued his voyage, leaving the village on the 5th of March following, carrying with him all the spoil he could. Hence he likewise led away some new prisoners, inhabitants there, with those in Panama, who had not paid their ransoms. But the two religious men, who had diverted the lady's money, were ransomed three days after by other persons, who had more compassion for them than they had showed for her.

About the middle of the way to Chagre, Captain Morgan commanded them to be mustered, and caused every one to be sworn, that they had concealed nothing, even not to the value of sixpence. This done, Captain Morgan knowing those lewd fellows would not stick to swear falsely for interest, he commanded every one to be searched very strictly, both in their clothes and satchels, and elsewhere. Yea, that this order might not be ill taken by his companions, he permitted himself to be searched, even to his very shoes. To this effect, by common consent, one was assigned out of every company to be searchers of the rest. The French pirates that assisted on this expedition disliked this new practice of searching; but, being outnumbered by the English, they were forced to submit as well as the rest. The search being over, they reëmbarked, and arrived at the castle of Chagre on the 9th of March.

THE MALAY PROAS[3]

James Fenimore Cooper

We had cleared the Straits of Sunda early in the morning, and had made a pretty fair run in the course of the day, though most of the time in thick weather. Just as the sun set, however, the horizon became clear, and we got a sight of two small sail, seemingly heading in toward the coast of Sumatra, proas by their rig and dimensions. They were so distant, and were so evidently steering for the land, that no one gave them much thought, or bestowed on them any particular attention. Proas in that quarter were usually distrusted by ships, it is true; but the sea is full of them, and far more are innocent than are guilty of any acts of violence. Then it became dark soon after these craft were seen, and night shut them in. An hour after the sun had set, the wind fell to a light air, that just kept steerage-way on the ship. Fortunately, the John was not only fast, but she minded her helm, as a light-footed girl turns in a lively dance. I never was in a better-steering ship, most especially in moderate weather.

Mr. Marble had the middle watch that night, and, of course, I was on deck from midnight until four in the morning. It proved misty most of the watch, and for quite an hour we had a light drizzling rain. The ship the whole time was close-hauled, carrying royals. As everybody seemed to have made up his mind to a quiet night, one without any reefing or furling, most of the watch were sleeping about the decks, or wherever they could get good quarters, and be least in the way. I do not know what kept me awake, for lads of my age are apt to get all the sleep they can; but I believe I was thinking of Clawbonny, and Grace, and Lucy; for the latter, excellent girl as she was, often crossed my mind in those days of youth and comparative innocence. Awake I was, and walking in the weather-gangway, in a sailor's trot. Mr. Marble, he I do believe was fairly snoozing on the hen-coops, being, like the sails, as one might say, barely "asleep." At that moment I heard a noise, one familiar to seamen; that of an oar falling in a boat. So completely was my mind bent on other and distant scenes, that at first I felt no surprise, as if we were in a harbor surrounded by craft of various sizes, coming and going at all hours. But a second thought destroyed this illusion, and I looked eagerly about me. Directly on our weather-bow,

3 From Afloat and Ashore.

distant, perhaps, a cable's length, I saw a small sail, and I could distinguish it sufficiently well to perceive it was a proa. I sang out "Sail ho! and close aboard!"

Mr. Marble was on his feet in an instant. He afterward told me that when he opened his eyes, for he admitted this much to me in confidence, they fell directly on the stranger. He was too much of a seaman to require a second look in order to ascertain what was to be done. "Keep the ship away—keep her broad off!" he called out to the man at the wheel. "Lay the yards square—call all hands, one of you. Captain Robbins, Mr. Kite, bear a hand up; the bloody proas are aboard us!" The last part of this call was uttered in a loud voice, with the speaker's head down the companion-way. It was heard plainly enough below, but scarcely at all on deck.

In the meantime everybody was in motion. It is amazing how soon sailors are wide awake when there is really anything to do! It appeared to me that all our people mustered on deck in less than a minute, most of them with nothing on but their shirts and trousers. The ship was nearly before the wind by the time I heard the captain's voice; and then Mr. Kite came bustling in among us forward, ordering most of the men to lay aft to the braces, remaining himself on the forecastle, and keeping me with him to let go the sheets. On the forecastle, the strange sail was no longer visible, being now abaft the beam; but I could hear Mr. Marble swearing there were two of them, and that they must be the very chaps we had seen to leeward, and standing in for the land at sunset. I also heard the captain calling out to the steward to bring him a powder-horn. Immediately after, orders were given to let fly all our sheets forward, and then I perceived that they were wearing ship. Nothing saved us but the prompt order of Mr. Marble to keep the ship away, by which means, instead of moving toward the proas, we instantly began to move from them. Although they went three feet to our two, this gave us a moment of breathing time.

As our sheets were all flying forward, and remained so for a few minutes, it gave me leisure to look about. I soon saw both proas, and glad enough was I to perceive that they had not approached materially nearer. Mr. Kite observed this also, and remarked that our movements had been so prompt as to "take the rascals aback." He meant they did not exactly know what we were at, and had not kept away with us.

At this instant, the captain and five or six of the oldest seamen began to cast loose all our starboard, or weather guns, four in all, and sixes. We had loaded these guns in the Straits of Banca, with grape and canister, in readiness for just such pirates as were now coming down upon us; and nothing was wanting but the priming

29

and a hot loggerhead. It seems two of the last had been ordered in the fire, when we saw the proas at sunset; and they were now in excellent condition for service, live coals being kept around them all night by command. I saw a cluster of men busy with the second gun from forward, and could distinguish the captain pointing to it.

"There cannot well be any mistake, Mr. Marble?" the captain observed, hesitating whether to fire or not.

"Mistake, sir? Lord, Captain Robbins, you might cannonade any of the islands astern for a week, and never hurt an honest man. Let 'em have it, sir; I'll answer for it, you do good."

This settled the matter. The loggerhead was applied, and one of our sixes spoke out in a smart report. A breathless stillness succeeded. The proas did not alter their course, but neared us fast. The captain levelled his night-glass, and I heard him tell Kite, in a low voice, that they were full of men. The word was now passed to clear away all the guns, and to open the arm-chest, to come at the muskets and pistols. I heard the rattling of the boarding-pikes, too, as they were cut adrift from the spanker-boom, and fell upon the decks. All this sounded very ominous, and I began to think we should have a desperate engagement first, and then have all our throats cut afterward.

I expected now to hear the guns discharged in quick succession, but they were got ready only, not fired. Kite went aft, and returned with three or four muskets, and as many pikes. He gave the latter to those of the people who had nothing to do with the guns. By this time the ship was on a wind, steering a good full, while the two proas were just abeam, and closing fast. The stillness that reigned on both sides was like that of death. The proas, however, fell a little more astern; the result of their own manœuvering, out of all doubt, as they moved through the water much faster than the ship, seeming desirous of dropping into our wake, with a design of closing under our stern, and avoiding our broadside. As this would never do, and the wind freshened so as to give us four or five knot way, a most fortunate circumstance for us, the captain determined to tack while he had room. The John behaved beautifully, and came round like a top. The proas saw there was no time to lose, and attempted to close before we could fill again; and this they would have done with ninety-nine ships in a hundred. The captain knew his vessel, however, and did not let her lose her way, making everything draw again as it might be by instinct. The proas tacked, too, and, laying up much nearer to the wind than we did, appeared as if about to close on our lee-bow. The question was, now, whether we could pass them or not before they got near enough to grapple. If the pirates got on board us, we were hopelessly gone; and

30

everything depended on coolness and judgment. The captain behaved perfectly well in this critical instant, commanding a dead silence, and the closest attention to his orders.

I was too much interested at this moment to feel the concern that I might otherwise have experienced. On the forecastle, it appeared to us all that we should be boarded in a minute, for one of the proas was actually within a hundred feet, though losing her advantage a little by getting under the lee of our sails. Kite had ordered us to muster forward of the rigging, to meet the expected leap with a discharge of muskets, and then to present our pikes, when I felt an arm thrown around my body, and was turned inboard, while another person assumed my place. This was Neb, who had thus coolly thrust himself before me, in order to meet the danger first. I felt vexed, even while touched with the fellow's attachment and self-devotion, but had no time to betray either feeling before the crews of the proas gave a yell, and discharged some fifty or sixty matchlocks at us. The air was full of bullets, but they all went over our heads. Not a soul on board the John was hurt. On our side, we gave the gentlemen the four sixes, two at the nearest and two at the stern-most proa, which was still near a cable's length distant. As often happens, the one seemingly farthest from danger, fared the worst. Our grape and canister had room to scatter, and I can at this distant day still hear the shrieks that arose from that craft! They were like the yells of fiends in anguish. The effect on that proa was instantaneous; instead of keeping on after her consort, she wore short round on her heel, and stood away in our wake, on the other tack, apparently to get out of the range of our fire.

I doubt if we touched a man in the nearest proa. At any rate, no noise proceeded from her, and she came up under our bows fast. As every gun was discharged, and there was not time to load them, all now depended on repelling the boarders. Part of our people mustered in the waist, where it was expected the proa would fall alongside, and part on the forecastle. Just as this distribution was made, the pirates cast their grapnel. It was admirably thrown, but caught only by a ratlin. I saw this, and was about to jump into the rigging to try what I could do to clear it, when Neb again went ahead of me, and cut the ratlin with his knife. This was just as the pirates had abandoned sails and oars, and had risen to haul up alongside. So sudden was the release, that twenty of them fell over by their own efforts. In this state the ship passed ahead, all her canvas being full, leaving the proa motionless in her wake. In passing, however, the two vessels were so near, that those aft in the John distinctly saw the swarthy faces of their enemies.

31

We were no sooner clear of the proas than the order was given, "Ready about!" The helm was put down, and the ship came into the wind in a minute. As we came square with the two proas, all our larboard guns were given to them, and this ended the affair. I think the nearest of the rascals got it this time, for away she went, after her consort, both running off toward the islands. We made a little show of chasing, but it was only a feint; for we were too glad to get away from them, to be in earnest. In ten minutes after we tacked the last time, we ceased firing, having thrown some eight or ten round-shot after the proas, and were close-hauled again, heading to the southwest.

THE WONDERFUL FIGHT OF THE EXCHANGE OF BRISTOL WITH THE PIRATES OF ALGIERS[4]

Samuel Purchas

In the yeere 1621, the first of November, there was one Iohn Rawlins, borne in Rochester, and dwelling three and twenty yeere in Plimmoth, imployed to the Strait of Gibraltar, by Master Richard, and Steven Treviles, Merchants of Plimmoth, and fraighted in a Barke, called the Nicholas of Plimmoth, of the burden of forty Tun, which had also in her company another ship of Plimmoth, called the George Benaventure of seventy Tun burthen, or thereabouts; which by reason of her greatnesse beyond the other, I will name the Admirall; and Iohn Rawlins Barke shall, if you please, be the Vice-admirall. These two according to the time of the yeere, had a faire passage, and by the eighteenth of the same moneth came to a place at the entring of the straits, named Trafflegar: but the next morning, being in the sight of Gibraltar, at the very mouth of the straits, the watch descried five saile of ships, who as it seemed, used all the means they could to come neere us, and we as we had cause, used the same means to go as farre from them: yet did their Admirall take in both his top sailes, that either we might not suspect them, or that his owne company might come up the closer together. At last perceiving us Christians, they fell from devices to apparent discovery of hostility, and making out against us: we againe suspecting them Pirats, tooke our course to escape from them, and made all the sailes we possibly could for Tirriff, or Gibraltar: but all we could doe, could not prevent their approach. For suddenly one of them came right over against us to wind-ward, and so fell upon our quarter: another came upon our luffe, and so threatened us there, and at last all five chased us, making great speed to surprise us.

Their Admirall was called Callfater, having upon her maine top-saile, two top-gallant sailes, one above another. But whereas we thought them all five to be Turkish ships of war, we afterwards understood, that two of them were their prizes, the one a smal ship of London, the other of the West-countrey, that came out of the Quactath laden with figges, and other Merchandise, but now subiect to the fortune of the Sea, and the captivity of Pirats. But to our

---

[4] From Purchas, His Pilgrims.

businesse. Three of these ships got much upon us, and so much that ere halfe the day was spent, the Admirall who was the best sailer, fetcht up the George Bonaventure, and made booty of it. The Vice-Admirall againe being neerest unto the lesser Barke, whereof Iohn Rawlins was Master, shewed him the force of a stronger arme, and by his Turkish name, called Villa-Rise, commanded him in like sort to strike his sailes, and submit to his mercy, which not to be gaine-saied nor prevented, was quickly done: and so Rawlins with his Barke was quickly taken, although the Reare-Admirall being the worst sayler of the three, called Reggiprise, came not in, till all was done.

The same day before night, the Admirall either loth to pester himselfe with too much company, or ignorant of the commodity that was to be made by the sale of English prisoners, or daring not to trust them in his company, for feare of mutinies, and exciting others to rebellion; set twelve persons who were in the George Bonaventure on the land, and divers other English, whom he had taken before, to trie their fortunes in an unknowne Countrey. But Villa-Rise, the Vice-Admirall that had taken Iohn Rawlins, would not so dispence with his men, but commanded him and five more of his company to be brought aboord his ship, leaving in his Barke three men and his boy, with thirteene Turkes and Moores, who were questionlesse sufficient to over-master the other, and direct the Barke to Harbour. Thus they sailed directly for Algier; but the night following, followed them with great tempest and foule weather, which ended not without some effect of a storme: for they lost the sight of Rawlins Barke, called the Nicholas, and in a manner lost themselves, though they seemed safe a shipboord, by fearefull coniecturing what should become of us: at last, by the two and twentieth of the same moneth, they, or we (chuse you whether) arrived at Algier, and came in safety within the Mould, but found not our other Barke there; nay, though we earnestly inquired after the same, yet heard we nothing to our satisfaction; but much matter was ministred to our discomfort and amazement. For although the Captaine and our over-seers, were loth we should have any conference with our Country-men; yet did we adventure to informe ourselves of the present affaires, both of the Towne, and the shipping: so that finding many English at worke in other ships, they spared not to tell us the danger we were in, and the mischiefes we must needs incurre, as being sure if we were not used like slaves, to be sold as slaves; for there had beene five hundred brought into the market for the same purpose, and above a hundred hansome youths compelled to turne Turkes, or made subiect to more viler prostitution, and all English: yet like good Christians, they bade us be of good cheere, and comfort ourselves in this, that Gods trials were gentle purgations, and these crosses were but to cleanse the drosse from the gold, and bring us out of the fire againe more cleare and lovely. Yet I must needs confesse, that they afforded us reason for this cruelty, as if they determined to be revenged of our last attempt to fire their ships in the Mould, and therefore protested to spare none whom they could surprise and take alive; but either to sell them for money, or torment them to serve their owne turnes. Now their customes and usages in both these was in this manner.

First, concerning the first. The Bashaw had the over-seeing of all prisoners, who were presented unto him at their first comming into the harbour, and to choose one out of every eight for a present or fee to himselfe: the rest were rated by the Captaines, and so sent to the Market to be sold; whereat if either there were repining, or any drawing backe, then certaine Moores and Officers attended either to beate you forward, or thrust you into the sides with Goades; and this was the manner of the selling of Slaves.

Secondly, concerning their enforcing them, either to turne Turke, or to attend their filthines and impieties, although it would make a Christians heart bleed to heare of the same, yet must the truth not be hid, nor the terror left untold. They commonly lay them on their naked backs or bellies, beating them so long, till they bleed at the nose and mouth; and if yet they continue constant, then they strike the teeth out of their heads, pinch them by their tongues, and use many other sorts of tortures to convert them; nay, many times they lay them their whole length in the ground like a grave, and so cover them with boords, threatening to starve them, if they will not turne; and so many even for feare of torment and death, make their tongues betray their hearts to a most fearefull wickednesse, and so are circumcised with new names, and brought to confesse a new Religion. Others againe, I must confesse, who never knew any God, but their own sensuall lusts and pleasures, thought that any religion would serve their turnes, and so for preferment or wealth very voluntarily renounced their faith, and became Renegadoes in despight of any counsell which seemed to intercept them: and this was the first newes wee encountred with at our comming first to Algier.

The 26. of the same moneth, Iohn Rawlins his Barke, with his other three men and a boy, came safe into the Mould, and so were put all together to be carried before the Bashaw, but that they tooke the Owners servant, and Rawlins Boy, and by force and torment compelled them to turne Turkes: then were they in all seven English, besides Iohn Rawlins, of whom the Bashaw tooke one, and sent the rest to their Captaines, who set a valuation upon them, and so the Souldiers hurried us like dogs into the Market, whereas men sell Hacknies in England. We were tossed up and downe to see who would give most for us; and although we had heavy hearts, and looked with sad countenances, yet many came to behold us, sometimes taking us by the hand, sometimes turning us round about, sometimes feeling our brawnes and naked armes, and so beholding our prices written on our breasts, they bargained for us accordingly, and at last we were all sold, and the Souldiers returned with the money to their Captaines.

Iohn Rawlins was the last who was sold, by reason of his lame hand, and bought by the Captaine that tooke him, even that dog Villa Rise, who better informing himselfe of his skill fit to be a Pilot, and his experience to bee an over-seer, bought him and his Carpenter at very easie rates. For as we afterwards understood by divers English Renegadoes, he paid for Rawlins but one hundred and fiftie Dooblets, which make of English money seven pound ten shilling. Thus was he and his Carpenter with divers other slaves sent into his ship to worke, and imployed about such affaires, as belonged to the well rigging and preparing the same. But the villanous Turkes perceiving his lame hand, and that he could not performe so much as other Slaves, quickly complained to their Patron, who as quickly apprehended the inconvenience; whereupon hee sent for him the next day, and told him he was unserviceable for his present purpose, and therefore unlesse he could procure fifteene pound of the English there for his ransome, he would send him up into the Countrey, where he should never see Christendome againe, and endure the extremity of a miserable banishment.

But see how God worketh all for the best for his servants, and confounded the presumption of Tyrants, frustrating their purposes, to make his wonders knowne to the sonnes of men, and releeves his people, when they least thinke of succour and releasement. Whilest Iohn Rawlins was thus terrified with the dogged answere of Villa Rise, the Exchange of Bristow,[5] a ship formerly surprised by the Pirats, lay all unrigged in the Harbour, till at last one Iohn Goodale, an English Turke, with his confederates, understanding shee was a good sailer, and might be made a proper Man of Warre, bought her from the Turkes that tooke her, and prepared her for their owne purpose. Now the Captaine that set them at worke, was also an English Renegado, by the name of Rammetham Rise, but by his Christian name Henrie Chandler, who resolved to make Goodale Master over her; and because they were both English Turkes, having the command notwithstanding of many Turkes and Moores, they

---

[5] Bristol.

concluded to have all English slaves to goe in her, and for their Gunners, English and Dutch Renegadoes, and so they agreed with the Patrons of nine English and one French Slave for their ransoms, who were presently imployed to rig and furnish the ship for a Man of Warre, and while they were thus busied, two of Iohn Rawlins men, who were taken with him, were also taken up to serve in this Man of Warre, their names, Iames Roe, and Iohn Davies, the one dwelling in Plimmoth, and the other in Foy, where the Commander of this ship was also borne, by which occasion they came acquainted, so that both the Captaine, and the Master promised them good usage, upon the good service they should performe in the voyage, and withall demanded of them, if they knew of any Englishman to be bought, that could serve as a Pilot, both to direct them out of Harbour, and conduct them in their voyage. For in truth neither was the Captaine a Mariner, nor any Turke in her of sufficiency to dispose of her through the Straites in securitie, nor oppose any enemie, that should hold it out bravely against them. Davies quickly replied, that as farre as he understood, Villa Rise would sell Iohn Rawlins his Master, and Commander of the Barke which was taken, a man every way sufficient for Sea affaires, being of great resolution and good experience; and for all he had a lame hand, yet had he a sound heart and noble courage for any attempt or adventure.

When the Captaine understood thus much, he imployed Davies to search for Rawlins, who at last lighting upon him, asked him if the Turke would sell him: Rawlins suddenly answered, that by reason of his lame hand he was willing to part with him; but because he had disbursed money for him, he would gaine something by him, and so prized him at three hundred Dooblets, which amounteth to fifteene pound English; which he must procure, or incurre sorer indurances. When Davies had certified this much, the Turkes a ship-boord conferred about the matter, and the Master whose Christen name was Iohn Goodale joyned with two Turkes, who were consorted with him, and disbursed one hundred Dooblets a piece, and so bought him of Villa Rise, sending him into the said ship, called the Exchange of Bristow, as well to supervise what had been done, as to order what was left undone, but especially to fit the sailes, and to accommodate the ship, all which Rawlins was very carefull and dilligent in, not yet thinking of any peculiar plot of deliverance, more than a generall desire to be freed from this Turkish slaverie, and inhumane abuses.

By the seventh of Ianuarie, the ship was prepared with twelve good cast Pieces, and all manner of munition and provision, which belonged to such a purpose, and the same day haled out of the Mould of Algier, with this company, and in this manner.

There were in her sixtie three Turkes and Moores, nine English slaves, and one French, foure Hollanders that were free men, to whom the Turkes promised one prise or other, and so to returne to Holland; or if they were disposed to goe backe againe for Algier, they should have great reward and no enforcement offered, but continue as they would, both their religion and their customes: and for their Gunners they had two of our Souldiers, one English and one Dutch Renegado; and thus much for the companie. For the manner of setting out, it was as usuall as in other ships, but that the Turkes delighted in the ostentous braverie of their Streamers, Banners, and Top-sayles; the ship being a handsome ship, and well built for any purpose. The Slaves and English were imployed under Hatches about the Ordnance, and other workes of order, and accommodating themselves: all which Iohn Rawlins marked, as supposing it an intolerable slaverie to take such paines, and be subiect to such dangers, and still to enrich other men and maintaine their voluptuous filthinesse and lives, returning themselves as Slaves, and living worse than their Dogs amongst them. Whereupon hee burst out into these, or the like abrupt speeches: "Oh Hellish slaverie to be thus subiect to Dogs! Oh, God strengthen my heart and hand, that something shall be done to ease us of these mischiefs, and deliver us from these cruell Mahumetan Dogs." The other Slaves pittying his distraction (as they thought) bad him speake softly, lest they should all fare the worse for his distemperature. "The worse (quoth Rawlins) what can be worse? I will either attempt my deliverance at one time, or another, or perish in the enterprise: but if you would be contented to hearken after a release, and joyne with me in the action, I would not doubt of facilitating the same, and shew you a way to make your credits thrive by some worke of amazement, and augment your glorie in purchasing your libertie." "I prethee be quiet (said they againe) and think not of impossibilities: yet if you can but open such a doore of reason and probabilitie, that we be not condemned for desperate and distracted persons, in pulling the Sunne as it were out of the Firmament, wee can but sacrifice our lives, and you may be sure of secrecie and faithfulnesse."

The fifteenth of Januarie, the morning water brought us neere Cape de Gatt, hard by the shoare, we having in our companie a smal Turkish ship of Warre, that followed us out of Algier the next day, and now ioyning with us, gave us notice of seven small vessels, sixe of them being Sallees, and one Pollack, who very quickly appeared in sight, and so we made toward them: but having more advantage

38

of the Pollack, then the rest, and loth to lose all, we both fetcht her up, and brought her past hope of recoverie, which when she perceived, rather then she would voluntarily come into the slaverie of these Mahumetans, she ran her selfe a shoare, and so all the men forsooke her. We still followed as neere as we durst, and for feare of splitting, let fall our anchors, sending out both our boates, wherein were many Musketeers, and some English and Dutch Renegadoes, who came aboord home at their Conge, and found three pieces of Ordnance, and foure Murtherers: but they straightway threw them all over-boord to lighten the ship, and so they got her off, being laden with Hides, and Logwood for dying, and presently sent her to Algier, taking nine Turkes, and one English Slave, out of one ship, and six out of the lesse, which we thought sufficient to man her.

In the rifling of this Catelaynia, our Turkes fell at variance one with another, and in such a manner, that we divided our selves, the lesser ship returned to Algier, and our Exchange tooke the opportunitie of the wind, and plyed out of the Streights, which reioyced Iohn Rawlins very much, as resolving on some Stratageme, when opportunities should serve. In the meane-while, the Turkes began to murmurre, and would not willingly goe into the Marr Granada, as the phrase is amongst them: notwithstanding the Moores being very superstitious, were contented to be directed by their Hoshea, who with us, signifieth a Witch, and is of great account and reputation amongst them, as not going in any great Vessell to Sea without one, and observing whatsoever he concludeth out of his Divination. The Ceremonies they use are many, and when they come into the Ocean, every second or third night they make their Conjuration; it beginneth and endeth with Prayer, using many Characters, and calling upon God by divers names: yet at this time, all that they did consisted in these particulars.

Upon the sight of two great ships, and as wee were afraid of their chasing us, they beeing supposed to bee Spanish men of Warre, a great silence is commanded in the ship, and when all is done, the company giveth as great a skreech; the Captaine comming to John Rawlins, and sometimes making him take in all his sayles, and sometimes causing him to hoyst them all out, as the Witch findeth by his Booke, and presages; then have they two Arrowes, and a Curtleaxe, lying upon a Pillow naked; the Arrowes are one for the Turkes, and the other for the Christians; then the Witch readeth, and the Captaine or some other taketh the Arrowes in their hand by the heads, and if the Arrow for the Christians commeth over the head of the Arrow for the Turkes, then doe they advance their sayles, and will not endure the fight, whatsoever they see: but if the Arrow of the Turkes is found in the opening of the hand upon the

Arrow of the Christians, then will they stay and encounter with any shippe whatsoever. The Curtleaxe is taken up by some Childe, that is innocent, or rather ignorant of the Ceremonie, and so layd downe againe; then doe they observe, whether the same side is uppermost, which lay before, and so proceed accordingly.

They also observe Lunatickes and Changelings, and the Coniurer writeth downe their Sayings in a Booke, groveling on the ground, as if he whispered to the Devil to tell him the truth, and so expoundeth the Letter, as it were by inspiration. Many other foolish Rites they have, whereupon they doe dote as foolishly.

Whilest he was busied, and made demonstration that all was finished, the people in the ship gave a great shout, and cryed out, "a sayle, a sayle," which at last was discovered to bee another man of Warre of Turkes. For he made toward us, and sent his Boat aboord us, to whom our Captain complained, that being becalmed by the Southerne Cape, and having made no Voyage, the Turkes denyed to goe any further Northward: but the Captaine resolved not to returne to Algier, except he could obtayne some Prize worthy his endurances, but rather to goe to Salle, and tell his Christians to victuall his ship; which the other Captaine apprehended for his honour, and so perswaded the Turkes to be obedient unto him; whereupon followed a pacification amongst us, and so that Turke tooke his course for the Streights, and wee put up Northward, expecting the good houre of some beneficiall bootie.

All this while our slavery continued, and the Turkes with insulting tyrannie set us still on worke in all base and servile actions, adding stripes and inhumane revilings, even in our greatest labour, whereupon Iohn Rawlins resolved to obtane his libertie, and surprize the ship; providing Ropes with broad spikes of Iron, and all the Iron Crowes, with which hee knew a way, upon consent of the rest, to ramme up or tye fast their Scuttels, Gratings, and Cabbins, yea, to shut up the Captaine himselfe with all his consorts, and so to handle the matter, that upon the watch-word given, the English being Masters of the Gunner roome, Ordnance, and Powder, they would eyther blow them into the Ayre, or kill them as they adventured to come downe one by one, if they should by any chance open their Cabbins. But because hee would proceed the better in his enterprise, as he had somewhat abruptly discovered himselfe to the nine English slaves, so he kept the same distance with the foure Hollanders, that were free men, till finding them comming somewhat toward them, he acquainted them with the whole Conspiracie, and they affecting the Plot, offered the adventure of their lives in the businesse. Then very warily he undermined the English Renegado, which was the Gunner, and three more his

Associats, who at first seemed to retract. Last of all were brought in the Dutch Renegadoes, who were also in the Gunner roome, for alwayes there lay twelve there, five Christians, and seven English, and Dutch Turkes: so that when another motion had settled their resolutions, and Iohn Rawlins his constancie had put new life as it were in the matter, the foure Hollanders very honestly, according to their promise, sounded the Dutch Renegadoes, who with easie perswasion gave their consent to so brave an Enterprize; whereupon Iohn Rawlins, not caring whether the English Gunners would yeeld or no, resolved in the Captaines morning watch, to make the attempt. But you must understand that where the English slaves lay, there hung up alwayes foure or five Crowes of Iron, being still under the carriages of the Peeces, and when the time approached being very darke, because Iohn Rawlins would have his Crow of Iron ready as other things were, and other men prepared in their severall places, in taking it out of the carriage, by chance, it hit on the side of the Peece, making such a noyse, that the Souldiers hearing it awaked the Turkes, and bade them come downe: whereupon the Botesane of the Turkes descended with a Candle, and presently searched all the slaves places, making much adoe of the matter, but finding neyther Hatchet nor Hammer, nor any thing else to move suspicion of the Enterprize, more then the Crow of Iron, which lay slipped downe under the carriages of the Peeces, they went quietly up againe, and certified the Captaine what had chanced, who satisfied himselfe, that it was a common thing to have a Crow of Iron slip from its place. But by this occasion wee made stay of our attempt, yet were resolved to take another or a better oportunitie.

For we sayled still more North-ward, and Rawlins had more time to tamper with his Gunners, and the rest of the English Renegadoes, who very willingly, when they considered the matter, and perpended the reasons, gave way unto the Proiect, and with a kind of joy seemed to entertayne the motives: only they made a stop at the first on-set, who should begin the enterprize, which was no way fit for them to doe, because they were no slaves, but Renegadoes, and so had always beneficiall entertaynment amongst them. But when it is once put in practice, they would be sure not to faile them, but venture their lives for God and their Countrey. But once againe he is disappointed, and a suspitious accident brought him to recollect his spirits anew, and studie on the danger of the enterprize, and thus it was. After the Renegado Gunner, had protested secrecie by all that might induce a man to bestow some beliefe upon him, he presently went up the Scottle, but stayed not aloft a quarter of an houre; nay he came sooner down, & in the Gunner roome sate by Rawlins, who tarryed for him where he left him: he was no sooner placed, and entred into some conference, but there entred into the place a furious Turke, with his Knife drawne, and presented it to Rawlins his body, who verily supposed, he intended to kill him, as suspitious that the Gunner had discovered something, whereat Rawlins was much moved, and hastily asked what the matter meant, and whether he would kill him, observing his companion's countenance to change colour, whereby his suspitious heart, condemned him for a Traytor: but at more leisure he sware the contrary, and afterward proved faithfull and industrious in the enterprize. For the present, he answered Rawlins in this manner, "no Master, be not afraid, I thinke hee doth but iest." With that John Rawlins gave backe a little and drew out his Knife, stepping also to the Gunners sheath and taking out his, whereby he had two Knives to one, which when the Turke perceived, he threw downe his Knife, saying, hee did but iest with him. But when the Gunner perceived, Rawlins tooke it so ill, hee whispered something in his eare, that at last satisfied him, calling Heaven to witnesse, that he never spake word of the Enterprize, nor ever would, either to the preiudice of the businesse, or danger of his person. Notwithstanding, Rawlins kept the Knives in his sleeve all night, and was somewhat troubled, for that hee had made so many acquainted with an action of such importance; but the next day, when hee perceived the Coast cleere, and that there was no cause of further feare, hee somewhat comforted himselfe.

All this while, Rawlins drew the Captaine to lye for the Northerne Cape, assuring him, that thereby he should not misse a prize, which accordingly fell out, as a wish would have it: but his drift was in truth to draw him from any supply, or help of Turkes, if God should give way to their Enterprize, or successe to the victorie: yet for the present the sixth of February, being twelve leagues from the Cape, wee descryed a sayle, and presently took the advantage of the wind in chasing her, and at last fetched her up, making her strike all her sayles, whereby wee knew her to be a Barke belonging to Tor Bay, neere Dartmouth, that came from Auerure laden with Salt. Ere we had fully dispatched, it chanced to be foule weather, so that we could not, or at least would not make out our Boat, but caused the Master of the Barke to let downe his, and come aboord with his Company, being in the Barke but nine men, and one Boy; and so the Master leaving his Mate with two men in the ship, came himselfe with five men, and the boy unto us, whereupon our Turkish Captain sent ten Turkes to man her, amongst whom were two Dutch, and one English Renegado, who were of our confederacie, and acquainted with the businesse.

But when Rawlins saw this partition of his friends; before they could hoyst out their Boat for the Barke, he made meanes to speake with them, and told them plainly, that he would prosecute the matter eyther that night, or the next and therefore whatsoever came of it they should acquaint the English with his resolution, and make toward England, bearing up the helme, whiles the Turkes slept, and suspected no such matter: for by Gods grace in his first watch about mid-night, he would shew them a light, by which they might understand, that the Enterprize was begunne, or at least in a good forwardnesse for the execution: and so the Boat was let downe, and they came to the Barke of Tor Bay, where the Masters Mate beeing left (as before you have heard) apprehended quickly the matter, and heard the Discourse with amazement. But time was precious, and not to be spent in disputing, or casting of doubts, whether the Turkes that were with them were able to master them, or no, beeing seven to sixe, considering they had the helme of the ship, and the Turkes being Souldiers, and ignorant of Sea Affaires, could not discover, whether they went to Algier or no; or if they did, they resolved by Rawlins example to cut their throats, or cast them over-boord: and so I leave them to make use of the Renegadoes instructions, and returne to Rawlins againe.

The Master of the Barke of Tor Bay, and his Company were quickly searched, and as quickly pillaged, and dismissed to the libertie of the shippe, whereby Rawlins had leisure to entertayne him with the lamentable newes of their extremities, and in a word, of every particular which was befitting to the purpose: yea, he told him, that that night he should lose the sight of them, for they would make the helme for England and hee would that night and evermore pray for their good successe, and safe deliverance.

When the Master of the Barke of Tor Bay had heard him out, and that his company were partakers of his Storie, they became all silent, not eyther diffident of his Discourse, or afraid of the attempt, but resolved to assist him. Yet to shew himselfe an understanding man, hee demanded of Rawlins, what weapons he had, and in what manner he would execute the businesse: to which he answered, that he had Ropes, and Iron Hookes to make fast the Scottels, Gratings, and Cabbines, he had also in the Gunner roome two Curtleaxes, and the slaves had five Crowes of Iron before them: Besides, in the scuffling they made no question of some of the Souldiers weapons. Then for the manner, hee told them, they were sure of the Ordnance, the Gunner roome, and the Powder, and so blocking them up, would eyther kill them as they came downe, or turne the Ordnance against their Cabbins, or blow them into the Ayre by one Strategeme or other; and thus were they contented on all sides, and resolved to the Enterprize.

43

The next morning, being the seventh of February, the Prize of Tor Bay was not to bee seene or found, whereat the Captaine began to storme and sweare, commanding Rawlins to search the Seas up and downe for her, who bestowed all that day in the businesse, but to little purpose: whereupon when the humour was spent, the Captaine pacified himselfe, as conceiting he should sure find her at Algier: but by the permission of the Ruler of all actions, that Algier was England, and all his wickednesse frustrated: for Rawlins beeing now startled, lest hee should returne in this humour for the Streights, on the eight of February went downe into the hold, and finding a great deale of water below, told the Captaine of the same, adding, that it did not come to the Pumpe, which he said very politickly, that he might remove the Ordnance. For when the Captaine askt him the reason, he told him the ship was too farre after the head: then hee commanded to use the best meanes he could to bring her in order: "sure then," quoth Rawlins, "wee must quit our Cables, and bring foure Peeces of Ordnance after, and that would bring the water to the Pumpe;" which was presently put in practice, so the Peeces beeing usually made fast thwart the ship, we brought two of them with their mouthes right before the Binnacle, and because the Renegadoe Flemmings would not begin, it was thus concluded: that the ship having three Deckes, wee that did belong to the Gunner roome should bee all there, and breake up the lower Decke. The English slaves, who always lay in the middle Decks, should doe the like, and watch the Scuttels: Rawlins himselfe prevayled with the Gunner, for so much Powder, as should prime the Peeces, and so told them all there was no better watch-word, nor meanes to begin, then upon the report of the Peece to make a cry and shout, for God, and King Iames, and Saint George for England!

When all things were prepared, and every man resolved, as knowing what hee had to doe, and the houre when it should happen, to be two in the afternoone, Rawlins advised the Master Gunner to speake to the Captaine, that the Souldiers might attend on the Poope, which would bring the ship after: to which the Captaine was very willing, and upon the Gunners information, the Souldiers gat themselves to the Poope, to the number of twentie, and five or sixe went into the Captaines Cabbin, where always lay divers Curtleaxes, and some Targets, and so wee fell to worke to pumpe the water, and carryed the matter fairely till the next day, which was spent as the former, being the ninth of February, and as God must have the prayse, the triumph of our victorie.

For by that time all things were prepared, and the Souldiers got upon the Poope as the day before: to avoid suspition, all that did belong to the Gunner-roome went downe, and the slaves in the middle decke attended their business, so that we could cast up our account in this manner. First, nine English slaves, besides Iohn Rawlins: five of the Tor Bay men, and one boy, foure English Renegadoes, and two French, foure Hollanders: in all four and twenty and a boy: so that lifting up our hearts and hands to God for the successe of the businesse, we were wonderfully incouraged; and setled our selves, till the report of the peece gave us warning of the enterprise. Now, you must consider, that in this company were two of Rawlins men, Iames Roe, and Iohn Davies, whom he brought out of England, and whom the fortune of the Sea brought into the same predicament with their Master. These were imployed about noone (being as I said, the ninth of February) to prepare their matches, while all the Turkes or at least most of them stood on the Poope, to weigh down the ship as it were, to bring the water forward to the Pumpe: the one brought his match lighted betweene two spoons, the other brought his in a little peece of a Can: and so in the name of God, the Turkes and Moores being placed as you have heard, and five and forty in number, and Rawlins having proined the Tuch-holes, Iames Roe gave fire to one of the peeces, about two of the clocke in the afternoone, and the confederates upon the warning, shouted most cheerefully: the report of the peece did teare and breake down all the Binnacle, and compasses, and the noise of the slaves made all the Souldiers amased at the matter, till seeing the quarter of the ship rent, and feeling the whole body to shake under them: understanding the ship was surprised, and the attempt tended to their utter destruction, never Beare robbed of her whelpes was so fell and mad: For they not onely cald us dogs, and cried out, Usance de Lamair, which is as much to say, the Fortune of the wars: but attempted to teare up the planckes, setting a worke hammers, hatchets, knives, the oares of the Boate, the Boat-hooke, their curtleaxes, and what else came to hand, besides stones and brickes in the Cooke-roome, all which they threw amongst us, attempting still and still to breake and rip up the hatches, and boords of the steering, not desisting from their former execrations, and horrible blasphemies and revilings.

When Iohn Rawlins perceived them so violent, and understood how the slaves had cleared the deckes of all the Turkes and Moores beneath, he set a guard upon the Powder, and charged their owne Muskets against them, killing them from divers scout-holes, both before and behind, and so lessened their number, to the ioy of all our hearts, whereupon they cried out, and called for the Pilot, and so Rawlins, with some to guard him, went to them, and understood them by their kneeling, that they cried for mercy, and to have their lives saved, and they would come downe, which he bade

45

them doe, and so they were taken one by one, and bound, yea killed with their owne Curtleaxes; which when the rest perceived, they called us English dogs, and reviled us with many opprobrious termes, some leaping over-boord, crying, it was the chance of war; some were manacled, and so throwne over-boord, and some were slaine and mangled with the Curtleaxes, till the ship was well cleared, and our selves assured of the victory.

At the first report of our Peece, and hurliburly in the decks, the Captaine was a writing in his Cabbin, and hearing the noyse, thought it some strange accident, and so came out with his Curtleaxe in his hand, presuming by his authority to pacifie the mischiefe: But when hee cast his eyes upon us, and saw that we were like to surprise the ship, he threw downe his Curtleaxe, and begged us to save his life, intimating unto Rawlins, how he had redeemed him from Villa-Rise, and ever since admitted him to place of command in the ship, besides honest usage in the whole course of the Voyage. All which Rawlins confessed, and at last condescended to mercy, and brought the Captaine and five more into England. The Captain was called Ramtham-Rise, but his Christen name, Henry Chandler, and as they say, was a Chandler's sonne in Southwarke. Iohn Goodale, was also an English Turke. Richard Clarke, in Turkish, Iafar; George Cooke, Ramdam; Iohn Browne, Mamme; William Winter, Mustapha; besides all the slaves and Hollanders, with other Renegadoes, who were willing to be reconciled to their true Saviour, as being formerly seduced with the hopes of riches, honour, preferment, and such like devillish baits, to catch the soules of mortall men, and entangle frailty in the fetters of horrible abuses, and imposturing deceit.

When all was done, and the ship cleared of the dead bodies, Iohn Rawlins assembled his men together, and with one consent gave the praise unto God, using the accustomed service on ship-boord, and for want of bookes lifted up their voyces to God, as he put into their hearts, or renewed their memories: then did they sing a Psalme, and last of all, embraced one another for playing the men in such a Deliverance, whereby our feare was turned into joy, and trembling hearts exhillirated, that we had escaped such inevitable dangers, and especially the slavery and terror of bondage, worse than death it selfe. The same night we washed our ship, put every thing in as good order as we could, repaired the broken quarter, set up the Binnacle, and bore up the Helme for England, where by Gods grace and good guiding, we arrived at Plimmoth, the thirteenth of February, and were welcommed like the recovery of the lost sheepe, or as you read of a loving mother, that runneth with embraces to entertaine her sonne from a long Voyage and escape of many dangers.

46

Not long after we understood of our confederats, that returned home in the Barke of Torbay, that they arrived in Pensance in Corne-wall the eleventh of February: and if any aske after their deliverance, considering there were ten Turkes sent to man her, I will tell you that too: the next day after they lost us, as you have heard and that the three Renegadoes had acquainted the Masters Mate, and the two English in her with Rawlins determination, and that they themselves would be true to them, and assist them in any enterprise: then if the worst came, there were but seven to sixe: but as it fell out, they had a more easie passage, then turmoile, or man-slaughter. For they made the Turkes beleeve, the wind was come faire, and that they were sayling to Algier, till they came within sight of England, which one of them amongst the rest discovered, saying plainely, that that land was not like Cape Vincent; "yes faith," said he, that was at the Helme, "and you will be contented, and goe downe into the hold, and trim the salt over to wind-ward, whereby the ship may beare full saile, you shall know and see more to morrow": Whereupon five of them went downe very orderly, the Renegadoes faining themselves asleep, who presently start up, and with the helpe of the two English, nailed downe the hatches, whereat the principall amongst them much repined, and began to grow into choller and rage, had it not quickly beene suppressed. For one of them stepped to him, and dasht out his braines, and threw him over-boord: the rest were brought to Excester, and either to be arraigned, according to the punishment of delinquents in such a kind, or disposed of, as the King and Counsell shall thinke meet and this is the story of this deliverance, and end of Iohn Rawlins Voyage. The Actors in this Comick Tragedie are most of them alive; The Turkes are in prison; the ship is to be seene, and Rawlins himselfe dare justifie the matter.

THE DAUGHTER OF THE GREAT MOGUL[6]

Daniel Defoe

In this time I pursued my voyage, coasted the whole Malabar shore, and met with no purchase but a great Portugal East India ship, which I chased into Goa, where she got out of my reach. I took several small vessels and barks, but little of value in them, till I entered the great Bay of Bengal, when I began to look about me with more expectation of success, though without prospect of what happened.

I cruised here about two months, finding nothing worth while; so I stood away to a port on the north point of the isle of Sumatra, where I made no stay; for here I got news that two large ships belonging to the Great Mogul were expected to cross the bay from Hoogly, in the Ganges, to the country of the King of Pegu, being to carry the granddaughter of the Great Mogul to Pegu, who was to be married to the king of that country, with all her retinue, jewels, and wealth.

This was a booty worth watching for, though it had been some months longer; so I resolved that we would go and cruise off Point Negaris, on the east side of the bay, near Diamond Isle; and here we plied off and on for three weeks, and began to despair of success; but the knowledge of the booty we expected spurred us on, and we waited with great patience, for we knew the prize would be immensely rich.

At length we spied three ships coming right up to us with the wind. We could easily see they were not Europeans by their sails, and began to prepare ourselves for a prize, not for a fight; but were a little disappointed when we found the first ship full of guns and full of soldiers, and in condition, had she been managed by English sailors, to have fought two such ships as ours were. However, we resolved to attack her if she had been full of devils as she was full of men.

Accordingly, when we came near them, we fired a gun with shot as a challenge. They fired again immediately three or four guns, but fired them so confusedly that we could easily see they did not understand their business; when we considered how to lay them on board, and so to come thwart them, if we could; but falling, for want of wind, open to them, we gave them a fair broadside. We could

---

[6] From The King of the Pirates.

48

easily see, by the confusion that was on board, that they were frightened out of their wits; they fired here a gun and there a gun, and some on that side that was from us, as well as those that were next to us. The next thing we did was to lay them on board, which we did presently, and then gave them a volley of our small shot, which, as they stood so thick, killed a great many of them, and made all the rest run down under their hatches, crying out like creatures bewitched. In a word, we presently took the ship, and having secured her men, we chased the other two. One was chiefly filled with women, and the other with lumber. Upon the whole, as the granddaughter of the Great Mogul was our prize in the first ship, so in the second was her women, or, in a word, her household, her eunuchs, all the necessaries of her wardrobe, of her stables, and of her kitchen; and in the last, great quantities of household stuff, and things less costly, though not less useful.

But the first was the main prize. When my men had entered and mastered the ship, one of our lieutenants called for me, and accordingly I jumped on board. He told me he thought nobody but I ought to go into the great cabin, or, at least, nobody should go there before me; for that the lady herself and all her attendance was there, and he feared the men were so heated they would murder them all, or do worse.

I immediately went to the great cabin door, taking the lieutenant that called me along with me, and caused the cabin door to be opened. But such a sight of glory and misery was never seen by buccaneer before. The queen (for such she was to have been) was all in gold and silver, but frightened and crying, and, at the sight of me, she appeared trembling, and just as if she was going to die. She sat on the side of a kind of a bed like a couch, with no canopy over it, or any covering; only made to lie down upon. She was, in a manner, covered with diamonds, and I, like a true pirate, soon let her see that I had more mind to the jewels than to the lady.

However, before I touched her, I ordered the lieutenant to place a guard at the cabin door, and fastening the door, shut us both in, which he did. The lady was young, and, I suppose, in their country esteem, very handsome, but she was not very much so in my thoughts. At first, her fright, and the danger she thought she was in of being killed, taught her to do everything that she thought might interpose between her and danger, and that was to take off her jewels as fast as she could, and give them to me; and I, without any great compliment, took them as fast as she gave them me, and put them into my pocket, taking no great notice of them or of her, which frighted her worse than all the rest, and she said something which I could not understand. However, two of the other ladies

49

came, all crying, and kneeled down to me with their hands lifted up. What they meant, I knew not at first; but by their gestures and pointings I found at last it was to beg the young queen's life, and that I would not kill her.

When the three ladies kneeled down to me, and as soon as I understood what it was for, I let them know I would not hurt the queen, nor let any one else hurt her, but that she must give me all her jewels and money. Upon this they acquainted her that I would save her life; and no sooner had they assured her of that but she got up smiling, and went to a fine Indian cabinet, and opened a private drawer, from whence she took another little thing full of little square drawers and holes. This she brings to me in her hand, and offered to kneel down to give it me. This innocent usage began to rouse some good-nature in me (though I never had much), and I would not let her kneel; but sitting down myself on the side of her couch or bed, made a motion to her to sit down too. But here she was frightened again, it seems, at what I had no thought of. But as I did not offer anything of that kind, only made her sit down by me, they began all to be easier after some time, and she gave me the little box or casket, I know not what to call it, but it was full of invaluable jewels. I have them still in my keeping, and wish they were safe in England; for I doubt not but some of them are fit to be placed on the king's crown.

Being master of this treasure, I was very willing to be good-humored to the persons; so I went out of the cabin, and caused the women to be left alone, causing the guard to be kept still, that they might receive no more injury than I would do them myself.

After I had been out of the cabin some time, a slave of the women's came to me, and made sign to me that the queen would speak with me again. I made signs back that I would come and dine with her majesty; and accordingly I ordered that her servants should prepare her dinner, and carry it in, and then call me. They provided her repast after the usual manner, and when she saw it brought in she appeared pleased, and more when she saw me come in after it; for she was exceedingly pleased that I had caused a guard to keep the rest of my men from her; and she had, it seems, been told how rude they had been to some of the women that belonged to her.

When I came in, she rose up, and paid me such respect as I did not well know how to receive, and not in the least how to return. If she had understood English, I could have said plainly, and in good rough words, "Madam, be easy; we are rude, rough-hewn fellows, but none of our men should hurt you, or touch you; I will be your guard and protection; we are for money indeed, and we shall

50

take what you have, but we will do you no other harm." But as I could not talk thus to her, I scarce knew what to say; but I sat down, and made signs to have her sit down and eat, which she did, but with so much ceremony that I did not know well what to do with it.

After we had eaten, she rose up again, and drinking some water out of a china cup, sat her down on the side of the couch as before. When she saw I had done eating, she went then to another cabinet, and pulling out a drawer, she brought it to me; it was full of small pieces of gold coin of Pegu, about as big as an English half-guinea, and I think there were three thousand of them. She opened several other drawers, and showed me the wealth that was in them, and then gave me the key of the whole.

We had revelled thus all day, and part of the next day, in a bottomless sea of riches, when my lieutenant began to tell me, we must consider what to do with our prisoners and the ships, for that there was no subsisting in that manner. Upon this we called a short council, and concluded to carry the great ship away with us, but to put all the prisoners—queen, ladies, and all the rest—into the lesser vessels, and let them go; and so far was I from ravishing this lady, as I hear is reported of me, that though I might rifle her of everything else, yet, I assure you, I let her go untouched for me, or, as I am satisfied, for any one of my men; nay, when we dismissed them, we gave her leave to take a great many things of value with her, which she would have been plundered of if I had not been so careful of her.

We had now wealth enough not only to make us rich, but almost to have made a nation rich; and to tell you the truth, considering the costly things we took here, which we did not know the value of, and besides gold and silver and jewels,—I say, we never knew how rich we were; besides which we had a great quantity of bales of goods, as well calicoes as wrought silks, which, being for sale, were perhaps as a cargo of goods to answer the bills which might be drawn upon them for the account of the bride's portion; all which fell into our hands, with a great sum in silver coin, too big to talk of among Englishmen, especially while I am living, for reasons which I may give you hereafter.

BARBAROSSA—KING OF THE CORSAIRS[7]

E. Hamilton Currey, R.N.

At the coming of spring Barbarossa was at sea again with thirty-two ships ready for any eventuality, his crews aflame with ardor for revenge against those by whom they had been so roughly handled. He chose for the scene of operations a place on the coast of Majorca some fifteen miles from Palma; from here he commanded the route of the Spaniards from their country to the African coast, and it was against this nation that he felt a great bitterness owing to recent events. Eagerly did the corsair and his men watch for the Spanish ships, the heavier vessels lying at anchor, but the light, swift galleys ranging and questing afar so that none might be missed. Very soon the vigilance of the Moslems was rewarded by the capture of a number of vessels, sent by Bernard de Mendoza laden with Turkish and Moorish slaves, destined to be utilized as rowers in the Spanish galleys. These men were hailed as a welcome reinforcement, and joyfully joined the forces of Kheyr-ed-Din when he moved on Minorca, captured the castle by a surprise assault, raided the surrounding country, and captured five thousand seven hundred Christians, amongst whom were eight hundred men who had been wounded in the attack on Tunis—all these unfortunates were sent to refill the bagnio of Algiers.

This private war of revenge was, however, destined soon to come to an end, as Soliman the Magnificent in this year became involved in disputes with the Venetian Republic, and recalled "that veritable man of the sea," as Barbarossa had been described by Ibrahim, to Constantinople.

In this city by the sea there had taken place a tragedy which, although it only involved the death of a single man, was nevertheless far-reaching in its consequences; for the man was none other than that great statesman Ibrahim, Grand Vizier, and the only trusted counsellor of the Padishah. He who had been originally a slave had risen step by step in the favor of his master until he arrived at the giddy eminence which he occupied at the time of his death. It is a somewhat curious commentary on the essentially democratic status of an autocracy that a man could thus rise to a position second only to that of the autocrat himself; and, in all probability, wielding quite as much power.

---

[7] From Sea Wolves of the Mediterranean.

Ibrahim had for years been treated by Soliman more as a brother than as a dependent, which, in spite of his Grand Viziership, he was in fact. They lived in the very closest communion, taking their meals together, and even sleeping in the same room, Soliman, a man of high intelligence himself, and a ruler who kept in touch with all the happenings which arose in his immense dominions, desiring always to have at hand the man whom he loved; from whom, with his amazing grip of political problems and endless fertility of resource, he was certain of sympathy and sound advice. But in an oriental despotism there are other forces at work besides those of la haute politique, and Ibrahim had one deadly enemy who was sworn to compass his destruction. The Sultana Roxalana was the light of the harem of the Grand Turk. This supremely beautiful woman, originally a Russian slave, was the object of the most passionate devotion on the part of Soliman; but she was as ambitious as she was lovely, and brooked no rival in the affections of Soliman, be that person man, woman, or child. In her hands the master of millions, the despot whose nod was death, became a submissive slave; the undisciplined passions of this headstrong woman swept aside from her path all those whom she suspected of sharing her influence, in no matter how remote a fashion. At her dictation had Soliman caused to be murdered his son Mustafa, a youth of the brightest promise, because, in his intelligence and his winning ways he threatened to eclipse Selim, the son of Roxalana herself.

This woman possessed a strong natural intelligence, albeit she was totally uneducated; she saw and knew that Ibrahim was all-powerful with her lover, and this roused her jealousy to fever-heat. She was not possessed of a cool judgment, which would have told her that Ibrahim was a statesman dealing with the external affairs of the Sublime Porte, and that with her and with her affairs he neither desired, nor had he the power, to interfere. What, however, the Sultana did know was that in these same affairs of State her opinion was dust in the balance when weighed against that of the Grand Vizier.

Soliman had that true attribute of supreme greatness, the unerring aptitude for the choice of the right man. He had picked out Ibrahim from among his immense entourage, and never once had he regretted his choice. As time went on and the intellect and power of the man became more and more revealed to his master, that sovereign left in his hands even such matters as despots are apt to guard most jealously. We have seen how, in spite of the murmurings of the whole of his capital, and the almost insubordinate attitude of his navy, he had persevered in the appointment of Kheyr-ed-Din

Barbarossa, because the judgment of Ibrahim was in favor of its being carried out. This, to Roxalana, was gall and wormwood; well she knew that, as long as the Grand Vizier lived, her sovereignty was at best but a divided one. There was a point at which her blandishments stopped short; this was when she found that her opinion did not coincide with that of the minister. She was, as we have seen in the instance of her son, not a woman to stick at trifles, and she decided that Ibrahim must die.

There could be no hole-and-corner business about this; he must die, and when his murder had been accomplished she would boldly avow to her lover what she had done and take the consequences, believing in her power over him to come scatheless out of the adventure. In those days, when human life was so cheap, she might have asked for the death of almost any one, and her whim would have been gratified by a lover who had not hesitated to put to death his own son at her dictation. But with Ibrahim it was another matter; he was the familiar of the Sultan, his alter ego in fact. It says much for the nerve of the Sultana that she dared so greatly on this memorable and lamentable occasion.

On March 5th, 1536, Ibrahim went to the royal seraglio, and, following his ancient custom, was admitted to the table of his master, sleeping after the meal at his side. At least so it was supposed, but none knew save those engaged in the murder what passed on that fatal night; the next day his dead body lay in the house of the Sultan.

Across the floor of jasper, in that palace which was a fitting residence for one rightly known as "The Magnificent," the blood of Ibrahim flowed to the feet of Roxalana. The disordered clothing, the terrible expression of the face of the dead man, the gaping wounds which he had received, bore witness that there had taken place a grim struggle before that iron frame and splendid intellect had been leveled with the dust. This much leaked out afterwards, as such things will leak out, and then the Sultana took Soliman into her chamber and gazed up into his eyes. The man was stunned by the immensity of the calamity which had befallen him and his kingdom, but his manhood availed him not against the wiles of this Circe. Ibrahim had been foully done to death in his own palace, and this woman clinging so lovingly round his neck now was the murderess. The heart's blood of his best friend was coagulating on the threshold of his own apartment when he forgave her by whom his murder had been accomplished. This was the vengeance of Roxalana, and who shall say that it was not complete?

The Ottoman Empire was the poorer by the loss of its greatest man, the jealousy of the Sultana was assuaged, the despot who had permitted this unavenged murder was still on the throne, thrall to the woman who had first murdered his son and then his friend and minister. But the deed carried with it the evil consequences which were only too likely to occur when so capable a head of the State was removed at so critical a time. Renewed strife was in the air, and endless squabbles between Venice and the Porte were taking place. With these we have no concern, but, in addition to other complaints, there were loud and continuous ones concerning the corsairs. Venice, "The Bride of the Sea," had neither rest nor peace; the pirates swarmed in Corfu, in Zante, in Candia, in Cephalonia, and the plunder and murder of the subjects of the Republic was the theme of the perpetual representations to the Sultan. The balance of advantage in this guerilla warfare was with the corsairs until Girolame Canale, a Venetian captain, seized one of the Moslem leaders known as "The Young Moor of Alexandria." The victory of Canale was somewhat an important one as he captured the galley of "The Young Moor" and four others; two more were sunk, and three hundred Janissaries and one thousand slaves fell into the hands of the Venetian commander. There being an absence of nice feeling on the part of the Venetians, the Janissaries were at once beheaded to a man.

The whole story is an illustration of the extraordinary relations existing among the Mediterranean States at this time. Soliman the Magnificent, Sultan of Turkey, had lent three hundred of his Janissaries, his own picked troops, to assist the corsairs in their depredations on Venetian commerce. Having done this, and the Janissaries having been caught and summarily and rightly put to death as pirates, the Sultan, as soon as he heard of what had occurred, sent an ambassador, one Yonis Bey, to Venice to demand satisfaction for the insult passed upon him by the beheading of his own soldiers turned pirates. The conclusion of the affair was that the Venetians released "The Young Moor of Alexandria" as soon as he was cured of the eight wounds which he had received in the conflict, and sent him back to Africa with such of his galleys as were left. There was one rather comical incident in connection with this affair, which was that when Yonis Bey was on his way from Constantinople to Venice he was chased by a Venetian fleet, under the command of the Count Grandenico, and driven ashore. The Count was profuse in his apologies when he discovered that he had been chasing a live ambassador; but the occurrence so exasperated Soliman that he increased his demands in consequence.

Barbarossa, who had spent his time harrying the Spaniards at sea ever since the fall of Tunis, was shortly to appear on the scene again. He received orders from the Sultan, and came as fast as a favoring wind would bring him. Kheyr-ed-Din had been doing well in the matter of slaves and plunder, but he knew that, with the backing of the Grand Turk, he would once again be in command of a fleet in which he might repeat his triumph of past years, and prove himself once more the indispensable "man of the sea."

Soon after his arrival his ambitions were gratified, and he found himself with a fleet of one hundred ships. Since the death of Ibrahim, and the incident which terminated with the dispatch of Yonis Bey to Venice, the relations between the Grand Turk and the Venetian Republic had become steadily worse, and at last the Sultan declared war. On May 17th, 1537, Soliman, accompanied by his two sons, Selim and Mohammed, left Constantinople. With the campaign conducted by the Sultan we are not concerned here; it was directed against the Ionian Islands, which had been in the possession of Venice since 1401. On August 18th Soliman laid siege to Corfu, and was disastrously beaten, re-embarking his men on September 7th, after losing thousands in a fruitless attack on the fortress. He returned to Constantinople utterly discomfited. It was the seventh campaign which the Sultan had conducted in person, but the first in which the ever-faithful Ibrahim had not been by his side.

This defeat at the hands of the Venetians was not, however, the only humiliation which he was destined to experience in this disastrous year; for once again Doria, that scourge of the Moslem, was loose upon the seas, and was making his presence felt in the immediate neighborhood of Corfu, where the Turks had been defeated. On July 17th Andrea had left the port of Messina with twenty-five galleys, had captured ten richly laden Turkish ships, gutted and burned them. Kheyr-ed-Din was at sea at the time, but the great rivals were not destined to meet on this occasion. Instead of Barbarossa, Andrea fell in with Ali-Chabelli, the lieutenant of Sandjak Bey of Gallipoli. On July 22nd the Genoese admiral and the Turkish commander from the Dardanelles met to the southward of Corfu, off the small island of Paxo, and a smart action ensued. It ended in the defeat of Ali-Chabelli, whose galleys were captured and towed by Doria into Paxo. That veteran fighter was himself in the thickest of the fray, and, conspicuous in his crimson doublet, had been an object of attention to the marksmen of Chabelli during the entire action. In spite of the receipt of a severe wound in the knee, the admiral refused to go below until victory was assured. He was surrounded at this time by a devoted band of nobles sworn to defend the person of their admiral or to die in his defense. His portrait has been sketched for us at this time by the Dominican Friar, Padre Alberto Guglielmotto, author of "La guerra dei Pirati e la marina Pontifica dal 1500 al 1560." The description runs thus: "Andrea Doria was of lofty stature, his face oval in shape, forehead broad and commanding, his neck was powerful, his hair short, his beard long and fan-shaped, his lips were thin, his eyes bright and piercing."

Once again had he defeated an officer of the Grand Turk; and it may be remarked that Ibrahim was probably quite right in the estimation, or rather in the lack of estimation, in which he held the sea-officers of his master, as they seem to have been deficient in every quality save that of personal valor, and in their encounters with Doria and the knights were almost invariably worsted. For the sake of Islam, for the prestige of the Moslem arms at sea, it was time that Barbarossa should take matters in hand once more.

The autumn of this year 1537 proved that the old Sea-wolf had lost none of his cunning, that his followers were as terrible as ever. What did it seem to matter that Venetian and Catalan, Genoese and Frenchman, Andalusian and the dwellers in the Archipelago, were all banded together in league against this common foe? Did not the redoubtable Andrea range the seas in vain, and were not all the efforts of the Knights of Saint John futile, when the son of the renegado from Mitylene and his Christian wife put forth from the Golden Horn? What was the magic of this man, it was asked despairingly, that none seemed able to prevail against him? Had it not been currently reported that Carlos Quinto, the great Emperor, had driven him forth from Tunis a hunted fugitive, broken and penniless, with never a galley left, without one ducat in his pocket? Was he so different, then, from all the rest of mankind that his followers would stick to him in evil report as well as in the height of his prosperity? Men swore and women crossed themselves at the mention of his name.

"Terrible as an army with banners," indeed, was Kheyr-ed-Din in this eventful summer: things had gone badly with the crescent flag, the Padishah was unapproachable in his palace, brooding perchance on that "might have been" had he not sold his honor and the life of his only friend to gratify the malice of a she-devil; those in attendance on the Sultan trembled, for the humor of the despot was black indeed.

But "the veritable man of the sea" was in some sort to console him for that which he had lost; as never in his own history—and there was none else with which it could be compared—had the Corsair King made so fruitful a raid. He ravaged the coasts of the Adriatic and the islands of the Archipelago, sweeping in slaves by the thousand, and by the end of the year he had collected eighteen thousand in the arsenal at Stamboul. Great was the jubilation in

Constantinople when the Admiralissimo himself returned from his last expedition against the infidel; stilled were the voices which hinted disaffection—who among them all could bring back four hundred thousand pieces of gold? What mariner could offer to the Grand Turk such varied and magnificent presents?

Upon his arrival Barbarossa asked permission to kiss the threshold of the palace of the Sultan, which boon being graciously accorded to him, he made his triumphal entry. Two hundred captives clad in scarlet robes carried cups of gold and flasks of silver; behind them came thirty others, each staggering under an enormous purse of sequins; yet another two hundred brought collars of precious stones or bales of the choicest goods; and a further two hundred were laden with sacks of small coin. Certainly if Soliman the Magnificent had lost a Grand Vizier he had succeeded in finding an admiral!

All through the earlier months of 1538 the dockyards of Constantinople hummed with a furious activity, for Soliman had decreed that the maritime campaign of this year was to begin with no less than one hundred and fifty ships. His admiral, however, did not agree with this decision; to the Viziers he raged and stormed. "Listen," he said, "O men of the land who understand naught of the happenings of the sea. By this time Saleh-Reis must have quitted Alexandria convoying to the Bosphorus twenty sail filled with the richest merchandise; should he fall in with the accursed Genoese, Doria, where then will be Saleh-Reis and his galleys and his convoy? I will tell you: the ships in Genoa, the galleys burned, Saleh-Reis and all his mariners chained to the rowers' bench."

The Viziers trembled as men did when Barbarossa stormed and turned upon them those terrible eyes which knew neither fear nor pity. "We be but men," they answered, "and our lord the Sultan has so ordained it."

"I have forty galleys," replied the corsair; "you have forty more. With these I will take the sea; but, mark you," he continued, softening somewhat, "you do right to fear the displeasure of the Sultan, and I also have no wish to encounter it; but vessels raised and equipped in a hurry will be of small use to me. In the name of Allah the compassionate and his holy Prophet give me my eighty galleys and let me go."

In Kheyr-ed-Din Barbarossa sound strategical instinct went hand in hand with the desperate valor of the corsair. To dally in the Golden Horn while so rich a prey was at sea to be picked up by his Christian foes was altogether opposed to his instincts: never to throw away a chance in the game of life had ever been his guiding principle.

Soliman, great man as he undoubtedly was, had not the adamantine hardness of character which enabled his admiral to risk all on the hazards of the moment; or possibly the Grand Turk was deficient in that clearness of strategical instinct which never in any circumstances foregoes a present advantage for something which may turn out well in a problematical future. Soliman, sore, sullen, and unapproachable, dwelt in his palace brooding over the misfortunes which had been his lot since the death of Ibrahim. Barbarossa, who so recently had lost practically all that he possessed, and who had reached an age at which most men have no hopes for the future, was as clear in intellect, as undaunted in spirit, as if he had been half a century younger: to be even once more with those by whom he had been defeated and dispossessed was the only thing now in his mind. The capture of Saleh-Reis and his convoy would be a triumph of which he could not bear to think. Further, it would add to the demoralization of the sea forces of the Sultan, which were sadly in need of some striking success after the defeats which had so recently been their portion. The Sultan had decided that one hundred and fifty ships were necessary; his admiral thought otherwise. There was too much at stake for him to dally at Constantinople; his fiery energy swept all before it, and in the end he had his way. On June 7th, 1538, he finally triumphed over the hesitations of the Viziers and put to sea with eighty sail.

The Sultan, from his kiosk, the windows of which opened on the Bosphorus, counted the ships.

"Only eighty sail; is that all?" he asked.

The trembling Viziers prostrated themselves before him.

"O our Lord, the Padishah," they cried, "Saleh-Reis comes from Alexandria with a rich convoy; somewhere lurking is Andrea Doria, the accursed; it was necessary, O Magnificent, to send succor."

There was a pause, in which the hearts of men beat as do those who know not but that the next moment may be their last on earth.

The Sultan stared from his window at the retreating ships in a silence like the silence of the grave. At last he turned:

"So be it," he answered briefly; "but see to it that reinforcements do not lag upon the road."

If there had been activity in the dockyards before it was as nothing to the strenuous work that was to be done henceforward.

Before starting on this expedition Kheyr-ed-Din had made an innovation in the manning of some of the most powerful of his galleys, which was of the utmost importance, and which was to add enormously to the success of his future maritime enterprises. The custom had always been that the Ottoman galleys had been rowed by Christians, captured and enslaved; of course the converse was true in the galleys of their foes. There were, for the size of the vessels, an enormous number of men carried in the galleys of the sixteenth century, and an average craft of this description would have on board some four hundred men; of these, however, the proportion would be two hundred and fifty slaves to one hundred and fifty fighting men. That which Kheyr-ed-Din now insisted upon was that a certain proportion of his most powerful units should be rowed by Moslem fighting men, so that on the day of battle the oarsmen could join in the fray instead of remaining chained to their benches, as was the custom with the slaves. It is, however, an extraordinary testimony to the influence which the corsair had attained in Constantinople that he had been able to effect this change in the composition of some of his crews; it must have been done with the active coöperation of the Sultan, as no authority less potent than that of the sovereign himself could have induced free men to undertake the terrible toil of rower in a galley. This was reserved for the unfortunate slave on either side owing to the intolerable hardship of the life, and results, in the pace at which a galley proceeded through the water, were usually obtained by an unsparing use of the lash on the naked bodies of the rowers.

This human material was used up in the most prodigal manner possible, as those in command had not the inducement of treating the rowers well, from that economic standpoint which causes a man to so use his beast of burden as to get the best work from him. In the galley, when a slave would row no more he was flung overboard and another was put in his place.

The admiral, however, even when backed by the Padishah, could not man a large fleet of galleys with Moslem rowers, and, as there was a shortage in the matter of propelling power, his first business was to collect slaves, and for this purpose he visited the islands of the Archipelago. The lot of the unhappy inhabitants of these was indeed a hard one. They were nearer to the seat of the Moslem power than any other Christians; they were in those days totally unable to resist an attack in force, and in consequence were swept off in their thousands.

Seven islands cover the entrance to the Gulf of Volo. The nearest to the coast is Skiathos, which is also the most important; it was defended by a castle built upon a rock. This castle was attacked by Barbarossa, who bombarded it for six days, carried it by assault, and massacred the garrison. He spared the lives of the inhabitants of the island, and by this means secured three thousand four hundred rowers for his galleys. He had to provide motor-power for the reinforcements which he expected. In July he was reinforced from Constantinople by ninety galleys, while from Egypt came Saleh-Reis, who had succeeded in avoiding the terrible Doria, with twenty more; the fleet was thus complete.

MORGAN AT PUERTO BELLO[8]

John Esquemeling

Some may think that the French having deserted Captain Morgan, the English alone could not have sufficient courage to attempt such great actions as before. But Captain Morgan, who always communicated vigor with his words, infused such spirit into his men, as put them instantly upon new designs. He inspired them with the belief that the sole execution of his orders would be a certain means of obtaining great riches, which so influenced their minds, that with inimitable courage they all resolved to follow him, as did also a certain pirate of Campechy, on this occasion joined with Captain Morgan, to seek new fortunes under his conduct. Thus Captain Morgan in a few days gathered a fleet of nine sail, either ships or great boats, wherein he had four hundred and sixty military men.

All things being ready, they put forth to sea, Captain Morgan imparting his design to nobody at present; he only told them on several occasions, that he doubted not to make a good fortune by that voyage, if strange occurrences happened not. They steered towards the continent, where they arrived in a few days near Costa Rica, all their fleet safe. No sooner had they discovered land but Captain Morgan declared his intentions to the captains, and presently after to the company. He told them he intended to plunder Puerto Bello by night, being resolved to put the whole city to the sack: and to encourage them he added, this enterprise could not fail, seeing he had kept it secret, without revealing it to anybody, whereby they could not have notice of his coming. To this proposition some answered, they had not a sufficient number of men to assault so strong and great a city. But Captain Morgan replied, "If our number is small, our hearts are great; and the fewer persons we are, the more union and better shares we shall have in the spoil." Hereupon, being stimulated with the hope of those vast riches they promised themselves from their success, they unanimously agreed to that design. Now, that my reader may better comprehend the boldness of this exploit, it may be necessary to say something beforehand of the city of Puerto Bello.

This city is in the province of Costa Rica, 10 deg. north latitude, fourteen leagues from the gulf of Darien, and eight

[8] From The Buccaneers of America.

62

westwards from the port called Nombre de Dios. It is judged the strongest place the king of Spain possesses in all the West Indies, except Havanna and Carthagena. Here are two castles almost impregnable, that defend the city, situate at the entry of the port, so that no ship or boat can pass without permission. The garrison consists of three hundred soldiers, and the town is inhabited by four hundred families. The merchants dwell not here, but only reside a while, when the galleons come from or go for Spain, by reason of the unhealthiness of the air, occasioned by vapors from the mountains; so that though their chief warehouses are at Puerto Bello, their habitations are at Panama, whence they bring the plate upon mules when the fair begins, and when the ships belonging to the company of negroes arrive to sell slaves.

Captain Morgan, who knew very well all the avenues of this city and the neighboring coasts, arrived in the evening with his men at Puerto de Naos, ten leagues to the west of Puerto Bello. Being come hither, they sailed up the river to another harbor called Puerto Pontin, where they anchored: here they put themselves into boats and canoes, leaving in the ships only a few men to bring them next day to the port. About midnight they came to a place called Estera longa Lemos, where they all went on shore and marched by land to the first posts of the city. They had in their company an Englishman, formerly a prisoner in those parts, who now served them for a guide. To him and three or four more they gave commission to take the sentinel, if possible, or kill him on the place: but they seized him so cunningly, as he had no time to give warning with his musket, or make any noise, and brought him, with his hands bound, to Captain Morgan, who asked him how things went in the city, and what forces they had; with other circumstances he desired to know. After every question they made him a thousand menaces to kill him, if he declared not the truth. Then they advanced to the city, carrying the said sentinel bound before them: having marched about a quarter of a league, they came to the castle near the city, which presently they closely surrounded, so that no person could get either in or out.

Being posted under the walls of the castle, Captain Morgan commanded the sentinel, whom they had taken prisoner, to speak to those within, charging them to surrender to his discretion; otherwise they should all be cut in pieces, without quarter. But disregarding these threats, they began instantly to fire, which alarmed the city; yet notwithstanding, though the governor and soldiers of the said castle made as great resistance as could be, they were forced to surrender. Having taken the castle, Morgan resolved to be as good as his word, putting the Spaniards to the sword,

63

thereby to strike a terror into the rest of the city. Whereupon, having shut up all the soldiers and officers as prisoners into one room, they set fire to the powder (whereof they found great quantity) and blew up the castle into the air, with all the Spaniards that were within. This done, they pursued the course of their victory, falling upon the city, which as yet was not ready to receive them. Many of the inhabitants cast their precious jewels and money into wells and cisterns, or hid them in places underground, to avoid as much as possible, being totally robbed. One of the party of pirates, assigned to this purpose, ran immediately to the cloisters, and took as many religious men and women as they could find. The governor of the city, not being able to rally the citizens, through their great confusion, retired to one of the castles remaining, and thence fired incessantly at the pirates: but these were not in the least negligent either to assault him, or defend themselves, so that amidst the horror of the assault, they made very few shots in vain; for aiming with great dexterity at the mouths of the guns, the Spaniards were certain to lose one or two men every time they charged each gun anew.

The fight continued very furious from break of day till noon; indeed, about this time of the day the case was very dubious which party should conquer, or be conquered. At last, the pirates perceiving they had lost many men, and yet advanced but little towards gaining either this, or the other castles, made use of fire-balls, which they threw with their hands, designing to burn the doors of the castles. But the Spaniards from the walls let fall great quantities of stones, and earthen pots full of powder, and other combustible matter, which forced them to desist. Captain Morgan seeing this desperate defence made by the Spaniards, began to despair of success. Hereupon, many faint and calm meditations came into his mind; neither could he determine which way to turn himself in that strait. Being thus puzzled, he was suddenly animated to continue the assault, by seeing the English colors put forth at one of the lesser castles, then entered by his men; of whom he presently after spied a troop coming to meet him, proclaiming victory with loud shouts of joy. This instantly put him on new resolutions of taking the rest of the castles, especially seeing the chiefest citizens were fled to them, and had conveyed thither great part of their riches, with all the plate belonging to the churches and divine service.

To this effect, he ordered ten or twelve ladders to be made in all haste, so broad, that three or four men at once might ascend them: these being finished, he commanded all the religious men and women, whom he had taken prisoners, to fix them against the walls

64

of the castle. This he had before threatened the governor to do, if he delivered not the castle: but his answer was, "he would never surrender himself alive." Captain Morgan was persuaded the governor would not employ his utmost force, on seeing the religious women and ecclesiastical persons exposed in the front of the soldiers to the greatest danger. Thus the ladders, as I have said, were at once put into the hands of religious persons of both sexes, and these were forced, at the head of the companies, to raise and apply them to the walls. But Captain Morgan was fully deceived in his judgment of this design; for the governor, who acted like a brave soldier in performance of his duty, used his utmost endeavor to destroy whomsoever came near the walls. The religious men and women ceased not to cry to him, and beg of him, by all the saints of heaven, to deliver the castle, and spare both his and their own lives; but nothing could prevail with his obstinacy and fierceness. Thus many of the religious men and nuns were killed before they could fix the ladders; which at last being done, though with great loss of their number, the pirates mounted them in great numbers, and with reckless valor, having fire-balls in their hands, and earthen pots full of powder; which, being now at the top of the walls, they kindled and cast down among the Spaniards.

This effort of the pirates was very great, insomuch that the Spaniards could not longer resist nor defend the castle, which was now entered. Hereupon they all threw down their arms, and craved quarter for their lives; only the governor of the city would crave no mercy, but killed many of the pirates with his own hands, and not a few of his own soldiers; because they did not stand to their arms. And though the pirates asked him if he would have quarter; yet he constantly answered, "By no means, I had rather die as a valiant soldier, than be hanged as a coward." They endeavored as much as they could to take him prisoner, but he defended himself so obstinately, that they were forced to kill him, notwithstanding all the cries and tears of his own wife and daughter, who begged him, on their knees, to demand quarter, and save his life. When the pirates had possessed themselves of the castle, which was about nightfall, they enclosed therein all the prisoners, placing the women and men by themselves, with some guards. The wounded were put in an apartment by themselves, that their own complaints might be the cure of their diseases; for no other was afforded them.

This done, they fell to eating and drinking, and as usual, to committing all manner of debauchery and excess, so that fifty courageous men might easily have retaken the city, and killed all the pirates. Next day, having plundered all they could find, they examined some of the prisoners (who had been persuaded by their

65

companions to say they were the richest of the town), charging them severely to discover where they had hid their riches and goods. Not being able to extort anything from them, they not being the right persons, it was resolved to torture them: this they did so cruelly, that many of them died on the rack, or presently after. Now the president of Panama being advertised of the pillage and ruin of Puerto Bello, he employed all his care and industry to raise forces to pursue and cast out the pirates thence; but these cared little for his preparations, having their ships at hand, and determining to fire the city, and retreat. They had now been at Puerto Bello fifteen days, in which time they had lost many of their men, both by the unhealthiness of the country, and their extravagant debaucheries.

Hereupon, they prepared to depart, carrying on board all the pillage they had got, having first provided the fleet with sufficient victuals for the voyage. While these things were doing Captain Morgan demanded of the prisoners a ransom for the city, or else he would burn it down, and blow up all the castles; withal, he commanded them to send speedily two persons, to procure the sum, which was 100,000 pieces-of-eight. To this effect two men were sent to the president of Panama, who gave him an account of all. The president, having now a body of men ready, set forth towards Puerto Bello, to encounter the pirates before their retreat; but, they, hearing of his coming, instead of flying away, went out to meet him at a narrow passage, which he must pass: here they placed a hundred men, very well armed, which at the first encounter put to flight a good party of those of Panama. This obliged the president to retire for that time, not being yet in a posture of strength to proceed farther. Presently after, he sent a message to Captain Morgan, to tell him, "that if he departed not suddenly with all his forces from Puerto Bello, he ought to expect no quarter for himself, nor his companions, when he should take them, as he hoped soon to do." Captain Morgan, who feared not his threats, knowing he had a secure retreat in his ships, which were at hand, answered, "he would not deliver the castles, before he had received the contribution-money he had demanded; which if it were not paid down, he would certainly burn the whole city, and then leave it, demolishing beforehand the castles, and killing the prisoners."

The governor of Panama perceived by this answer that no means would serve to mollify the hearts of the pirates, nor reduce them to reason: whereupon, he determined to leave the inhabitants of the city to make the best agreement they could. In a few days more the miserable citizens gathered the contributions required, and brought 100,000 pieces-of-eight to the pirates for their ransom. The president of Panama was much amazed that four hundred men could take such a great city, with so many strong castles, especially having no ordnance, wherewith to raise batteries, and, knowing the citizens of Puerto Bello had always great repute of being good soldiers themselves, who never wanted courage in their own defence. His astonishment was so great, that he sent to Captain Morgan, desiring some small pattern of those arms wherewith he had taken with such vigor so great a city. Captain Morgan received this messenger very kindly, and with great civility; and gave him a pistol, and a few small bullets, to carry back to the president his master; telling him, withal, "he desired him to accept that slender pattern of the arms wherewith he had taken Puerto Bello, and keep them for a twelvemonth; after which time he promised to come to Panama, and fetch them away."[9] The governor returned the present very soon to Captain Morgan, giving him thanks for the favor of lending him such weapons as he needed not; and, withal, sent him a ring of gold, with this message, "that he desired him not to give himself the labor of coming to Panama, as he had done to Puerto Bello: for he did assure him, he should not speed so well here, as he had done there."

After this, Captain Morgan (having provided his fleet with all necessaries, and taken with him the best guns of the castles, nailing up the rest) set sail from Puerto Bello with all his ships, and arriving in a few days at Cuba, he sought out a place wherein he might quickly make the dividend of their spoil. They found in ready money 250,000 pieces-of-eight, besides other merchandise; as cloth, linen, silks, etc. With this rich purchase they sailed thence to their common place of rendezvous, Jamaica. Being arrived, they passed here some time in all sorts of vices and debaucheries, according to their custom; spending very prodigally what others had gained with no small labor and toil.

---

[9] This promise was kept. See The Capture of Panama (footnote).

THE WAYS OF THE BUCCANEERS[10]

John Masefield after John Esquemeling

Throughout the years of buccaneering, the buccaneers often put to sea in canoes and periaguas, just as Drake put to sea in his three pinnaces. Life in an open boat is far from pleasant, but men who passed their leisure cutting logwood at Campeachy, or hoeing tobacco in Jamaica, or toiling over gramma grass under a hot sun after cattle, were not disposed to make the worst of things. They would sit contentedly upon the oar bench, rowing with a long, slow stroke for hours together without showing signs of fatigue. Nearly all of them were men of more than ordinary strength, and all of them were well accustomed to the climate. When they had rowed their canoa to the Main they were able to take it easy till a ship came by from one of the Spanish ports. If she seemed a reasonable prey, without too many guns, and not too high charged, or high built, the privateers would load their muskets, and row down to engage her. The best shots were sent into the bows, and excused from rowing, lest the exercise should cause their hands to tremble. A clever man was put to the steering oar, and the musketeers were bidden to sing out whenever the enemy yawed, so as to fire her guns. It was in action, and in action only, that the captain had command over his men. The steersman endeavored to keep the masts of the quarry in a line, and to approach her from astern. The marksmen from the bows kept up a continual fire at the vessel's helmsmen, if they could be seen, and at any gun-ports which happened to be open. If the helmsmen could not be seen from the sea, the canoas aimed to row in upon the vessel's quarters, where they could wedge up the rudder with wooden chocks or wedges. They then laid her aboard over the quarter, or by the after chains, and carried her with their knives and pistols. The first man to get aboard received some gift of money at the division of the spoil.

When the prize was taken, the prisoners were questioned, and despoiled. Often, indeed, they were stripped stark naked, and granted the privilege of seeing their finery on a pirate's back. Each buccaneer had the right to take a shift of clothes out of each prize captured. The cargo was then rummaged, and the state of the ship looked to, with an eye to using her as a cruiser. As a rule, the prisoners were put ashore on the first opportunity, but some buccaneers had a way of selling their captives into slavery. If the

---

[10] From Buccaneer Customs on the Spanish Main.

ship were old, leaky, valueless, in ballast, or with a cargo useless to the rovers, she was either robbed of her guns, and turned adrift with her crew, or run ashore in some snug cove, where she could be burnt for the sake of the iron-work. If the cargo were of value, and, as a rule, the ships they took had some rich thing aboard them, they sailed her to one of the Dutch, French or English settlements, where they sold her freight for what they could get—some tenth or twentieth of its value. If the ship were a good one, in good condition, well found, swift, and not of too great draught (for they preferred to sail in small ships), they took her for their cruiser as soon as they had emptied out her freight. They sponged and loaded her guns, brought their stores aboard her, laid their mats upon her deck, secured the boats astern, and sailed away in search of other plunder. They kept little discipline aboard their ships. What work had to be done they did, but works of supererogation they despised and rejected as a shade unholy. The night watches were partly orgies. While some slept, the others fired guns and drank to the health of their fellows. By the light of the binnacle, or by the light of the slush lamps in the cabin, the rovers played a hand at cards, or diced each other at "seven and eleven," using a pannikin as dice-box. While the gamblers cut and shuffled, and the dice rattled in the tin, the musical sang songs, the fiddlers set their music chuckling, and the seaboots stamped approval. The cunning dancers showed their science in the moonlight, avoiding the sleepers if they could. In this jolly fashion were the nights made short. In the daytime, the gambling continued with little intermission; nor had the captain any authority to stop it. One captain, in the histories, was so bold as to throw the dice and cards overboard, but, as a rule, the captain of a buccaneer cruiser was chosen as an artist, or navigator, or as a lucky fighter. He was not expected to spoil sport. The continual gambling nearly always led to fights and quarrels. The lucky dicers often won so much that the unlucky had to part with all their booty. Sometimes a few men would win all the plunder of the cruise, much to the disgust of the majority, who clamored for a redivision of the spoil. If two buccaneers got into a quarrel they fought it out on shore at the first opportunity, using knives, swords, or pistols, according to taste. The usual way of fighting was with pistols, the combatants standing back to back, at a distance of ten or twelve paces, and turning round to fire at the word of command. If both shots missed, the question was decided with cutlasses, the man who drew first blood being declared the winner. If a man were proved to be a coward he was either tied to the mast, and shot, or mutilated, and sent ashore. No cruise came to an end until the company declared themselves satisfied with the amount of plunder taken. The question, like all other important questions, was debated round the mast, and decided by vote.

At the conclusion of a successful cruise, they sailed for Port Royal, with the ship full of treasure, such as vicuna wool, packets of pearls from the Hatch, jars of civet or of ambergris, boxes of "marmalett" and spices, casks of strong drink, bales of silk, sacks of chocolate and vanilla, and rolls of green cloth and pale blue cotton which the Indians had woven in Peru, in some sandy village near the sea, in sight of the pelicans and the penguins. In addition to all these things, they usually had a number of the personal possessions of those they had taken on the seas. Lying in the chests for subsequent division were swords, silver-mounted pistols, daggers chased and inlaid, watches from Spain, necklaces of uncut jewels, rings and bangles, heavy carved furniture, "cases of bottles" of delicately cut green glass, containing cordials distilled of precious mints, with packets of emeralds from Brazil, bezoar stones from Patagonia, paintings from Spain, and medicinal gums from Nicaragua. All these things were divided by lot at the main-mast as soon as the anchor held. As the ship, or ships, neared port, her men hung colors out—any colors they could find—to make their vessel gay. A cup of drink was taken as they sailed slowly home to moorings, and as they drank they fired off the cannon, "bullets and all," again and yet again, rejoicing as the bullets struck the water. Up in the bay, the ships in the harbor answered with salutes of cannon; flags were dipped and hoisted in salute; and so the anchor dropped in some safe reach, and the division of the spoil began.

After the division of the spoil in the beautiful Port Royal harbor, in sight of the palm-trees and the fort with the colors flying, the buccaneers packed their gear, and dropped over the side into a boat. They were pulled ashore by some grinning black man with a scarlet scarf about his head and the brand of a hot iron on his shoulders. At the jetty end, where the Indians lounged at their tobacco and the fishermen's canoas rocked, the sunburnt pirates put ashore. Among the noisy company which always gathers on a pier they met with their companions. A sort of Roman triumph followed, as the "happily returned" lounged swaggeringly towards the taverns. Eager hands helped them to carry in their plunder. In a few minutes the gang was entering the tavern, the long, cool room with barrels round the walls, where there were benches and a table and an old blind fiddler jerking his elbow at a jig. Noisily the party ranged about the table, and sat themselves upon the benches, while the drawers, or potboys, in their shirts, drew near to take the orders. I wonder if the reader has ever heard a sailor in the like circumstance, five minutes after he has touched his pay, address a company of parasites in an inn with the question: "What's it going to be?"

70

A TRUE ACCOUNT OF THREE NOTORIOUS PIRATESA[11]

Howard Pyle, Ed.

I

Captain Teach alias Black-beard

Edward Teach was a Bristol man born, but had sailed some time out of Jamaica, in privateers, in the late French war; yet though he had often distinguished himself for his uncommon boldness and personal courage, he was never raised to any command, till he went a-pirating, which, I think, was at the latter end of the year 1716, when Captain Benjamin Hornygold put him into a sloop that he had made prize of, and with whom he continued in consortship till a little while before Hornygold surrendered.

In the spring of the year 1717 Teach and Hornygold sailed from Providence, for the main of America, and took in their way a billop from the Havana, with 120 barrels of flour, as also a sloop from Bermuda, Thurbar master, from whom they took only some gallons of wine, and then let him go; and a ship from Madeira to South Carolina, out of which they got plunder to a considerable value.

After cleaning on the coast of Virginia, they returned to the West Indies, and in the latitude of 24, made prize of a large French Guineaman, bound to Martinico, which, by Hornygold's consent, Teach went aboard of as captain, and took a cruise in her. Hornygold returned with his sloop to Providence, where, at the arrival of Captain Rogers, the governor, he surrendered to mercy, pursuant to the king's proclamation.

Aboard of this Guineaman Teach mounted forty guns, and named her the Queen Ann's Revenge; and cruising near the island of St. Vincent, took a large ship, called the Great Allen, Christopher Taylor, commander; the pirates plundered her of what they thought fit, put all the men ashore upon the island above mentioned, and set fire to the ship.

A few days after Teach fell in with the Scarborough, man-of-war, of thirty guns, who engaged him for some hours; but she,

---

[11] A contemporary narrative. From The Buccaneers of America.

71

finding the pirate well-manned, and having tried her strength, gave over the engagement and returned to Barbadoes, the place of her station, and Teach sailed towards the Spanish America.

In this way he met with a pirate sloop of ten guns, commanded by one Major Bonnet, lately a gentleman of good reputation and estate in the island of Barbadoes, whom he joined; but in a few days after, Teach, finding that Bonnet knew nothing of a maritime life, with the consent of his own men, put in another captain, one Richards, to command Bonnet's sloop, and took the Major on board his own ship, telling him, that as he had not been used to the fatigues and care of such a post, it would be better for him to decline it and live easy, at his pleasure, in such a ship as his, where he would not be obliged to perform the necessary duties of a sea-voyage.

At Turniff, ten leagues short of the Bay of Honduras, the pirates took in fresh water, and while they were at anchor there, they saw a sloop coming in, whereupon Richards, in the sloop called the Revenge, slipped his cable and run out to meet her; who, upon seeing the black flag hoisted, struck his sail and came to under the stern of Teach, the commodore. She was called the Adventure, from Jamaica, David Harriot, master. They took him and his men aboard the great ship, and sent a number of other hands with Israel Hands, master of Teach's ship, to man the sloop for the piratical account.

The 9th of April they weighed from Turniff, having lain there about a week, and sailed to the bay, where they found a ship and four sloops; three of the latter belonged to Jonathan Bernard, of Jamaica, and the other to Captain James. The ship was of Boston, called the Protestant Cæsar, Captain Wyar, commander. Teach hoisted his black colors and fired a gun, upon which Captain Wyar and all his men left their ship and got ashore in their boat. Teach's quartermaster and eight of his crew took possession of Wyar's ship, and Richards secured all the sloops, one of which they burnt out of spite to the owner. The Protestant Cæsar they also burnt, after they had plundered her, because she belonged to Boston, where some men had been hanged for piracy, and the three sloops belonging to Bernard they let go.

From hence the rovers sailed to Turkill, and then to the Grand Caimanes, a small island about thirty leagues to the westward of Jamaica, where they took a small turtler, and so to the Havana, and from thence to the Bahama Wrecks; and from the Bahama Wrecks they sailed to Carolina, taking a brigantine and two sloops in their way, where they lay off the bar of Charles Town for five or six days. They took here a ship as she was coming out, bound for London, commanded by Robert Clark, with some passengers on board for

England. The next day they took another vessel coming out of Charles Town, and also two pinks coming into Charles Town; likewise a brigantine with fourteen negroes aboard; all of which, being done in the face of the town, struck so great a terror to the whole province of Carolina, having just before been visited by Vane, another notorious pirate, that they abandoned themselves to despair, being in no condition to resist their force. There were eight sail in the harbor, ready for the sea, but none dared to venture out, it being almost impossible to escape their hands. The inward bound vessels were under the same unhappy dilemma, so that the trade of this place was totally interrupted. What made these misfortunes heavier to them was a long, expensive war the colony had had with the natives, which was but just ended when these robbers infested them.

Teach detained all the ships and prisoners, and, being in want of medicines, resolved to demand a chest from the government of the province. Accordingly, Richards, the captain of the Revenge sloop, with two or three more pirates, were sent up along with Mr. Marks, one of the prisoners whom they had taken in Clark's ship, and very insolently made their demands, threatening that if they did not send immediately the chest of medicines and let the pirate ambassadors return, without offering any violence to their persons, they would murder all their prisoners, send up their heads to the governor, and set the ships they had taken on fire.

Whilst Mr. Marks was making application to the council, Richards and the rest of the pirates walked the streets publicly in the sight of all people, who were fired with the utmost indignation, looking upon them as robbers and murderers, and particularly the authors of their wrongs and oppressions, but durst not so much as think of executing their revenge for fear of bringing more calamities upon themselves, and so they were forced to let the villains pass with impunity. The government was not long in deliberating upon the message, though it was the greatest affront that could have been put upon them, yet, for the saving so many men's lives (among them Mr. Samuel Wragg, one of the council), they complied with the necessity and sent aboard a chest, valued at between three and four hundred pounds, and the pirates went back safe to their ships.

Black-beard (for so Teach was generally called, as we shall hereafter show), as soon as he had received the medicines and his brother rogues, let go the ships and the prisoners, having first taken out of them in gold and silver about £1,500 sterling, besides provisions and other matters.

From the bar of Charles Town they sailed to North Carolina, Captain Teach in the ship, which they called the man-of-war,

73

Captain Richards and Captain Hands in the sloops, which they termed privateers, and another sloop serving them as a tender. Teach began now to think of breaking up the company and securing the money and the best of the effects for himself and some others of his companions he had most friendship for, and to cheat the rest. Accordingly, on pretense of running into Topsail inlet to clean, he grounded his ship, and then, as if it had been done undesignedly and by accident, he orders Hands' sloop to come to his assistance and get him off again, which he, endeavoring to do, ran the sloop on shore near the other, and so were both lost. This done, Teach goes into the tender sloop, with forty hands, and leaves the Revenge there, then takes seventeen others and maroons them upon a small sandy island, about a league from the main, where there was neither bird, beast, or herb for their subsistence, and where they must have perished if Major Bonnet had not, two days after, taken them off.

Teach goes up to the governor of North Carolina, with about twenty of his men, and they surrender to his Majesty's proclamation, and receive certificates thereof from his Excellency; but it did not appear that their submitting to this pardon was from any reformation of manners, but only to await a more favorable opportunity to play the same game over again; which he soon after effected, with greater security to himself, and with much better prospect of success, having in this time cultivated a very good understanding with Charles Eden, Esq., the governor above mentioned.

The first piece of service this kind governor did to Black-beard was to give him a right to the vessel which he had taken when he was a-pirating in the great ship called the Queen Ann's Revenge, for which purpose a court of vice-admiralty was held at Bath Town, and, though Teach had never any commission in his life, and the sloop belonging to the English merchants, and taken in time of peace, yet was she condemned as a prize taken from the Spaniards by the said Teach. These proceedings show that governors are but men.

Before he sailed upon his adventures, he married a young creature of about sixteen years of age, the governor performing the ceremony. As it is a custom to marry here by a priest, so it is there by a magistrate; and this, I have been informed, made Teach's fourteenth wife whereof about a dozen might be still living.

In June, 1718, he went to sea upon another expedition, and steered his course towards Bermudas. He met with two or three English vessels in his way, but robbed them only of provisions, stores, and other necessaries, for his present expense; but near the island before mentioned, he fell in with two French ships, one of them was laden with sugar and cocoa, and the other light, both bound to Martinico. The ship that had no lading he let go, and putting all the men of the loaded ship aboard her, he brought home the other with her cargo to North Carolina, where the governor and the pirates shared the plunder.

When Teach and his prize arrived he and four of his crew went to his Excellency and made affidavit that they found the French ship at sea without a soul on board her; and then a court was called, and the ship condemned. The governor had sixty hogsheads of sugar for his dividend, and one Mr. Knight, who was his secretary and collector for the province, twenty, and the rest was shared among the other pirates.

The business was not yet done; the ship remained, and it was possible one or other might come into the river that might be acquainted with her, and so discover the roguery. But Teach thought of a contrivance to prevent this, for, upon a pretence that she was leaky, and that she might sink, and so stop up the mouth of the inlet or cove where she lay, he obtained an order from the governor to bring her out into the river and set her on fire, which was accordingly executed, and she was burnt down to the water's edge, her bottom sunk, and with it their fears of her ever rising in judgment against them.

Captain Teach, alias Black-beard, passed three or four months in the river, sometimes lying at anchor in the coves, at other times sailing from one inlet to another, trading with such sloops as he met for the plunder he had taken, and would often give them presents for stores and provisions he took from them; that is, when he happened to be in a giving humor; at other times he made bold with them, and took what he liked, without saying "By your leave," knowing well they dared not send him a bill for the payment. He often diverted himself with going ashore among the planters, where he revelled night and day. By these he was well received, but whether out of love or fear I cannot say. Sometimes he used them courteously enough, and made them presents of rum and sugar in recompense of what he took from them; but, as for liberties, which it is said he and his companions often took with the wives and daughters of the planters, I cannot take upon me to say whether he paid them ad valorem or no. At other times he carried it in a lordly manner towards them, and would lay some of them under contribution; nay, he often proceeded to bully the governor, not that I can discover the least cause of quarrel between them, but it seemed only to be done to show he dared do it.

The sloops trading up and down this river being so frequently pillaged by Black-beard, consulted with the traders and some of the best planters what course to take. They saw plainly it would be in vain to make an application to the governor of North Carolina, to whom it properly belonged to find some redress; so that if they could not be relieved from some other quarter, Black-beard would be like to reign with impunity; therefore, with as much secrecy as possible, they sent a deputation to Virginia, to lay the affair before the governor of that colony, and to solicit an armed force from the men-of-war lying there to take or destroy this pirate.

This governor consulted with the captains of the two men-of-war, viz., the Pearl and Lime, who had lain in St. James's river about ten months. It was agreed that the governor should hire a couple of small sloops, and the men-of-war should man them. This was accordingly done, and the command of them given to Mr. Robert Maynard, first lieutenant of the Pearl, an experienced officer, and a gentleman of great bravery and resolution, as will appear by his gallant behavior in this expedition. The sloops were well manned, and furnished with ammunition and small arms, but had no guns mounted.

About the time of their going out the governor called an assembly, in which it was resolved to publish a proclamation, offering certain rewards to any person or persons who, within a year after that time, should take or destroy any pirate. The original proclamation, being in our hands, is as follows:—

By his Majesty's Lieutenant-Governor and Commander-in-Chief
of the Colony and Dominion of Virginia.

A PROCLAMATION,

Publishing the Rewards given for apprehending or killing Pirates.

Whereas, by an Act of Assembly, made at a Session of Assembly, begun at the capital in Williamsburg, the eleventh day of November, in the fifth year of his Majesty's reign, entitled, An Act to Encourage the Apprehending and Destroying of Pirates: It is, amongst other things, enacted, that all and every person, or persons, who, from and after the fourteenth day of November, in the Year of our Lord one thousand seven hundred and eighteen, and before the fourteenth day of November, which shall be in the Year of our Lord one thousand seven hundred and nineteen, shall take any pirate, or pirates, on the sea or land, or, in case of resistance, shall kill any such pirate, or pirates, between the degrees of thirty-four and thirty-nine of northern latitude, and within one hundred leagues of the continent of Virginia, or within the provinces of Virginia, or North Carolina, upon the conviction, or making due proof of the killing of all and every such pirate, and pirates, before the Governor and Council, shall be entitled to have, and receive out of the public money, in the hands of the Treasurer of this Colony, the several rewards following: that is to say, for Edward Teach, commonly called Captain Teach, or Black-beard, one hundred pounds; for every other commander of a pirate ship, sloop, or vessel, forty pounds; for every lieutenant, master, or quartermaster, boatswain, or carpenter, twenty pounds; for every other inferior officer, fifteen pounds; and for every private man taken on board such ship, sloop, or vessel, ten pounds; and that for every pirate which shall be taken by any ship, sloop, or vessel, belonging to this colony, or North Carolina, within the time aforesaid, in any place whatsoever, the like rewards shall be paid according to the quality and condition of such pirates. Wherefore, for the encouragement of all such persons as shall be willing to serve his Majesty, and their country, in so just and honourable an undertaking as the suppressing a sort of people who may be truly called enemies to mankind: I have thought fit, with the advice and consent of his Majesty's Council, to issue this Proclamation, hereby declaring the said rewards shall be punctually and justly paid, in current money of Virginia, according to the directions of the said Act. And I do order and appoint this proclamation to be published by the sheriffs at their respective country houses, and by all ministers and readers in the several churches and chapels throughout this colony.

Given at our Council-Chamber at Williamsburgh, this 24th day of November, 1718, in the fifth year of his Majesty's reign.

GOD SAVE THE KING.

A. Spotswood.

The 17th of November, 1718, the lieutenant sailed from Kicquetan, in James river in Virginia, and the 31st, in the evening, came to the mouth of Okerecock inlet, where he got sight of the pirate. This expedition was made with all imaginable secrecy, and the officer managed with all the prudence that was necessary, stopping all boats and vessels he met with in the river from going up, and thereby preventing any intelligence from reaching Black-beard, and receiving at the same time an account from them all of the place where the pirate was lurking. But notwithstanding this caution, Black-beard had information of the design from his Excellency of the province; and his secretary, Mr. Knight, wrote him a letter particularly concerning it, intimating "that he had sent him four of his men, which were all he could meet with in or about town, and so bid him be upon his guard." These men belonged to Black-beard, and were sent from Bath Town to Okerecock inlet, where the sloop lay, which is about twenty leagues.

Black-beard had heard several reports, which happened not to be true, and so gave the less credit to this advice; nor was he convinced till he saw the sloops. Then it was time to put his vessel in a posture of defense. He had no more than twenty-five men on board, though he gave out to all the vessels he spoke with that he had forty. When he had prepared for battle he sat down and spent the night in drinking with the master of a trading sloop, who, it was thought, had more business with Teach than he should have had.

Lieutenant Maynard came to an anchor, for the place being shoal, and the channel intricate, there was no getting in where Teach lay that night; but in the morning he weighed, and sent his boat ahead of the sloops to sound, and coming within gun-shot of the pirate, received his fire; whereupon Maynard hoisted the king's colors, and stood directly towards him with the best way that his sails and oars could make. Black-beard cut his cable, and endeavored to make a running fight, keeping a continual fire at his enemies with his guns. Mr. Maynard, not having any, kept a constant fire with small arms, while some of his men labored at their oars. In a little time Teach's sloop ran aground, and Mr. Maynard's, drawing more water than that of the pirate, he could not come near him; so he anchored within half gun-shot of the enemy, and, in order to lighten his vessel, that he might run him aboard, the lieutenant ordered all his ballast to be thrown overboard, and all the water to be staved, and then weighed and stood for him; upon which Black-beard hailed him in this rude manner: "Damn you for villains, who are you; and from whence came you?" The lieutenant made him answer, "You may see by our colors we are no pirates." Black-beard bid him send his boat on board that he might see who he was; but Mr. Maynard replied thus: "I cannot spare my boat, but I will come aboard of you as soon as I can with my sloop." Upon this

Black-beard took a glass of liquor, and drank to him with these words: "Damnation seize my soul if I give you quarter, or take any from you." In answer to which Mr. Maynard told him "that he expected no quarter from him, nor should he give him any."

By this time Black-beard's sloop fleeted as Mr. Maynard's sloops were rowing towards him, which being not above a foot high in the waist, and consequently the men all exposed, as they came near together (there being hitherto little or no execution done on either side), the pirate fired a broadside charged with all manner of small shot. A fatal stroke to them!—the sloop the lieutenant was in having twenty men killed and wounded, and the other sloop nine. This could not be helped, for there being no wind, they were obliged to keep to their oars, otherwise the pirate would have got away from him, which it seems, the lieutenant was resolute to prevent.

After this unlucky blow Black-beard's sloop fell broadside to the shore; Mr. Maynard's other sloop, which was called the Ranger, fell astern, being for the present disabled. So the lieutenant, finding his own sloop had way and would soon be on board of Teach, he ordered all his men down, for fear of another broadside, which must have been their destruction and the loss of their expedition. Mr. Maynard was the only person that kept the deck, except the man at the helm, whom he directed to lie down snug, and the men in the hold were ordered to get their pistols and their swords ready for close fighting, and to come up at his command; in order to which two ladders were placed in the hatchway for the more expedition. When the lieutenant's sloop boarded the other Captain Teach's men threw in several new-fashioned sort of grenades, viz., case-bottles filled with powder and small shot, slugs, and pieces of lead or iron, with a quick-match in the mouth of it, which, being lighted without side, presently runs into the bottle to the powder, and, as it is instantly thrown on board, generally does great execution besides putting all the crew into a confusion. But, by good Providence, they had not that effect here, the men being in the hold. Black-beard, seeing few or no hands aboard, told his men "that they were all knocked to head, except three or four; and therefore," says he, "let's jump on board and cut them to pieces."

Whereupon, under the smoke of one of the bottles just mentioned, Black-beard enters with fourteen men over the bows of Maynard's sloop, and were not seen by him until the air cleared. However, he just then gave a signal to his men, who all rose in an instant, and attacked the pirates with as much bravery as ever was done upon such an occasion. Black-beard and the lieutenant fired the first shots at each other, by which the pirate received a wound, and then engaged with swords, till the lieutenant's unluckily broke, and stepping back to cock a pistol, Black-beard, with his cutlass, was striking at that instant that one of Maynard's men gave him a terrible wound in the neck and throat, by which the lieutenant came off with only a small cut over his fingers.

They were now closely and warmly engaged, the lieutenant and twelve men against Black-beard and fourteen, till the sea was tinctured with blood round the vessel. Black-beard received a shot into his body from the pistol that Lieutenant Maynard discharged, yet he stood his ground, and fought with great fury till he received five-and-twenty wounds, and five of them by shot. At length, as he was cocking another pistol, having fired several before, he fell down dead; by which time eight more out of the fourteen dropped, and all the rest, much wounded, jumped overboard and called out for quarter, which was granted, though it was only prolonging their lives a few days. The sloop Ranger came up and attacked the men that remained in Black-beard's sloop with equal bravery, till they likewise cried for quarter.

Here was an end of that courageous brute, who might have passed in the world for a hero had he been employed in a good cause.

The lieutenant caused Black-beard's head to be severed from his body, and hung up at the boltsprit end; then he sailed to Bath Town, to get relief for his wounded men.

In rummaging the pirate's sloop, they found several letters and written papers, which discovered the correspondence between Governor Eden, the secretary and collector, and also some traders at New York, and Black-beard. It is likely he had regard enough for his friends to have destroyed these papers before action, in order to hinder them from falling into such hands, where the discovery would be of no use either to the interest or reputation of these fine gentlemen, if it had not been his fixed resolution to have blown up together, when he found no possibility of escaping.

When the lieutenant came to Bath Town, he made bold to seize from the governor's storehouse the sixty hogsheads of sugar, and from honest Mr. Knight, twenty; which it seems was their dividend of the plunder taken in the French ship. The latter did not survive this shameful discovery, for, being apprehensive that he might be called to an account for these trifles, fell sick, it is thought, with the fright, and died in a few days.

After the wounded men were pretty well recovered, the lieutenant sailed back to the men-of-war in James River, in Virginia, with Black-beard's head still hanging at the boltsprit end, and fifteen prisoners, thirteen of whom were hanged, it appearing, upon trial, that one of them, viz., Samuel Odell, was taken out of the trading sloop but the night before the engagement. This poor fellow was a little unlucky at his first entering upon his new trade, there appearing no less than seventy wounds upon him after the action; notwithstanding which he lived and was cured of them all. The other person that escaped the gallows was one Israel Hands, the master of Black-beard's sloop, and formerly captain of the same, before the Queen Ann's Revenge was lost in Topsail inlet.

The aforesaid Hands happened not to be in the fight, but was taken afterwards ashore at Bath Town, having been sometime before disabled by Black-beard, in one of his savage humors, after the following manner: One night, drinking in his cabin with Hands, the pilot, and another man, Black-beard, without any provocation, privately draws out a small pair of pistols, and cocks them under the table, which being perceived by the man, he withdrew and went upon deck, leaving Hands, the pilot, and the captain together. When the pistols were ready he blew out the candle, and, crossing his hands, discharged them at his company; Hands, the master, was shot through the knee and lamed for life, the other pistol did no execution. Being asked the meaning of this, he only answered by damning them, that "if he did not now and then kill one of them, they would forget who he was."

Hands being taken, was tried and condemned, but just as he was about to be executed a ship arrived at Virginia with a proclamation for prolonging the time of his Majesty's pardon to such of the pirates as should surrender by a limited time therein expressed. Notwithstanding the sentence, Hands pleaded the pardon, and was allowed the benefit of it, and was alive some time ago in London, begging his bread.

Now that we have given some account of Teach's life and actions, it will not be amiss that we speak of his beard, since it did not a little contribute towards making his name so terrible in those parts.

Plutarch and other grave historians have taken notice that several great men amongst the Romans took their surnames from certain odd marks in their countenances—as Cicero, from a mark, or vetch, on his nose—so our hero, Captain Teach, assumed the cognomen of Black-beard, from that large quantity of hair which, like a frightful meteor, covered his whole face, and frightened America more than any comet that has appeared there a long time.

This beard was black, which he suffered to grow of an extravagant length; as to breadth, it came up to his eyes. He was accustomed to twist it with ribbons, in small tails, after the manner of our Ramilie wigs, and turn them about his ears. In time of action he wore a sling over his shoulders, with three brace of pistols hanging in holsters like bandoliers, and stuck lighted matches under his hat, which, appearing on each side of his face, his eyes naturally looking fierce and wild, made him altogether such a figure that imagination cannot form an idea of a fury from hell to look more frightful.

If he had the look of a fury, his humors and passions were suitable to it.

In the commonwealth of pirates, he who goes the greatest length of wickedness is looked upon with a kind of envy amongst them as a person of a more extraordinary gallantry, and is thereby entitled to be distinguished by some post, and if such a one has but courage, he must certainly be a great man. The hero of whom we are writing was thoroughly accomplished this way, and some of his frolics of wickedness were so extravagant, as if he aimed at making his men believe he was a devil incarnate; for being one day at sea, and a little flushed with drink, "Come," says he, "let us make a hell of our own, and try how long we can bear it." Accordingly he, with two or three others, went down into the hold, and closing up all the hatches, filled several pots full of brimstone and other combustible matter, and set it on fire, and so continued till they were almost suffocated, when some of the men cried out for air. At length he opened the hatches, not a little pleased that he held out the longest.

The night before he was killed he sat up and drank till the morning with some of his own men and the master of a merchantman; and having had intelligence of the two sloops coming to attack him, as has been before observed, one of his men asked him, in case anything should happen to him in the engagement with the sloops, whether his wife knew where he had buried his money? He answered, "That nobody but himself and the devil knew where it was, and the longest liver should take all."

Those of his crew who were taken alive told a story which may appear a little incredible; however, we think it will not be fair to omit it since we had it from their own mouths. That once upon a cruise they found out that they had a man on board more than their crew; such a one was seen several days amongst them, sometimes below and sometimes upon deck, yet no man in the ship could give an account who he was, or from whence he came, but that he disappeared a little before they were cast away in their great ship; but it seems they verily believed it was the devil.

One would think these things should induce them to reform their lives, but so many reprobates together, encouraged and spirited one another up in their wickedness, to which a continual course of drinking did not a little contribute, for in Black-beard's journal, which was taken, there were several memorandums of the following nature found writ with his own hand: Such a day rum all out; our company somewhat sober; a damned confusion amongst us; rouges a-plotting; great talk of separation; so I looked sharp for a prize; such a day took one with a great deal of liquor on board, so kept the company hot, damned hot, then all things went well again.

Thus it was these wretches passed their lives, with very little pleasure or satisfaction in the possession of what they violently take away from others, and sure to pay for it at last by an ignominious death.

The names of the pirates killed in the engagement, are as follows:—

Edward Teach, commander; Philip Morton, gunner; Garret Gibbens, boatswain; Owen Roberts, carpenter; Thomas Miller, quartermaster; John Husk, Joseph Curtice, Joseph Brooks (1), Nath. Jackson. All the rest, except the two last, were wounded, and afterwards hanged in Virginia:—John Carnes, Joseph Brooks (2), James Blake, John Gills, Thomas Gates, James White, Richard Stiles, Cæsar, Joseph Philips, James Robbins, John Martin, Edward Salter, Stephen Daniel, Richard Greensail, Israel Hands, pardoned, Samuel Odel, acquitted.

There were in the pirate sloops, and ashore in a tent near where the sloops lay, twenty-five hogsheads of sugar, eleven tierces, and one hundred and forty-five bags of cocoa, a barrel of indigo, and a bale of cotton; which, with what was taken from the governor and secretary, and the sale of the sloop, came to £2,500, besides the rewards paid by the governor of Virginia, pursuant to his proclamation; all which was divided among the companies of the two ships, Lime and Pearl, that lay in James River; the brave fellows that took them coming in for no more than their dividend amongst the rest, and were paid it not till four years afterwards.

II

Captain William Kid

We are now going to give an account of one whose name is better known in England than most of those whose histories we have already related; the person we mean is Captain Kid, whose public trial and execution here rendered him the subject of all conversation, so that his actions have been chanted about in ballads; however, it is now a considerable time since these things passed, and though the people knew in general that Captain Kid was hanged, and that his crime was piracy, yet there were scarce any, even at that time, who were acquainted with his life or actions, or could account for his turning pirate.

In the beginning of King William's war, Captain Kid commanded a privateer in the West Indies, and by several adventurous actions acquired the reputation of a brave man, as well as an experienced seaman. About this time the pirates were very troublesome in those parts, wherefore Captain Kid was recommended by the Lord Bellamont, then governor of Barbadoes, as well as by several other persons, to the Government here, as a person very fit to be entrusted with the command of a Government ship, and to be employed in cruising upon the pirates, as knowing those seas perfectly well, and being acquainted with all their lurking places; but what reasons governed the politics of those times I cannot tell, but this proposal met with no encouragement here, though it is certain it would have been of great consequence to the subject, our merchants suffering incredible damages by those robbers.

Upon this neglect the Lord Bellamont and some others, who knew what great captures had been made by the pirates, and what a prodigious wealth must be in their possession, were tempted to fit out a ship at their own private charge, and to give the command of it to Captain Kid; and to give the thing a great reputation, as well as to keep their seamen under the better command, they procured the King's Commission for the said Captain Kid, of which the following is an exact copy:—

"William Rex,—William the Third, by the grace of God, King of England, Scotland, France, and Ireland, Defender of the Faith, &c. To our trusty and well-beloved Captain William Kid, Commander of the ship the Adventure galley, or to any other the commander of the same for the time being, greeting; Whereas we are informed, that Captain Thomas Too, John Ireland, Captain Thomas Wake, and Captain William Maze, or Mace, and other subjects, natives or inhabitants of New York, and elsewhere, in our plantations in America, have associated themselves, with divers others, wicked and ill-disposed persons, and do, against the law of nations, commit many and great piracies, robberies, and depredations on the seas upon the parts of America, and in other parts, to the great hindrance and discouragement of trade and navigation, and to the great danger and hurt of our loving subjects, our allies, and all others, navigating the seas upon their lawful occasions. Now know ye, that we being desirous to prevent the aforesaid mischiefs, and, as much as in us lies, to bring the said pirates, freebooters and sea-rovers to justice, have thought fit, and do hereby give and grant to the said William Kid (to whom our Commissioners for exercising the office of Lord High Admiral of England, have granted a commission as a private man-of-war, bearing date December 11, 1695), and unto the commander of the said ship for the time being, and unto the officers, mariners, and others, which shall be under your command, full power and authority to apprehend, seize, and take into your custody as well the said Captain Thomas Too, John Ireland, Captain Thomas Wake, and Captain William Maze, or Mace, as all such pirates, freebooters and sea-rovers, being either our subjects, or of other nations associated with them, which you shall meet with upon the seas or coasts of America, or upon any other seas or coasts, with all their ships and vessels; and all such merchandises, money, goods, and wares as shall be found on board, or with them, in case they shall willingly yield themselves; but if they will not yield without fighting, then you are by force to compel them to yield. And we do also require you to bring, or cause to be brought, such pirates, freebooters, or sea-rovers, as you shall seize, to a legal trial, to the end they may be proceeded against according to the law in such cases. And we do hereby command all our officers, ministers, and other our loving subjects whatsoever, to be aiding and assisting to you in the premises. And we do hereby enjoin you to keep an exact journal of your proceedings in the execution of the premises, and set down the names of such pirates, and of their officers and company, and the names of such ships and vessels as you shall by virtue of these presents take and seize, and the quantities of arms, ammunition, provision, and lading of such ships, and the true value of the same, as near as you judge. And we do hereby strictly charge and command you as you will answer the contrary at your peril, that you do not, in any manner, offend or molest our friends or allies, their ships, or subjects, by colour or pretence of these presents, or the authority thereby granted. In witness whereof we have caused our Great Seal of England to be affixed to these presents. Given at our Court of Kensington, the 26th day of January, 1695, in the seventh year of our reign."

Captain Kid had also another commission, which was called a Commission of Reprisals; for it being then war time, this commission was to justify him in the taking of French merchant ships, in case he should meet with any.

With these two commissions he sailed out of Plymouth in May, 1696, in the Adventure galley of thirty guns and eighty men. The place he first designed for was New York; in his voyage thither he took a French banker, but this was no act of piracy, he having a commission for that purpose, as we have just observed.

When he arrived at New York he put up articles for engaging more hands, it being necessary to his ship's crew, since he proposed to deal with a desperate enemy. The terms he offered were that every man should have a share of what was taken, reserving for himself and owners forty shares. Upon which encouragement he soon increased his company to a hundred and fifty-five men.

With this company he sailed first for Madeira, where he took in wine and some other necessaries; from thence he proceeded to Bonavist, one of the Cape de Verde islands, to furnish the ship with salt, and from thence went immediately to St. Jago, another of the Cape de Verde islands, in order to stock himself with provisions. When all this was done he bent his course to Madagascar, the known rendezvous of pirates. In his way he fell in with Captain Warren, commodore of three men-of-war; he acquainted them with his design, kept them company two or three days, and then leaving them made the best way for Madagascar, where he arrived in February, 1696, just nine months from his departure from Plymouth.

It happened that at this time the pirate ships were most of them out in search of prey, so that, according to the best intelligence Captain Kid could get, there was not one of them at this time about the island, wherefore, having spent some time in watering his ship and taking in more provisions, he thought of trying his fortune on the coast of Malabar, where he arrived in the month of June following, four months from his reaching Madagascar. Hereabouts he made an unsuccessful cruise, touching sometimes at the island of Mahala, sometimes at that of Joanna, between Malabar and Madagascar. His provisions were every day wasting, and his ship began to want repair; wherefore, when he was at Joanna, he found means of borrowing a sum of money from some Frenchmen who had lost their ship, but saved their effects, and with this he purchased materials for putting his ship in good repair.

It does not appear all this while that he had the least design of turning pirate, for near Mahala and Joanna both he met with several Indian ships richly laden, to which he did not offer the least

86

violence, though he was strong enough to have done what he pleased with them; and the first outrage or depredation I find he committed upon mankind was after his repairing his ship and leaving Joanna. He touched at a place called Mabbee, upon the Red Sea, where he took some Guinea corn from the natives, by force.

After this he sailed to Bab's Key, a place upon a little island at the entrance of the Red Sea. Here it was that he first began to open himself to his ship's company, and let them understand that he intended to change his measures; for, happening to talk of the Moca fleet which was to sail that way, he said, "We have been unsuccessful hitherto; but courage, my boys, we'll make our fortunes out of this fleet." And finding that none of them appeared averse to it he ordered a boat out, well manned, to go upon the coast to make discoveries, commanding them to take a prisoner and bring to him, or get intelligence any way they could. The boat returned in a few days, bringing him word that they saw fourteen or fifteen ships ready to sail, some with English, some with Dutch, and some with Moorish colors.

We cannot account for this sudden change in his conduct, otherwise than by supposing that he first meant well, while he had hopes of making his fortune by taking of pirates; but now, weary of ill-success, and fearing lest his owners, out of humor at their great expenses, should dismiss him, and he should want employment, and be marked out for an unlucky man—rather, I say, than run the hazard of poverty, he resolved to do his business one way, since he could not do it another.

He therefore ordered a man continually to watch at the mast-head, lest this fleet should go by them; and about four days after, towards evening it appeared in sight, being convoyed by one English and one Dutch man-of-war. Kid soon fell in with them, and, getting into the midst of them, fired at a Moorish ship which was next him; but the men-of-war, taking the alarm, bore down upon Kid, and, firing upon him, obliged him to sheer off, he not being strong enough to contend with them. Now he had begun hostilities he resolved to go on, and therefore he went and cruised along the coast of Malabar. The first prize he met was a small vessel belonging to Aden; the vessel was Moorish, and the owners were Moorish merchants, but the master was an Englishman; his name was Parker. Kid forced him and a Portuguese that was called Don Antonio, which were all the Europeans on board, to take on with them; the first he designed as a pilot, and the last as an interpreter. He also used the men very cruelly, causing them to be hoisted up by the arms, and drubbed with a naked cutlass, to force them to discover whether they had money on board, and where it lay; but as

87

they had neither gold nor silver on board he got nothing by his cruelty; however, he took from them a bale of pepper, and a bale of coffee, and so let them go.

A little time after he touched at Carawar, a place upon the same coast, where, before he arrived, the news of what he had done to the Moorish ship had reached them; for some of the English merchants there had received an account of it from the owners, who corresponded with them; wherefore, as soon as Kid came in, he was suspected to be the person who committed this piracy, and one Mr. Harvey and Mr. Mason, two of the English factory, came on board and asked for Parker and Antonio, the Portuguese, but Kid denied that he knew any such persons, having secured them both in a private place in the hold, where they were kept for seven or eight days, that is till Kid sailed from thence.

However, the coast was alarmed, and a Portuguese man-of-war was sent out to cruise. Kid met with her, and fought her about six hours, gallantly enough; but finding her too strong to be taken, he quitted her, for he was able to run away from her when he would. Then he went to a place called Porco, where he watered the ship, and bought a number of hogs of the natives to victual his company.

Soon after this he came up with a Moorish ship, the master whereof was a Dutchman, called Schipper Mitchel, and chased her under French colors, which, they observing, hoisted French colors too. When he came up with her he hailed her in French, and they, having a Frenchman on board, answered him in the same language; upon which he ordered them to send their boat on board. They were obliged to do so, and having examined who they were, and from whence they came, he asked the Frenchman, who was a passenger, if he had a French pass for himself? The Frenchman gave him to understand that he had. Then he told the Frenchman he must pass for captain, and "by G—d," says he, "you are the captain." The Frenchman durst not refuse doing as he would have him. The meaning of this was, that he would seize the ship as fair prize, and as if she had belonged to French subjects, according to a commission he had for that purpose; though, one would think, after what he had already done, that he need not have recourse to a quibble to give his actions a color.

In short, he took the cargo and sold it some time after; yet still he seemed to have some fears upon him lest these proceedings should have a bad end, for, coming up with a Dutch ship some time, when his men thought of nothing but attacking her, Kid opposed it; upon which a mutiny arose, and the majority being for taking the said ship, and arming themselves to man the boat to go and seize her, he told them, such as did, never should come on board him

88

again, which put an end to the design, so that he kept company with the said ship some time, without offering her any violence. However, this dispute was the occasion of an accident, upon which an indictment was afterwards grounded against Kid; for Moor, the gunner, being one day upon deck, and talking with Kid about the said Dutch ship, some words arose between them, and Moor told Kid that he had ruined them all; upon which Kid, calling him dog, took up a bucket and struck him with it, which, breaking his skull, he died the next day.

But Kid's penitential fit did not last long, for, coasting along Malabar, he met with a great number of boats, all which he plundered. Upon the same coast he also lighted upon a Portuguese ship, which he kept possession of a week, and then, having taken out of her some chests of Indian goods, thirty jars of butter, with some wax, iron, and a hundred bags of rice, he let her go.

Much about the same time he went to one of the Malabar islands for wood and water, and his cooper, being ashore, was murdered by the natives; upon which Kid himself landed, and burnt and pillaged several of their houses, the people running away; but having taken one, he caused him to be tied to a tree, and commanded one of his men to shoot him; then putting to sea again he took the greatest prize which fell into his hands while he followed his trade. This was a Moorish ship of four hundred tons, richly laden, named the Queda, merchant, the master whereof was an Englishman—he was called Wright, for the Indians often make use of English or Dutch men to command their ships, their own mariners not being so good artists in navigation. Kid chased her under French colors, and, having come up with her, he ordered her to hoist out her boat and to send on board of him, which, being done, he told Wright he was his prisoner; and informing himself concerning the said ship, he understood there were no Europeans on board except two Dutch, and one Frenchman, all the rest being Indians or Armenians, and that the Armenians were part owners of the cargo. Kid gave the Armenians to understand that if they would offer anything that was worth his taking for their ransom, he would hearken to it; upon which they proposed to pay him twenty thousand rupees, not quite three thousand pounds sterling; but Kid judged this would be making a bad bargain, wherefore he rejected it, and setting the crew on shore at different places on the coast, he soon sold as much of the cargo as came to near ten thousand pounds. With part of it he also trafficked, receiving in exchange provisions or such other goods as he wanted. By degrees he disposed of the whole cargo, and when the division was made it came to about two hundred pounds a man, and, having reserved forty shares to himself, his dividend amounted to about eight thousand pounds sterling.

The Indians along the coast came on board and trafficked with all freedom, and he punctually performed his bargains, till about the time he was ready to sail; and then, thinking he should have no further occasion for them, he made no scruple of taking their goods and setting them on shore without any payment in money or goods, which they little expected; for as they had been used to deal with pirates, they always found them men of honor in the way of trade—a people, enemies to deceit, and that scorned to rob but in their own way.

Kid put some of his men on board the Queda, merchant, and with this ship and his own sailed for Madagascar. As soon as he was arrived and had cast anchor there came on board of him a canoe, in which were several Englishmen who had formerly been well acquainted with Kid. As soon as they saw him they saluted him and told him they were informed he was come to take them, and hang them, which would be a little unkind in such an old acquaintance. Kid soon dissipated their doubts by swearing he had no such design, and that he was now in every respect their brother, and just as bad as they, and, calling for a cup of bomboo, drank their captain's health.

These men belonged to a pirate ship, called the Resolution, formerly the Mocco, merchant, whereof one Captain Culliford was commander, and which lay at an anchor not far from them. Kid went on board with them, promising them his friendship and assistance, and Culliford in his turn came on board of Kid; and Kid, to testify his sincerity in iniquity, finding Culliford in want of some necessaries, made him a present of an anchor and some guns, to fit him out for the sea again.

The Adventure galley was now so old and leaky that they were forced to keep two pumps continually going, wherefore Kid shifted all the guns and tackle out of her into the Queda, merchant, intending her for his man-of-war; and as he had divided the money before, he now made a division of the remainder of the cargo. Soon after which the greatest part of the company left him, some going on board Captain Culliford, and others absconding in the country, so that he had not above forty men left.

He put to sea and happened to touch at Amboyna, one of the Dutch spice islands, where he was told that the news of his actions had reached England, and that he was there declared a pirate.

The truth of it is, his piracies so alarmed our merchants that some motions were made in Parliament, to inquire into the commission that was given him, and the persons who fitted him out.

90

These proceedings seemed to lean a little hard upon the Lord Bellamont, who thought himself so much touched thereby that he published a justification of himself in a pamphlet after Kid's execution. In the meantime it was thought advisable, in order to stop the course of these piracies, to publish a proclamation, offering the king's free pardon to all such pirates as should voluntarily surrender themselves, whatever piracies they had been guilty of at any time, before the last day of April, 1699. That is to say, for all piracies committed eastward of the Cape of Good Hope, to the longitude and meridian of Socatora and Cape Camorin. In which proclamation Avery[12] and Kid were excepted by name.

When Kid left Amboyna he knew nothing of this proclamation, for certainly had he had notice of his being excepted in it he would not have been so infatuated to run himself into the very jaws of danger; but relying upon his interest with the Lord Bellamont, and fancying that a French pass or two he found on board some of the ships he took would serve to countenance the matter, and that part of the booty he got would gain him new friends—I say, all these things made him flatter himself that all would be hushed, and that justice would but wink at him. Wherefore he sailed directly for New York, where he was no sooner arrived but by the Lord Bellamont's orders he was secured with all his papers and effects. Many of his fellow-adventurers who had forsook him at Madagascar, came over from thence passengers, some to New England, and some to Jersey, where, hearing of the king's proclamation for pardoning of pirates, they surrendered themselves to the governor of those places. At first they were admitted to bail, but soon after were laid in strict confinement, where they were kept for some time, till an opportunity happened of sending them with their captain over to England to be tried.

Accordingly, a Sessions of Admiralty being held at the Old Bailey, in May, 1701, Captain Kid, Nicholas Churchill, James How, Robert Lumley, William Jenkins, Gabriel Loff, Hugh Parrot, Richard Barlicorn, Abel Owens, and Darby Mullins, were arraigned for piracy and robbery on the high seas, and all found guilty except three: these were Robert Lumley, William Jenkins, and Richard Barlicorn, who, proving themselves to be apprentices to some of the officers of the ship, and producing their indentures in court, were acquitted.

The three above mentioned, though they were proved to be concerned in taking and sharing the ship and goods mentioned in

---

[12] Avery was called "The King of the Pirates." See "The Daughter of the Great Mogul."

the indictment, yet, as the gentlemen of the long robe rightly distinguished, there was a great difference between their circumstances and the rest; for there must go an intention of the mind and a freedom of the will to the committing an act of felony or piracy. A pirate is not to be understood to be under constraint, but a free agent; for, in this case, the bare act will not make a man guilty, unless the will make it so.

Kid was tried upon an indictment of murder also—viz., for killing Moor, the gunner—and found guilty of the same.

As to Captain Kid's defense, he insisted much upon his own innocence, and the villainy of his men. He said he went out in a laudable employment, and had no occasion, being then in good circumstances, to go a-pirating; that the men often mutinied against him, and did as they pleased; that he was threatened to be shot in his cabin, and that ninety-five left him at one time, and set fire to his boat, so that he was disabled from bringing his ship home, or the prizes he took, to have them regularly condemned, which he said were taken by virtue of a commission under the broad seal, they having French passes. The captain called one Colonel Hewson to his reputation, who gave him an extraordinary character, and declared to the court that he had served under his command, and been in two engagements with him against the French, in which he fought as well as any man he ever saw; that there were only Kid's ship and his own against Monsieur du Cass, who commanded a squadron of six sail, and they got the better of him. But this being several years before the facts mentioned in the indictment were committed, proved of no manner of service to the prisoner on his trial.

As to the friendship shown to Culliford, a notorious pirate, Kid denied, and said he intended to have taken him, but his men, being a parcel of rogues and villains, refused to stand by him, and several of them ran away from his ship to the said pirate. But the evidence being full and particular against him, he was found guilty as before mentioned.

When Kid was asked what he had to say why sentence should not pass against him, he answered that "he had nothing to say, but that he had been sworn against by perjured, wicked people." And when sentence was pronounced, he said, "My lord, it is a very hard sentence. For my part I am the innocentest person of them all, only I have been sworn against by perjured persons."

Wherefore, about a week after, Captain Kid, Nicholas Churchill, James How, Gabriel Loff, Hugh Parrot, Abel Owen, and Darby Mullins, were executed at Execution Dock, and afterwards hung up in chains, at some distance from each other down the river, where their bodies hung exposed for many years.

III

Captain Bartholomew Roberts and His Crew

Bartholomew Roberts sailed in an honest employ from London, aboard of the Princess, Captain Plumb, commander, of which ship he was second mate. He left England November, 1719, and arrived at Guinea about February following and being at Anamaboe, taking in slaves for the West Indies, was taken in the said ship by Captain Howel Davis. In the beginning he was very averse to this sort of life, and would certainly have escaped from them had a fair opportunity presented itself; yet afterwards he changed his principles, as many besides him have done upon another element, and perhaps for the same reason too, viz., preferment; and what he did not like as a private man he could reconcile to his conscience as a commander.

Davis having been killed in the Island of Princes whilst planning to capture it with all its inhabitants, the company found themselves under the necessity of filling up his post, for which there appeared two or three candidates among the select part of them that were distinguished by the title of Lords—such were Sympson, Ashplant, Anstis, &c.—and on canvassing this matter, how shattered and weak a condition their government must be without a head, since Davis had been removed in the manner before mentioned, my Lord Dennis proposed, it is said, over a bowl, to this purpose:

"That it was not of any great signification who was dignified with title, for really and in good truth all good governments had, like theirs, the supreme power lodged with the community, who might doubtless depute and revoke as suited interest or humor. We are the original of this claim," says he, "and should a captain be so saucy as to exceed prescription at any time, why, down with him! It will be a caution after he is dead to his successors of what fatal consequence any sort of assuming may be. However, it is my advice that while we are sober we pitch upon a man of courage and skilled in navigation, one who by his council and bravery seems best able to defend this commonwealth, and ward us from the dangers and tempests of an unstable element, and the fatal consequences of anarchy; and such a one I take Roberts to be—a fellow, I think, in all respects worthy your esteem and favor."

This speech was loudly applauded by all but Lord Sympson, who had secret expectations himself, but on this disappointment grew sullen and left them, swearing "he did not care who they chose captain so it was not a papist, for against them he had conceived an

93

irreconcilable hatred, for that his father had been a sufferer in Monmouth's rebellion."

Roberts was accordingly elected, though he had not been above six weeks among them. The choice was confirmed both by the Lords and Commoners, and he accepted of the honor, saying that, since he had dipped his hands in muddy water and must be a pirate, it was better being a commander than a common man.

As soon as the government was settled, by promoting other officers in the room of those that were killed by the Portuguese, the company resolved to avenge Captain Davis's death, he being more than ordinarily respected by the crew for his affability and good nature, as well as his conduct and bravery upon all occasions; and, pursuant to this resolution, about thirty men were landed, in order to make an attack upon the fort, which must be ascended to by a steep hill against the mouth of the cannon. These men were headed by one Kennedy, a bold, daring fellow, but very wicked and profligate; they marched directly up under the fire of their ship guns, and as soon as they were discovered, the Portuguese quitted their post and fled to the town, and the pirates marched in without opposition, set fire to the fort, and threw all the guns off the hill into the sea, which after they had done they retreated quietly to their ship.

But this was not looked upon as a sufficient satisfaction for the injury they received, therefore most of the company were for burning the town, which Roberts said he would yield to if any means could be proposed of doing it without their own destruction, for the town had a securer situation than the fort, a thick wood coming almost close to it, affording cover to the defendants, who, under such an advantage, he told them, it was to be feared, would fire and stand better to their arms; beside, that bare houses would be but a slender reward for their trouble and loss. This prudent advice prevailed; however, they mounted the French ship they seized at this place with twelve guns, and lightened her, in order to come up to the town, the water being shoal, and battered down several houses; after which they all returned on board, gave back the French ship to those that had most right to her, and sailed out of the harbor by the light of two Portuguese ships, which they were pleased to set on fire there.

Roberts stood away to the southward, and met with a Dutch Guineaman, which he made prize of, but, after having plundered her, the skipper had his ship again. Two days after he took an English ship, called the Experiment, Captain Cornet, at Cape Lopez; the men went all into the pirate service, and having no occasion for the ship they burnt her and then steered for St. Thome, but meeting with nothing in their way, they sailed for Annabona, and there watered, took in provisions, and put it to a vote of the company whether their next voyage should be to the East Indies or to Brazil. The latter being resolved on, they sailed accordingly, and in twenty-eight days arrived at Ferdinando, an uninhabited island on that coast. Here they watered, boot-topped their ship, and made ready for the designed cruise.

Upon this coast our rovers cruised for about nine weeks, keeping generally out of sight of land, but without seeing a sail, which discouraged them so that they determined to leave the station and steer for the West Indies; and, in order thereto, stood in to make the land for the taking of their departure; and thereby they fell in unexpectedly with a fleet of forty-two sail of Portuguese ships off the bay of Los Todos Santos, with all their lading in, for Lisbon, several of them of good force, who lay-to waiting for two men-of-war of seventy guns each, their convoy. However, Roberts thought it should go hard with him, but he would make up his market among them, and thereupon mixed with the fleet, and kept his men hid till proper resolutions could be formed. That done, they came close up to one of the deepest, and ordered her to send the master on board quietly, threatening to give them no quarter if any resistance or signal of distress was made. The Portuguese, being surprised at these threats, and the sudden flourish of cutlasses from the pirates, submitted without a word, and the captain came on board. Roberts saluted him after a friendly manner telling him that they were gentlemen of fortune, but that their business with him was only to be informed which was the richest ship in that fleet; and if he directed them right he should be restored to his ship without molestation, otherwise he must expect immediate death.

Whereupon this Portuguese master pointed to one of forty guns and a hundred and fifty men, a ship of greater force than the Rover; but this no ways dismayed them; they were Portuguese, they said, and so immediately steered away for him. When they came within hail, the master whom they had prisoner was ordered to ask "how Seignior Captain did?" and to invite him on board, "for that he had a matter of consequence to impart to him;" which being done, he returned for answer that "he would wait upon him presently," but by the bustle that immediately followed, the pirates perceived that they were discovered, and that this was only a deceitful answer to gain time to put their ship in a posture of defense; so without further delay they poured in a broadside, boarded, and grappled her. The dispute was short and warm, wherein many of the Portuguese fell, and two only of the pirates. By this time the fleet was alarmed: signals of top-gallant sheets flying and guns fired to give notice to the men-of-war, who rid still at an anchor, and made but scurvy haste out to their assistance; and if what the pirates themselves related to be true, the commanders of those ships were blameable to the highest degree, and unworthy the title, or so much as the name, of men. For Roberts, finding the prize to sail heavy, and yet resolving not to lose her, lay by for the headmost of them, which much outsailed the other, and prepared for battle, which was ignominiously declined, though of such superior force; for, not daring to venture on the pirate alone, he tarried so long for his consort as gave them both time leisurely to make off.

They found this ship exceedingly rich, being laden chiefly with sugar, skins, and tobacco, and in gold forty thousand moidores, besides chains and trinkets of considerable value; particularly a cross set with diamonds designed for the king of Portugal, which they afterwards presented to the governor of Caiana, by whom they were obliged.

Elated with this booty, they had nothing now to think of but some safe retreat where they might give themselves up to all the pleasures that luxury and wantonness could bestow; and for the present pitched upon a place called the Devil's Islands in the river of Surinam, on the coast of Caiana, where they arrived, and found the civilest reception imaginable, not only from the governor and factory, but their wives, who exchanged wares, and drove a considerable trade with them.

They seized in this river a sloop, and by her gained intelligence that a brigantine had also sailed in company with her from Rhode Island, laden with provisions for the coast—a welcome cargo! They growing short in the sea store, and, as Sancho says, "No adventures to be made without belly-timber." One evening, as they were rummaging their mine of treasure, the Portuguese prize, this expected vessel was descried at the masthead, and Roberts, imagining nobody could do the business so well as himself, takes forty men in the sloop, and goes in pursuit of her; but a fatal accident followed this rash, though inconsiderable adventure, for Roberts, thinking of nothing less than bringing in the brigantine that afternoon, never troubled his head about the sloop's provision, nor inquired what there was on board to subsist such a number of men; but out he sails after his expected prize, which he not only lost further sight of, but after eight days' contending with contrary winds and currents, found themselves thirty leagues to leeward. The current still opposing their endeavors, and perceiving no hopes of beating up to their ship, they came to an anchor, and inconsiderately sent away the boat to give the rest of the company notice of their condition, and to order the ship to them; but too soon—even the next day—their wants made them sensible of their infatuation, for their water was all expended, and they had taken no thought how they should be supplied till either the ship came or the boat returned, which was not likely to be under five or six days. Here, like Tantalus, they almost famished in sight of the fresh streams and lakes, being drove to such extremity at last that they were forced to tear up the floor of the cabin and patch up a sort of tub or tray with rope-yarns to paddle ashore and fetch off immediate supplies of water to preserve life.

After some days the long-wished-for boat came back, but with the most unwelcome news in the world; for Kennedy, who was lieutenant, and left, in absence of Roberts, to command the privateer and prize, was gone off with both. This was mortification with a vengeance, and you may imagine they did not depart without some hard speeches from those that were left and had suffered by their treachery. And that there need be no further mention of this Kennedy, I shall leave Captain Roberts to vent his wrath in a few oaths and execrations, and follow the other, whom we may reckon from that time as steering his course towards Execution Dock.

Kennedy was now chosen captain of the revolted crew, but could not bring his company to any determined resolution. Some of them were for pursuing the old game, but the greater part of them seemed to have inclinations to turn from those evil courses, and get home privately, for there was no act of pardon in force; therefore they agreed to break up, and every man to shift for himself, as he should see occasion. The first thing they did was to part with the great Portuguese prize, and having the master of the sloop (whose name, I think, was Cane) aboard, who, they said, was a very honest fellow—for he had humored them upon every occasion—told them of the brigantine that Roberts went after; and when the pirates first took him he complimented them at any odd rate, telling them they were welcome to his sloop and cargo, and wished that the vessel had been larger and the loading richer for their sakes. To this good-natured man they gave the Portuguese ship, which was then above half loaded, three or four negroes, and all his own men, who returned thanks to his kind benefactors, and departed.

Captain Kennedy, in the Rover, sailed to Barbadoes, near which island they took a very peaceable ship belonging to Virginia. The commander was a Quaker, whose name was Knot; he had neither pistol, sword, nor cutlass on board; and Mr. Knot appearing so very passive to all they said to him, some of them thought this a good opportunity to go off; and accordingly eight of the pirates went aboard, and he carried them safe to Virginia. They made the Quaker a present of ten chests of sugar, ten rolls of Brazil tobacco, thirty moidores, and some gold dust, in all to the value of about £250. They also made presents to the sailors, some more, some less, and lived a jovial life all the while they were upon their voyage, Captain Knot giving them their way; nor, indeed, could he help himself, unless he had taken an opportunity to surprise them when they were either drunk or asleep, for awake they wore arms aboard the ship and put him in a continual terror, it not being his principle (or the sect's) to fight, unless with art and collusion. He managed these weapons well till he arrived at the Capes; and afterwards four of the pirates went off in a boat, which they had taken with them for the more easily making their escapes, and made up the bay towards Maryland, but were forced back by a storm into an obscure place of the country, where, meeting with good entertainment among the planters, they continued several days without being discovered to be pirates. In the meantime Captain Knot, leaving four others on board his ship who intended to go to North Carolina, made what haste he could to discover to Mr. Spotswood, the governor, what sort of passengers he had been forced to bring with him, who, by good fortune, got them seized; and search being made after the others, who were revelling about the country, they were also taken, and all tried, convicted, and hanged; two Portuguese Jews, who were taken on the coast of Brazil and whom they brought with them to Virginia, being the principal evidences. The latter had found means to lodge part of their wealth with the planters, who never brought it to account. But Captain Knot surrendered up everything that belonged to them that were taken aboard, even what they presented to him, in lieu of such things as they had plundered him of in their passage, and obliged his men to do the like.

Some days after the taking of the Virginiaman last mentioned, in cruising in the latitude of Jamaica, Kennedy took a sloop bound thither from Boston, loaded with bread and flour; aboard of this sloop went all the hands who were for breaking the gang, and left those behind that had a mind to pursue further adventures. Among the former was Kennedy, their captain, of whose honor they had such a despicable notion that they were about to throw him overboard when they found him in the sloop, as fearing he might betray them all at their return to England; he having in his childhood been bred a pick-pocket, and before he became a pirate a house-breaker; both professions that these gentlemen have a very mean opinion of. However, Captain Kennedy, by taking solemn oaths of fidelity to his companions, was suffered to proceed with them.

In this company there was but one that pretended to any skill in navigation (for Kennedy could neither write nor read, he being preferred to the command merely for his courage, which indeed he had often signalized, particularly in taking the Portuguese ship), and he proved to be a pretender only; for, shaping their course to Ireland, where they agreed to land, they ran away to the north-west coast of Scotland, and there were tossed about by hard storms of wind for several days without knowing where they were, and in great danger of perishing. At length they pushed the vessel into a little creek and went all ashore, leaving the sloop at an anchor for the next comers.

The whole company refreshed themselves at a little village about five miles from the place where they left the sloop, and passed there for shipwrecked sailors, and no doubt might have travelled on without suspicion, but the mad and riotous manner of their living on the road occasioned their journey to be cut short, as we shall observe presently.

Kennedy and another left them here, and, travelling to one of the seaports, shipped themselves for Ireland, and arrived there in safety. Six or seven wisely withdrew from the rest, travelled at their leisure, and got to their much-desired port of London without being disturbed or suspected, but the main gang alarmed the country wherever they came, drinking and roaring at such a rate that the people shut themselves up in their houses, in some places not daring to venture out among so many mad fellows. In other villages they treated the whole town, squandering their money away as if, like Æsop, they wanted to lighten their burthens. This expensive manner of living procured two of their drunken stragglers to be knocked on the head, they being found murdered in the road and their money taken from them. All the rest, to the number of seventeen, as they drew nigh to Edinburgh, were arrested and thrown into gaol upon suspicion of they knew not what; however, the magistrates were not long at a loss for proper accusations, for two of the gang offering themselves for evidences were accepted of, and the others were brought to a speedy trial, whereof nine were convicted and executed.

Kennedy having spent all his money, came over from Ireland and kept a public-house on Deptford Road, and now and then it was thought, made an excursion abroad in the way of his former profession, till one of his household gave information against him for a robbery, for which he was committed to Bridewell; but because she would not do the business by halves she found out a mate of a ship that Kennedy had committed piracy upon, as he foolishly confessed to her. This mate, whose name was Grant, paid Kennedy a visit in Bridewell, and knowing him to be the man, procured a warrant, and had him committed to the Marshalsea prison.

The game that Kennedy had now to play was to turn evidence himself; accordingly he gave a list of eight or ten of his comrades, but, not being acquainted with their habitations, one only was taken, who, though condemned, appeared to be a man of a fair character, was forced into their service, and took the first opportunity to get from them, and therefore received a pardon; but Walter Kennedy, being a notorious offender, was executed July 19, 1721, at Execution Dock.

The rest of the pirates who were left in the ship Rover stayed not long behind, for they went ashore to one of the West India islands. What became of them afterwards I cannot tell, but the ship was found at sea by a sloop belonging to St. Christophers, and carried into that island with only nine negroes aboard.

Thus we see what a disastrous fate ever attends the wicked, and how rarely they escape the punishment due to their crimes, who, abandoned to such a profligate life, rob, spoil, and prey upon mankind, contrary to the light and law of nature, as well as the law of God. It might have been hoped that the examples of these deaths would have been as marks to the remainder of this gang, how to shun the rocks their companions had split on; that they would have surrendered to mercy, or divided themselves for ever from such pursuits, as in the end they might be sure would subject them to the same law and punishment, which they must be conscious they now equally deserved; impending law, which never let them sleep well unless when drunk. But all the use that was made of it here, was to commend the justice of the court that condemned Kennedy, for he was a sad dog, they said, and deserved the fate he met with.

But to go back to Roberts, whom we left on the coast of Caiana, in a grievous passion at what Kennedy and the crew had done, and who was now projecting new adventures with his small company in the sloop; but finding hitherto they had been but as a rope of sand, they formed a set of articles to be signed and sworn to for the better conservation of their society, and doing justice to one another, excluding all Irishmen from the benefit of it, to whom they had an implacable aversion upon the account of Kennedy. How, indeed, Roberts could think that an oath would be obligatory where defiance had been given to the laws of God and man, I cannot tell, but he thought their greatest security lay in this—"that it was every one's interest to observe them, if they minded to keep up so abominable a combination."

The following is the substance of articles as taken from the pirates' own informations:—

I

Every man has a vote in affairs of moment, has equal title to the fresh provisions or strong liquors at any time seized, and may use them at pleasure, unless a scarcity (no uncommon thing among them) make it necessary for the good of all to vote a retrenchment.

II

Every man to be called fairly in turn by list, on board of prizes, because, over and above their proper share, they were on these occasions allowed a shift of clothes. But if they defrauded the company to the value of a dollar, in plate, jewels, or money, marooning was their punishment. (This was a barbarous custom of putting the offender on shore, on some desolate or uninhabited cape or island, with a gun, a few shot, a bottle of water, a bottle of powder, to subsist with or starve.) If the robbery was only between one another, they contented themselves with slitting the ears and nose of him that was guilty, and set him on shore, not in an uninhabited place, but somewhere where he was sure to encounter hardships.

III

No person to game at cards or dice for money.

IV

The lights and candles to be put out at eight o'clock at night. If any of the crew after that hour still remained inclined for drinking, they were to do it on the open deck. (Which Roberts believed would give a check to their debauches, for he was a sober man himself, but found at length that all his endeavors to put an end to this debauch proved ineffectual.)

V

To keep their piece, pistols, and cutlass clean, and fit for service. (In this they were extravagantly nice, endeavoring to outdo one another in the beauty and richness of their arms, giving sometimes at an auction—at the mast—£30 or £40 a pair for pistols. These were slung in time of service, with different colored ribbons, over their shoulders, in a way peculiar to these fellows, in which they took great delight.)

VI

No boy or woman to be allowed amongst them. If any man were found seducing any of the latter sex, and carried her to sea disguised, he was to suffer death. (So that when any fell into their hands, as it chanced in the Onslow, they put a sentinel immediately over her to prevent ill consequences from so dangerous an instrument of division and quarrel; but then here lies the roguery—they contend who shall be sentinel, which happens generally to one of the greatest bullies.)

VII

To desert the ship or their quarters in battle, was punished with death or marooning.

VIII

No striking one another on board, but every man's quarrel to be ended on shore, at sword and pistol. Thus the quartermaster of the ship, when the parties will not come to any reconciliation, accompanies them on shore with what assistance he thinks proper, and turns the disputants back to back at so many paces distance. At the word of command they turn and fire immediately, or else the piece is knocked out of their hands. If both miss, they come to their cutlasses, and then he is declared victor who draws the first blood.

IX

No man to talk of breaking up their way of living till each had shared £1,000. If, in order to this, any man should lose a limb, or become a cripple in their service, he was to have 800 dollars out of the public stock, and for lesser hurts proportionably.

X

The captain and quartermaster to receive two shares of a prize; the master, boatswain, and gunner, one share and a half, the other officers one and a quarter.

XI

The musicians to have rest on the Sabbath-day, but the other six days and nights none without special favor.

These, we are assured, were some of Roberts's articles, but as they had taken care to throw overboard the original they had signed and sworn to, there is a great deal of room to suspect the remainder contained something too horrid to be disclosed to any, except such as were willing to be sharers in the iniquity of them. Let them be what they will, they were together the test of all newcomers, who were initiated by an oath taken on a Bible, reserved for that purpose only, and were subscribed to in presence of the worshipful Mr. Roberts. And in case any doubt should arise concerning the construction of these laws, and it should remain a dispute whether the party had infringed them or no, a jury was appointed to explain them, and bring in a verdict upon the case in doubt.

Since we are now speaking of the laws of this company, I shall go on, and, in as brief a manner as I can, relate the principal customs and government of this roguish commonwealth, which are pretty near the same with all pirates.

For the punishment of small offences which are not provided for by the articles, and which are not of consequence enough to be left to a jury, there is a principal officer among the pirates, called the quartermaster, of the men's own choosing, who claims all authority this way, excepting in time of battle. If they disobey his command, are quarrelsome and mutinous with one another, misuse prisoners, plunder beyond his order, and in particular, if they be negligent of their arms, which he musters at discretion, he punishes at his own arbitrament, with drubbing or whipping, which no one else dare do without incurring the lash from all the ship's company. In short, this officer is trustee for the whole, is the first on board any prize, separating for the company's use what he pleases, and returning what he thinks fit to the owners, excepting gold and silver, which they have voted not returnable.

After a description of the quartermaster and his duty, who acts as a sort of civil magistrate on board a pirate ship, I shall consider their military officer, the captain; what privileges he exerts in such anarchy and unruliness of the members. Why, truly very little—they only permit him to be captain, on condition that they may be captain over him; they separate to his use the great cabin, and sometimes vote him small parcels of plate and china (for it may be noted that Roberts drank his tea constantly), but then every man, as the humor takes him, will use the plate and china, intrude into his apartment, swear at him, seize a part of his victuals and drink, if they like it, without his offering to find fault or contest it. Yet Roberts, by a better management than usual, became the chief director in everything of moment; and it happened thus:—The rank of captain being obtained by the suffrage of the majority, it falls on one superior for knowledge and boldness—pistol proof, as they call it—who can make those fear who do not love him. Roberts is said to have exceeded his fellows in these respects, and when advanced, enlarged the respect that followed it by making a sort of privy council of half a dozen of the greatest bullies, such as were his competitors, and had interest enough to make his government easy; yet even those, in the latter part of his reign, he had run counter to in every project that opposed his own opinion; for which, and because he grew reserved and would not drink and roar at their rate, a cabal was formed to take away his captainship, which death did more effectually.

The captain's power is uncontrollable in chase or in battle, drubbing, cutting, or even shooting any one who dares deny his command. The same privilege he takes over prisoners, who receive good or ill usage mostly as he approves of their behavior, for though the meanest would take upon them to misuse a master of a ship, yet he would control herein when he sees it, and merrily over a bottle give his prisoners this double reason for it: first, that it preserved his precedence; and secondly, that it took the punishment out of the hands of a much more rash and mad set of fellows than himself. When he found that rigor was not expected from his people (for he often practiced it to appease them), then he would give strangers to understand that it was pure inclination that induced him to a good treatment of them, and not any love or partiality to their persons; for, says he, "there is none of you but will hang me, I know, whenever you can clinch me within your power."

And now, seeing the disadvantages they were under for pursuing their plans, viz., a small vessel ill repaired, and without provisions or stores, they resolved, one and all, with the little supplies they could get, to proceed for the West Indies, not doubting to find a remedy for all these evils and to retrieve their loss.

In the latitude of Deseada, one of the islands, they took two sloops, which supplied them with provisions and other necessaries, and a few days afterwards took a brigantine belonging to Rhode Island, and then proceeded to Barbadoes, off of which island they fell in with a Bristol ship of ten guns, in her voyage out, from whom they took abundance of clothes, some money, twenty-five bales of goods, five barrels of powder, a cable, hawser, ten casks of oatmeal, six casks of beef, and several other goods, besides five of their men; and after they had detained her three days let her go, who, being bound for the aforesaid island, she acquainted the governor with what had happened as soon as she arrived.

Whereupon a Bristol galley that lay in the harbor was ordered to be fitted out with all imaginable expedition, of 20 guns and 80 men, there being then no man-of-war upon that station, and also a sloop with 10 guns and 40 men. The galley was commanded by one Captain Rogers, of Bristol, and the sloop by Captain Graves, of that island, and Captain Rogers, by a commission from the governor, was appointed commodore.

The second day after Rogers sailed out of the harbor he was discovered by Roberts, who, knowing nothing of their design, gave them chase. The Barbadoes ships kept an easy sail till the pirates came up with them, and then Roberts gave them a gun, expecting they would have immediately struck to his piratical flag; but instead thereof, he was forced to receive the fire of a broadside, with three huzzas at the same time, so that an engagement ensued; but Roberts, being hardly put to it, was obliged to crowd all the sail the sloop would bear to get off. The galley, sailing pretty well, kept company for a long while, keeping a constant fire, which galled the pirate; however, at length, by throwing over their guns and other heavy goods, and thereby lightening the vessel, they, with much ado, got clear; but Roberts could never endure a Barbadoes man afterwards, and when any ships belonging to that island fell in his way, he was more particularly severe to them than others.

Captain Roberts sailed in the sloop to the island of Dominico, where he watered and got provisions of the inhabitants, to whom he gave goods in exchange. At this place he met with thirteen Englishmen, who had been set ashore by a French Guard de la Coste, belonging to Martinico, taken out of two New England ships that had been seized as prizes by the said French sloop. The men willingly entered with the pirates, and it proved a seasonable recruiting.

They stayed not long here, though they had immediate occasion for cleaning their sloop, but did not think this a proper place; and herein they judged right, for the touching at this island had like to have been their destruction, because they, having resolved to go away to the Granada Islands for the aforesaid purpose, by some accident it came to be known to the French colony, who, sending word to the governor of Martinico, he equipped and manned two sloops to go in quest of them. The pirates sailed directly for the Granadilloes, and hall'd into a lagoon at Corvocoo, where they cleaned with unusual dispatch, staying but a little above a week, by which expedition they missed of the Martinico sloops only a few hours, Roberts sailing overnight and the French arriving the next morning. This was a fortunate escape, especially considering that it was not from any fears of their being discovered that they made so much haste from the island, but, as they had the impudence themselves to own, for the want of wine and women.

Thus narrowly escaped, they sailed for Newfoundland, and arrived upon the banks the latter end of June, 1720. They entered the harbor of Trepassi with their black colors flying, drums beating, and trumpets sounding. There were two-and-twenty vessels in the harbor, which the men all quitted upon the sight of the pirate, and fled ashore. It is impossible particularly to recount the destruction and havoc they made here, burning and sinking all the shipping except a Bristol galley, and destroying the fisheries and stages of the poor planters without remorse or compunction; for nothing is so deplorable as power in mean and ignorant hands—it makes men wanton and giddy, unconcerned at the misfortunes they are imposing on their fellow-creatures, and keeps them smiling at the mischiefs that bring themselves no advantage. They are like madmen that cast fire-brands, arrows, and death, and say, Are not we in sport?

106

NARRATIVE OF THE CAPTURE OF THE SHIP DERBY, 1735

Captain Anselm

I fell in with the Land of Madagascar, the Latitude of about 24 Degrees, 13 Minutes North: And some time before I had made it, I met with nothing but light Airs of Winds, and Calms, and continued so long. My People dropping down with the Scurvy, I took a small Still that I had, and distill'd Salt Water into Fresh. I allow'd them as much Pease and Flower as they could eat, that they might not eat any Salt Provision, tho' I boil'd it in fresh Water. I had been very liberal with my fresh Provision in my Passage, to my People, and the Passage so long, that I had hardly any left, and that only a few Fowls; and myself and Officers too had been much out of Order. At last, being got to the Northward of Augustin Bay, seeing my poor People fall down so very fast, it gave me very great Concern for them, but still was willing, in Hopes of Change of Wind, for Johanna. But the small Airs trifled with me, and what there were Northerly, a Current setting to the Southward, that what to do I could not well tell. To go into Augustin Bay I was very unwilling: I had two Boats came off to me, the People talking tolerable good English. At last, my Doctor, Sharp, told me there were above Thirty People down with the Scurvy, and all the rest, even some of the Petty Officers, were touch'd with the same. If I did not soon put into Port, I plainly found I should have been in a bad Condition, for Men; I consulted with my Officers, to go into Augustin Bay, and we agreed, and bore away for it. Soon after, the Wind came Southerly, and I bore away for Johanna. A fine Passage I had, and anchor'd the next Day about Four in the Afternoon, being Sept. 13. I thank God I brought all my People in alive, and that is as much I can say of a good many of them. I had a Tent made ashore for them, and supplied them all that ever I could, and the Doctors assisting with every thing in their Way for their speedy Recovery. After I had been here a Fortnight, the Winds in the Day-time set in very fresh from the N. N. W. to the N. N. E. Finding the People recover so very slowly, what to do I could not tell. To go out with my People as bad as when they came in, I was not willing, but resolv'd to have Patience one Week more. I consulted with Mr. Rogers, my Chief-Mate, and told him that we must consider the Condition of the People, and how we met the Winds and Currents before we came in. The People of the Island told me, that this was about the time of

Year for the Northerly Winds and Southerly Currents, and I told him I thought it better to trim all our Casks, and fill what Water we could, fearing of a long Passage, if our Stay was a little longer. Mr. Rogers was of my Opinion. This I must say, I found the Cask not so well used in the Hold, as they ought to have been, which caus'd the Coopers more Work; neither did I make a little Noise about it, because I had more Words with my Chief and Second Mate, about my Third and Fourth Mate, than any thing else.

Having all my Water aboard, about 80 Tun, 25 Head of Oxen, &c., I sail'd the 13th of October, with several of my Men not recover'd; some I buried at Johanna, and some after, to the Number of Ten, or thereabouts. Having a fine Gale, I made all the Sail I could, except Studding-sails, which I thought needless. The Wind veer'd to the Northward, and I was resolved to make the Mallabar Course as soon as possible, for the Advantage of the Land and Sea Winds. I had one Passenger aboard, a sad troublesome wicked Fellow, whose Behaviour was so bad, that I could hardly forbear using him ill. I forbid my Officers keeping Company with him; but Mr. B——s would do it at all Events. I turn'd him once off the Quarter-Deck for being with him there, yet that did not avail. I came out one Night about half an Hour past Ten, my second Mate's Watch, and this B——s's Turn to sleep; and seeing a Light in his Cabin, I sent Mr. Cuddon, the second Mate, to him, to know how he would be able to sit up one Watch, and keep his own. Upon this B——s came up half way the Steerage-Ladder, with his Pipe in his Hand, and talk'd to me very pertly; and that was not the first time. This put me into a Passion, to be so talk'd to by a Boy, that I did dismiss him for two or three Days, and then re-stated him, which was more than he deserv'd, for keeping Company with him for whom the worst of Names is good enough, and those who recommended him to his Commission. B——s was told of this by Mr. Rogers, by my Orders, and I told him of it on the Quarter-Deck, and told him at the same time I was resolv'd to tell the Gentlemen at Home of ——; and ask'd him what he imagin'd they would think of him for keeping such swearing drunken Company. This was before I dismiss'd him.

Before I came in with the Land, hearing much talk of Angria,[13] by Capt. Scarlet, and Mr. Rogers, and of his great Force (for I had very little Notion of him before) I took care to put the Ship in a proper Posture of Defence: Powder-Chests on the Quarter-Deck, Poop, and Forecastle, a Puncheon fill'd with Water in the Main-top, a Hogshead in the Fore-top, and a Barrel in the Mizen-top, all fill'd

[13] A noted pirate.

with Water: Chests with good Coverings in the Tops for Grenado-Shells; all the small Arms, with 50 new ones in Readiness. My Ship being too deep to get the Gun-room Ports open, as the Gunner inform'd me, the Ship sending, and the Sea washing above the Tops of the Ports; I got those Guns into the Great Cabin; Quarter-Bills over the Guns; the Rewards and Close-quarters, &c. at the Mizen-mast, Shot-lockers and Shot in their proper Station; Pluggs for Shot-holes; and every thing that I could think of: and gave particular Orders to my Gunner, Carpenter, and Boatswain, to have every thing in their way, in Readiness, the two lower Yards flung with the Top-chains. Not being easy in my Mind about these Gun-room Stern-Ports, I sent Mr. Rogers, it being smooth Water, to open one of the Gun-room Stern-Ports, to see, if we could, on Occasion, get Guns out there, but he brought me Word it could not be done with Safety, the Ship being so deep. A few Days before I made the Land, the Winds used to vere and haul, that Offing in an Hour I could hardly up from E. N. E. to S. E. but the Winds chiefly kept to the Northward. I was very desirous to make the Land, not knowing how far the Southwest Currents might set me to the Westward. At noon, being Dec. 12, I made the Land of Goa, in the Latitude of 15 Degrees North. My Chief Mate wanted me to go into Goa, but I was resolved not, but to make the best of my Way for Bombay. The next Morning, having a fine Six-Knot-Gale, about Nine o' Clock Mr. Rogers told me, he saw Gereah, and desired me to haul further off Shore, and said, if Angria and his Grabbs should see us in his River, he would send them out after us. I asked him, if his Grabbs came out of Sight of Land. He told me they were afraid to do that, fearing the Bombay Vessels should get between them and the Shore, and keep them out of their Ports. To prevent running into Danger, I kept out of Sight of Land: I thought it better to do so, since it would make but a few Days Difference in getting at Bombay; making no Doubt I should get there the last of the Month, as doubtless we should, if we had not met with our sad Misfortune.

When it was too late, I was acquainted by those taken in the Severn, that Mr. Rogers inform'd me wrong; for Angria sometimes keeps the Shore aboard, and sometimes goes directly out to Sea 60 Leagues off. It was too late to reflect; neither could I blame myself, knowing I had done every thing to the best of my Judgment: But had I been better inform'd, it is my Opinion we might have escaped those cursed Dogs, by keeping in Shore, and taken the Advantage of the Land and Sea Winds.

I have since repented that we did not go into Goa; but God knows whether a Man goes too fast or too slow; for I had certainly a very suitable Cargo for that Place; But my earnest Desire was to get to Bombay, the Season of the Year being far advanc'd.

December 26, being my second Mate's Morning Watch, about Five o' Clock he came to me, and told me he saw Nine Sail of Gallivats. I got up, and found them to be Five Top-mast Vessels, and Four Gallivats, not above two Miles from us. I order'd all Hands to be call'd, and down with the Cabins in the Steerage, which was done in an Instant, and every body to their respective Quarters. They came up with us apace, having but light Airs of Winds, and found them to be Angria's Fleet. I had the Transome in the great Cabin, and the Balcony in the Round-house cut away, for traversing the Stern-Chase Guns. They came up with me very boldly within Pistol-shot. Before Six, they began firing upon us, throwing their Shot in at our Stern, raking us afore and aft. I order'd everything to be got ready for going about, to give them my Broad-side, when my Chief-Mate Mr. Rogers, and my Third Mate Mr. Burroughs came to me, and begg'd that I would not put about, for if I did, they would certainly board us. As to my Part, being a Stranger to this Coast and Angria, knowing my Chief Mate had been often this Way, and my Third Mate had sail'd in the Gallies, I was over prevail'd upon not to tack about. As the Enemy kept under my Stern, playing their Shot in very hot upon us, and destroying my Rigging so fast, I soon after endeavour'd to wear the Ship upon the Enemy; but the Wind dying away to a Calm, she would not regard her Helm, but lay like a Log in the Water. By Eight o' Clock most of my Rigging was destroy'd, and the Long-boat taking Fire a-stern, was forc'd to cut her away. The Yaul being stove by their shot, we launch'd her overboard. By Nine, the Top-chain that flung the Main-yard, was shot away, with Geer and Geer-Blocks. The Main-yard came next down, with the Sails almost torn to Pieces with the Shot. As fast as our People knotted and spliced the Rigging, it was shot away in their Hands. The Water-Tubs in the Tops were shot to pieces, and the Boatswain's Mate's Leg shot off in the Main-top. One of the Foremast-Men's Leg was shot off in the Fore-top, and one wounded. By Ten, the Mizen-mast was shot by the Board. Wanting People to cut the Mast-Rigging, &c. from her Side, found them appear very thin upon Deck, and desired my younger Mates to drive them out of their Holes. Word was then brought me, that my Chief Mate's Leg was shot off, but that he was in good Heart. All this time it was a Calm, and our Guns of the Broad-side of no Service, not being able, during the Engagement, to bring one Gun to bear upon them. They kept throwing their shot so thick in at our Stern, with a continual Fire, and we return'd it as fast as we could load and fire. About One, my Main-mast was shot by the Board, and the Fall of that stove the Pinnace on the Booms. The Loss of my Main-mast gave me a very great Concern, and seeing the Condition of the Fore-mast, the Fore-yard half way down, and the Top-sail Yard-arm sprung in several Places, the Head of the Top-gallant-Mast shot away, render'd that Mast quite useless. I could not see which way it was in the Power of Men to save us from these Dogs. However, I made myself as easy as could be expected, and kept my Thoughts to myself. Tho' the Shot were like Hail about my Ears, I thank God I escaped them, neither did they give me much Uneasiness as to my Person. The Grabbs perceiving their great Advantage by the Fall of our Main-mast, &c. tho' all the time before within Musket-Shot, come up boldly within Call, throwing in at our Stern Double-round and Partridge as fast as they could load and fire; we doing the same with Bolts, &c. We saw a great many Holes in their Sails. Soon after this, they lodg'd two Double-head-Shot, and a large Stone in the Fore-mast, the Shrowds of which were mostly gone. I often sent Capt. Scarlet to Mr. Cudden, to encourage the People, and to take care to cool his Guns, and not fire in Haste, but take good Aim. We received two Double-headed-Shot in the Bread-room, which were soon plugg'd up, and one Shot under the Larboard Chesstree, but so low in the Water, that could not get at it, and the Ship prov'd leaky. I had a Pack of sad cowardly, ignorant Dogs as ever came into a Ship. As to my common Sailors, who were not above Twelve Seamen, with the Officers, they stood by me. It was all owing to my Misfortune on the Mouse, that I was so poorly Mann'd. As to my Third Mate, B——s, he did not seem to stomach what he was about; he was sometimes on the Quarter-Deck (not being able to use any Guns but the Stern-Chase) and every Shot the Enemy fir'd, he cowardly trembled, with his Head almost down to the Deck. This Captain Scarlet has often declared to the Gentlemen at Bombay, and before those that are now coming Home. I had six Men kill'd, and six their Legs shot off, with several others wounded by their Partridge-Shot, &c. Had our People kept the Deck like Men, there must have been several more kill'd and wounded. About Three, I heard a great Call for Shot, and desired Capt. Scarlet to go to Mr. Cuddon, and tell him not to fire in Waste.

We lay now just like a Wreck in the Sea, and at our Wits Ends. Our Shot being almost spent, we had a Hole cut in the Well to try to come at the Company's. We continued on with Double-round and Partridge, and Bolts, &c. with a Double Allowance of Powder to each Gun, doing the utmost we could to save the Ship. The Tiller-rope was now shot away, tho' of no Service before. The Carpenter told me the Ship made a great deal of Water, and had above two Foot in her Hold. The Caulker afterwards told me she had three Foot. I saw nothing we could do more than firing our Stern-Chase. There was a sad Complaint for Shot; however we fir'd Bolts. I call'd out to the People to have good Hearts, and went into the Round-house to encourage them there. It was very hard we could stand no Chance for a Mast of theirs, nor no lucky Shot to disable some of them, in all the Number that we fir'd. As to our small Arms, they were of little Service, they keeping their Men so close. The Rigging of the Foremast being gone, and that fetching so much way, I expected it to go every Minute; and about Seven in the Evening, the Ship falling off into the Trough of the Sea, the Foremast came by the Board. It was now about Four o' Clock, when Mr. Thomas Rogers, my Chief Mate, sent my Steward to desire to speak with me. When I went to him, he spoke to me to this Purpose. "Sir," says he, "I am inform'd what Condition the Ship is in; as her Masts are gone, you had better not be obstinate, in standing out longer; it will only be the Means of making more Objects, of murdering more Men, and all to no Purpose, but to be used worse by the Enemy, for it is impossible to get away. Therefore you had better surrender." To the best of my Knowledge, I hardly made him any Answer; nor had I, before he sent to me, the least Thoughts of surrendering, which I declare before God and Man; tho' I was well convinc'd within myself, that it was impossible to save the Ship. I went up to my old Station the Quarter-Deck, and took several Turns, as usual, and proceeded in the Engagement. I begun to consider what Mr. Rogers told me, and the Condition of the Ship, and argue within myself the Impossibility of doing any more (for if a Gale had sprung up, it could be of no Service) and all the time from the Fall of our Main-mast, the Enemy were got so near, that I could hear them talk, and my Second Mate did the same. As to our Masts, they had gain'd their Ends, and their only Business now was to fire at the Hull. There was no Hopes of their leaving us, considering the condition they had brought us to, and it could not be long before we sunk: for as they lay so near us, and so low in Water, our Shot must doubtless fly over them. At last I was of Mr. Rogers's Opinion, that it was only sacrificing the Men to no Purpose; for they had so large a Mark of us, they could not miss us; and during all the Engagement, as they play'd their Shot so hot at our Stern, it is surprizing there were not many more Men Kill'd. I then sent for my Second and Third Mate, and told them Mr. Rogers's Opinion and my own. They both agreed to it, and consented to the surrendering of the Ship. So we submitted to the Enemy, finding it in vain to proceed. By my Watch it was Five o' Clock. My Second and Third Mate went in to the Steerage to forbid firing, and myself in the Round-House, did the same. Every Body seem'd to be very well satisfied as to the surrendering Part, and no Objection was made. Colours we had none to strike; those and the Ensign-Staff were shot to Pieces; and what was left of the Ensign being made fast to the Main-Shrouds, went with the Mast. Capt.

Scarlet went into the Round-House, and call'd the Enemy on board, and told them we had no Boats. They sent their Dingey aboard with Four Men for me and my chief Officers. They left Two of the Four aboard the Derby. Myself and my Second Mate went in the Dingey aboard the Grabb. We were gone an Hour and a half good, if not more; then we return'd in a Gallivat with 50 or 60 Men, but not a Soul went aboard the Derby, till we return'd. Then came aboard more Gallivats and more Men, and secured the Arms, &c. and drove our People up, some to the Pumps, and some to clear the Rigging off the Ship's Side. They transkipt to their Grabbs what Treasure could be got at, and the next Day turn'd out the Remainder, with myself, Scarlet, Cuddon, the two Ladies, and my Servants, into one of the Grabbs.

FRANCIS LOLONOIS

The Slave Who Became a Pirate King[14]

John Esquemeling

Francis Lolonois was a native of that territory in France which is called Les Sables d'Olone, or The Sands of Olone. In his youth he was transported to the Caribbee islands, in quality of servant, or slave, according to custom. Having served his time, he came to Hispaniola; here he joined for some time with the hunters, before he began his robberies upon the Spaniards.

At first he made two or three voyages as a common mariner, wherein he behaved himself so courageously as to gain the favor of the governor of Tortuga, Monsieur de la Place; insomuch that he gave him a ship, in which he might seek his fortune, which was very favorable to him at first; for in a short time he got great riches. But his cruelties against the Spaniards were such, that the fame of them made him so well known through the Indies, that the Spaniards, in his time, would choose rather to die, or sink fighting, than surrender, knowing they should have no mercy at his hands. But Fortune, being seldom constant, after some time turned her back; for in a huge storm he lost his ship on the coast of Campechy. The men were all saved, but coming upon dry land, the Spaniards pursued them, and killed the greatest part, wounding also Lolonois. Not knowing how to escape, he saved his life by a stratagem; mingling sand with the blood of his wounds, with which besmearing his face, and other parts of his body, and hiding himself dextrously among the dead, he continued there till the Spaniards quitted the field.

They being gone, he retired to the woods and bound up his wounds as well as he could. These being pretty well healed, he took his way to Campechy, having disguised himself in a Spanish habit; here he enticed certain slaves, to whom he promised liberty if they would obey him and trust to his conduct. They accepted his promises, and stealing a canoe, they went to sea with him. Now the Spaniards, having made several of his companions prisoners, kept them close in a dungeon, while Lolonois went about the town and saw what passed. These were often asked, "What is become of your

[14] The Buccaneers of America.

114

captain?" To whom they constantly answered, "He is dead:" which rejoiced the Spaniards, who made thanks to God for their deliverance from such a cruel pirate. Lolonois, having seen these rejoicings for his death, made haste to escape, with the slaves above-mentioned, and came safe to Tortuga, the common refuge of all sorts of wickedness, and the seminary, as it were, of pirates and thieves. Though now his fortune was low, yet he got another ship with craft and subtlety, and in it twenty-one men. Being well provided with arms and necessaries, he set forth for Cuba, on the south whereof is a small village, called De los Cayos. The inhabitants drive a great trade in tobacco, sugar, and hides, and all in boats, not being able to use ships, by reason of the little depth of that sea.

Lolonois was persuaded he should get here some considerable prey; but by the good fortune of some fishermen who saw him, and the mercy of God, they escaped him: for the inhabitants of the town dispatched immediately a vessel overland to the Havannah, complaining that Lolonois was come to destroy them with two canoes. The governor could hardly believe this, having received letters from Campechy that he was dead: but, at their importunity, he sent a ship for their relief, with ten guns and ninety men, well armed; giving them this express command, "that they should not return into his presence without having totally destroyed those pirates." To this effect he gave them a negro to serve for a hangman, and orders, "that they should immediately hang every one of the pirates, excepting Lolonois, their captain, whom they should bring alive to the Havannah." This ship arrived at Cayos, of whose coming the pirates were advertised beforehand, and instead of flying, went to seek it in the river Estera, where she rode at anchor. The pirates seized some fishermen, and forced them by night to show them the entry of the port, hoping soon to obtain a greater vessel than their two canoes, and thereby to mend their fortune. They arrived, after two in the morning, very nigh the ship; and the watch on board the ship asking them, whence they came, and if they had seen any pirates abroad. They caused one of the prisoners to answer, they had seen no pirates, nor anything else. Which answer made them believe that they were fled upon hearing of their coming.

But they soon found the contrary, for about break of day the pirates assaulted the vessel on both sides, with their two canoes, with such vigor, that though the Spaniards behaved themselves as they ought, and made as good defense as they could, making some use of their great guns, yet they were forced to surrender, being beaten by the pirates, with sword in hand, down under the hatches. From hence Lolonois commanded them to be brought up, one by one, and in this order caused their heads to be struck off. Among the rest came up the negro, designed to be the pirates' executioner; this fellow implored mercy at his hands very dolefully, telling Lolonois he was constituted hangman of that ship, and if he would spare him, he would tell him faithfully all that he should desire. Lolonois, making him confess what he thought fit, commanded him to be murdered with the rest. Thus he cruelly and barbarously put them all to death, reserving only one alive, whom he sent back to the governor of the Havannah, with this message in writing: "I shall never henceforward give quarter to any Spaniard whatsoever; and I have great hopes I shall execute on your own person the very same punishment I have done upon them you sent against me. Thus I have retaliated the kindness you designed to me and my companions." The governor, much troubled at this bad news, swore, in the presence of many, that he would never grant quarter to any pirate that should fall into his hands. But the citizens of the Havannah desired him not to persist in the execution of that rash and rigorous oath, seeing the pirates would certainly take occasion from thence to do the same, and they had an hundred times more opportunity of revenge than he; that being necessitated to get their livelihood by fishery, they should hereafter always be in danger of their lives. By these reasons he was persuaded to bridle his anger, and remit the severity of his oath.

Now Lolonois had got a good ship, but very few provisions and people in it; to purchase both which he resolved to cruise from one port to another. Doing thus, for some time, without success, he determined to go to the port of Maracaibo. Here he surprised a ship laden with plate, and other merchandises, outward bound, to buy cocoa-nuts. With this prize he returned to Tortuga, where he was received with joy by the inhabitants; they congratulating his happy success, and their own private interest. He stayed not long there, but designed to equip a fleet sufficient to transport five hundred men, and necessaries. Thus provided, he resolved to pillage both cities, towns, and villages, and finally, to take Maracaibo itself. For this purpose he knew the island of Tortuga would afford him many resolute and courageous men, fit for such enterprises: besides, he had in his service several prisoners well acquainted with the ways and places designed upon.

Of this design Lolonois giving notice to all the pirates, whether at home or abroad, he got together, in a little while, above four hundred men; beside which, there was then in Tortuga another pirate, named Michael de Basco, who, by his piracy, had got riches sufficient to live at ease, and go no more abroad; having, withal, the office of major of the island. But seeing the great preparations that

Lolonois made for this expedition, he joined him, and offered him, that if he would make him his chief captain by land (seeing he knew the country very well, and all its avenues) he would share in his fortunes, and go with him. They agreed upon articles to the great joy of Lolonois, knowing that Basco had done great actions in Europe, and had the repute of a good soldier. Thus they all embarked in eight vessels, that of Lolonois being the greatest, having ten guns of indifferent carriage.

All things being ready, and the whole company on board, they set sail together about the end of April, being, in all, six hundred and sixty persons. They steered for that part called Bayala, north of Hispaniola: here they took into their company some French hunters, who voluntarily offered themselves, and here they provided themselves with victuals and necessaries for their voyage.

From hence they sailed again the last of July, and steered directly to the eastern cape of the isle called Punta d'Espada. Hereabouts espying a ship from Puerto Rico, bound for New Spain, laden with cocoa-nuts, Lolonois commanded the rest of the fleet to wait for him near Savona, on the east of Cape Punta d'Espada, he alone intending to take the said vessel. The Spaniards, though they had been in sight full two hours, and knew them to be pirates, yet would not flee, but prepared to fight, being well armed, and provided. The combat lasted three hours, and then they surrendered. This ship had sixteen guns, and fifty fighting men aboard: they found in her 120,000 weight of cocoa, 40,000 pieces-of-eight, and the value of 10,000 more, in jewels. Lolonois sent the vessel presently to Tortuga to be unladed, with orders to return as soon as possible to Savona, where he would wait for them: meanwhile, the rest of the fleet being arrived at Savona, met another Spanish vessel coming from Coman, with military provisions to Hispaniola, and money to pay the garrisons there. This vessel they also took, without any resistance, though mounted with eight guns. In it were 7,000 weight of powder, a great number of muskets, and like things, with 12,000 pieces-of-eight.

These successes encouraged the pirates, they seeming very lucky beginnings, especially finding their fleet pretty well recruited in a little time: for the first ship arriving at Tortuga, the governor ordered it to be instantly unladen, and soon after sent back, with fresh provisions, and other necessaries, to Lolonois. This ship he chose for himself, and gave that which he commanded to his comrade, Anthony du Puis. Being thus recruited with men in lieu of them he had lost in taking the prizes, and by sickness, he found himself in a good condition to set sail for Maracaibo, in the province of Neuva Venezuela, in the latitude of 12 deg. 10 min. north. This island is twenty leagues long, and twelve broad. To this port also belong the islands of Onega and Monges. The east side thereof is called Cape St. Roman, and the western side Cape of Caquibacoa: the gulf is called, by some, the Gulf of Venezuela, but the pirates usually call it the Bay of Maracaibo.

At the entrance of this gulf are two islands extending from east to west; that towards the east is called Isla de las Vigilias, or the Watch Isle; because in the middle is a high hill, on which stands a watch-house. The other is called Isla de la Palomas, or the Isle of Pigeons. Between these two islands runs a little sea, or rather lake of fresh water, sixty leagues long, and thirty broad; which disgorging itself into the ocean, dilates itself about the said two islands. Between them is the best passage for ships, the channel being no broader than the flight of a great gun, of about eight pounds. On the Isle of Pigeons standeth a castle, to impede the entry of vessels, all being necessitated to come very nigh the castle, by reason of two banks of sand on the other side, with only fourteen feet water. Many other banks of sand there are in this lake; as that called El Tablazo, or the Great Table, no deeper than ten feet, forty leagues within the lake; others there are, that have no more than six, seven, or eight feet in depth: all are very dangerous, especially to mariners unacquainted with them. West hereof is the city of Maracaibo, very pleasant to the view, its houses being built along the shore, having delightful prospects all round: the city may contain three or four thousand persons, slaves included, all which make a town of reasonable bigness. There are judged to be about eight hundred persons able to bear arms, all Spaniards. Here are one parish church, well built and adorned, four monasteries, and one hospital. The city is governed by a deputy governor, substituted by the governor of the Caraccas. The trade here exercised is mostly in hides and tobacco. The inhabitants possess great numbers of cattle, and many plantations, which extend thirty leagues in the country, especially towards the great town of Gibraltar, where are gathered great quantities of cocoa-nuts, and all other garden fruits, which serve for the regale and sustenance of the inhabitants of Maracaibo, whose territories are much drier than those of Gibraltar. Hither those of Maracaibo send great quantities of flesh, they making returns in oranges, lemons, and other fruits; for the inhabitants of Gibraltar want flesh, their fields not being capable of feeding cows or sheep.

Before Maracaibo is a very spacious and secure port, wherein may be built all sorts of vessels, having great convenience of timber, which may be transported thither at little charge. Nigh the town lies also a small island called Borrica, where they feed great numbers of goats, which cattle the inhabitants use more for their skins than their flesh or milk; they slighting these two, unless while they are tender and young kids. In the fields are fed some sheep, but of a very small size. In some islands of the lake, and in other places hereabouts, are many savage Indians, called by the Spaniards bravoes, or wild: these could never be reduced by the Spaniards, being brutish, and untameable. They dwell mostly towards the west side of the lake, in little huts built on trees growing in the water; so to keep themselves from innumerable mosquitoes, or gnats, which infest and torment them night and day. To the east of the said lake are whole towns of fishermen, who likewise live in huts built on trees, as the former. Another reason of this dwelling, is the frequent inundations; for after great rains, the land is often overflown for two or three leagues, there being no less than twenty-five great rivers that feed this lake. The town of Gibraltar is also frequently drowned by these, so that the inhabitants are constrained to retire to their plantations.

Gibraltar, situate at the side of the lake about forty leagues within it, receives its provisions of flesh, as has been said, from Maracaibo. The town is inhabited by about 1,500 persons, whereof four hundred may bear arms; the greatest part of them keep shops, wherein they exercise one trade or another. In the adjacent fields are numerous plantations of sugar and cocoa, in which are many tall and beautiful trees, of whose timber houses may be built, and ships. Among these are many handsome and proportionable cedars, seven or eight feet about, of which they can build boats and ships, so as to bear only one great sail; such vessels being called piraguas. The whole country is well furnished with rivers and brooks, very useful in droughts, being then cut into many little channels to water their fields and plantations. They plant also much tobacco, well esteemed in Europe, and for its goodness is called there tobacco de sacerdotes, or priest's tobacco. They enjoy nigh twenty leagues of jurisdiction, which is bounded by very high mountains perpetually covered with snow. On the other side of these mountains is situate a great city called Merida, to which the town of Gibraltar is subject. All merchandise is carried hence to the aforesaid city on mules, and that but at one season of the year, by reason of the excessive cold in those high mountains. On the said mules returns are made in flour of meal, which comes from towards Peru, by the way of Estaffe.

Lolonois arriving at the gulf of Venezuela, cast anchor with his whole fleet out of sight of the Vigilia or Watch Isle; next day very early he set sail thence with all his ships for the lake of Maracaibo, where they cast anchor again; then they landed their men, with design to attack first the fortress that commanded the bar, therefore called de la barra. This fort consisted only of several great baskets of earth placed on a rising ground, planted with sixteen great guns, with several other heaps of earth round about for covering their men: the pirates having landed a league off this fort, advanced by degrees towards it; but the governor having espied their landing, had placed an ambuscade to cut them off behind, while he should attack them in front. This the pirates discovered, and getting before, they defeated it so entirely, that not a man could retreat to the castle: this done, Lolonois, with his companions, advanced immediately to the fort, and after a fight of almost three hours, with the usual desperation of this sort of people, they became masters thereof, without any other arms than swords and pistols: while they were fighting, those who were the routed ambuscade, not being able to get into the castle, retired into Maracaibo in great confusion and disorder, crying "The pirates will presently be here with two thousand men and more." The city having formerly been taken by this kind of people, and sacked to the uttermost, had still an idea of that misery; so that upon these dismal news they endeavored to escape towards Gibraltar in their boats and canoes, carrying with them all the goods and money they could. Being come to Gibraltar, they told how the fortress was taken, and nothing had been saved, nor any persons escaped.

The castle thus taken by the pirates, they presently signified to the ships their victory, that they should come farther in without fear of danger: the rest of that day was spent in ruining and demolishing the said castle. They nailed the guns, and burnt as much as they could not carry away, burying the dead, and sending on board the fleet the wounded. Next day, very early, they weighed anchor, and steered directly towards Maracaibo, about six leagues distant from the fort; but the wind failing that day, they could advance little, being forced to await the tide. Next morning they came in sight of the town, and prepared for landing under the protection of their own guns, fearing the Spaniards might have laid an ambuscade in the woods. They put their men into canoes, brought for that purpose, and landed, shooting meanwhile furiously with their great guns. Of those in the canoes, half only went ashore, the other half remained aboard. They fired from the ships as fast as possible, towards the woody part of the shore, but could discover nobody; then they entered the town, whose inhabitants were retired to the woods, and Gibraltar, with their wives children and families. Their houses they left well provided with victuals, as flour, bread, pork, brandy, wines, and poultry, and with these the pirates fell to making good cheer, for in four weeks before they had no opportunity of filling their stomachs with such plenty.

They instantly possessed themselves of the best houses in the town, and placed sentinels wherever they thought necessary;—the great church served them for their main guard. Next day they sent out an hundred and sixty men to find out some of the inhabitants in the woods thereabouts. These returned the same night, bringing with them 20,000 pieces-of-eight, several mules laden with household goods and merchandise, and twenty prisoners, men, women, and children. Some of these were put to the rack, to make them confess where they had hid the rest of the goods; but they could extort very little from them. Lolonois, who valued not murdering, though in cold blood, ten or twelve Spaniards, drew his cutlass, and hacked one to pieces before the rest, saying, "If you do not confess and declare where you have hid the rest of your goods, I will do the like to all your companions." At last, amongst these horrible cruelties and inhuman threats, one promised to show the place where the rest of the Spaniards were hid. But those that were fled, having intelligence of it, changed place, and buried the remnant of their riches underground, so that the pirates could not find them out, unless some of their own party should reveal them. Besides, the Spaniards flying from one place to another every day, and often changing woods, were jealous even of each other, so that the father durst scarce trust his own son.

After the pirates had been fifteen days in Maracaibo, they resolved for Gibraltar; but the inhabitants having received intelligence thereof, and that they intended afterwards to go to Merida, gave notice of it to the governor there, who was a valiant soldier, and had been an officer in Flanders. His answer was, "he would have them take no care, for he hoped in a little while to exterminate the said pirates." Whereupon he came to Gibraltar with four hundred men well armed, ordering at the same time the inhabitants to put themselves in arms, so that in all he made eight hundred fighting men. With the same speed he raised a battery toward the sea, mounted with twenty guns, covered with great baskets of earth: another battery he placed in another place, mounted with eight guns. This done, he barricaded a narrow passage to the town through which the pirates must pass, opening at the same time another one through much dirt and mud into a wood which was totally unknown to the pirates.

The pirates, ignorant of these preparations, having embarked all their prisoners and booty, took their way towards Gibraltar. Being come in sight of the place, they saw the royal standard hanging forth, and that those of the town designed to defend their homes. Lolonois seeing this, called a council of war what they ought to do, telling his officers and mariners, "That the difficulty of the enterprise was very great, seeing the Spaniards had had so much time to put themselves in a posture of defense, and had got a good body of men together, with much ammunition; but notwithstanding," said he, "have a good courage; we must either defend ourselves like good soldiers, or lose our lives with all the riches we have got. Do as I shall do who am your captain: at other times we have fought with fewer men than we have in our company at present, and yet we have overcome greater numbers than there possibly can be in this town: the more they are, the more glory and the greater riches we shall gain." The pirates supposed that all the riches of the inhabitants of Maracaibo were transported to Gibraltar, or at least the greatest part. After this speech, they all promised to follow, and obey him. Lolonois made answer, "'Tis well; but know ye, withal, that the first man who shall show any fear, or the least apprehension thereof, I will pistol him with my own hands."

With this resolution they cast anchor nigh the shore, near three-quarters of a league from the town: next day before sun-rising, they landed three hundred and eighty men well provided, and armed every one with a cutlass, and one or two pistols, and sufficient powder and bullet for thirty charges. Here they all shook hands in testimony of good courage, and began their march, Lolonois speaking thus, "Come, my brethren, follow me, and have good courage." They followed their guide, who, believing he led them well, brought them to the way which the governor had barricaded. Not being able to pass that way, they went to the other newly made in the wood among the mire, which the Spaniards could shoot into at pleasure; but the pirates, full of courage, cut down the branches of trees and threw them on the way, that they might not stick in the dirt. Meanwhile, those of Gibraltar fired with their great guns so furiously, they could scarce hear nor see for the noise and smoke. Being passed the wood, they came on firm ground, where they met with a battery of six guns, which immediately the Spaniards discharged upon them, all loaded with small bullets and pieces of iron; and the Spaniards sallying forth, set upon them with such fury, as caused the pirates to give way, few of them caring to advance towards the fort, many of them being already killed and wounded. This made them go back to seek another way; but the Spaniards having cut down many trees to hinder the passage, they could find none, but were forced to return to that they had left. Here the Spaniards continued to fire as before, nor would they sally out of their batteries to attack them any more. Lolonois and his companions not being able to climb up the bastion of earth, were compelled to use an old stratagem, wherewith at last they deceived and overcame the Spaniards.

Lolonois retired suddenly with all his men, making show as if he fled; hereupon the Spaniards crying out "They flee, they flee, let us follow them," sallied forth with great disorder to the pursuit. Being drawn to some distance from the batteries, which was the pirates only design, they turned upon them unexpectedly with sword in hand, and killed above two hundred men; and thus fighting their way through those who remained, they possessed themselves of the batteries. The Spaniards that remained abroad, giving themselves over for lost, fled to the woods: those in the battery of eight guns surrendered themselves, obtaining quarter for their lives. The pirates being now become masters of the town, pulled down the Spanish colors and set up their own, taking prisoners as many as they could find. These they carried to the great church, where they raised a battery of several great guns, fearing lest the Spaniards that were fled should rally, and come upon them again; but next day, being all fortified, their fears were over. They gathered the dead to bury them, being above five hundred Spaniards, besides the wounded in the town, and those that died of their wounds in the woods. The pirates had also above one hundred and fifty prisoners, and nigh five hundred slaves, many women and children.

Of their own companions only forty were killed, and almost eighty wounded, whereof the greatest part died through the bad air, which brought fevers and other illness. They put the slain Spaniards into two great boats, and carrying them a quarter of a league to sea, they sunk the boats; this done, they gathered all the plate, household stuff, and merchandise they could, or thought convenient to carry away. The Spaniards who had anything left had hid it carefully; but the unsatisfied pirates, not contented with the riches they had got, sought for more goods and merchandise, not sparing those who lived in the fields, such as hunters and planters. They had scarce been eighteen days on the place, when the greatest part of the prisoners died for hunger. For in the town were few provisions, especially of flesh, though they had some, but no sufficient quantity of flour of meal, and this the pirates had taken for themselves, as they also took the swine, cows, sheep, and poultry, without allowing any share to the poor prisoners. For these they only provided some small quantity of mules' and asses' flesh; and many who could not eat of that loathsome provision died for hunger, their stomachs not being accustomed to such sustenance. Of the prisoners many also died under the torment they sustained to make them discover their money or jewels; and of these, some had none, nor knew of none, and others denying what they knew, endured such horrible deaths.

Finally, after having been in possession of the town four entire

123

weeks, they sent four of the prisoners to the Spaniards that were fled to the woods, demanding of them a ransom for not burning the town. The sum demanded was 10,000 pieces-of-eight, which if not sent, they threatened to reduce it to ashes. For bringing in this money, they allowed them only two days; but the Spaniards not having been able to gather so punctually such a sum, the pirates fired many parts of the town; whereupon the inhabitants begged them to help quench the fire, and the ransom should be readily paid. The pirates condescended, helping as much as they could to stop the fire; but, notwithstanding all their best endeavors, one part of the town was ruined, especially the church belonging to the monastery was burned down. After they had received the said sum, they carried aboard all the riches they had got, with a great number of slaves which had not paid the ransom; for all the prisoners had sums of money set upon them, and the slaves were also commanded to be redeemed. Thence they returned to Maracaibo, where being arrived, they found a general consternation in the whole city, to which they sent three or four prisoners to tell the governor and inhabitants, "they should bring them 30,000 pieces-of-eight aboard their ships, for a ransom of their houses, otherwise they should be sacked anew and burned."

Among these debates a party of pirates came on shore, and carried away the images, pictures, and bells of the great church, aboard the fleet. The Spaniards who were sent to demand the sum aforesaid returned, with orders to make some agreement; who concluded with the pirates to give for their ransom and liberty 20,000 pieces-of-eight, and five hundred cows, provided that they should commit no further hostilities, but depart thence presently after payment of money and cattle. The one and the other being delivered, the whole fleet set sail, causing great joy to the inhabitants of Maracaibo, to see themselves quit of them: but three days after they renewed their fears with admiration, seeing the pirates appear again, and re-enter the port with all their ships: but these apprehensions vanished, upon hearing one of the pirate's errand, who came ashore from Lolonois, "to demand a skilful pilot to conduct one of the greatest ships over the dangerous bank that lieth at the very entry of the lake." Which petition, or rather command, was instantly granted.

They had now been full two months in these towns, wherein they committed those cruel and insolent actions we have related. Departing thence, they took their course to Hispaniola, and arrived there in eight days, casting anchor in a port called Isla de la Vacca, or Cow Island. This island is inhabited by French buccaneers, who mostly sell the flesh they hunt to pirates and others, who now and then put in there to victual, or trade. Here they unladed their whole cargazon of riches, the usual storehouse of the pirates being commonly under the shelter of the buccaneers. Here they made a dividend of all their prizes and gains, according to the orders and degree of every one, as has been mentioned before. Having made an exact calculation of all their plunder, they found in ready money 260,000 pieces-of-eight: this being divided, every one received for his share in money, as also in silk, linen, and other commodities, to the value of 100 pieces-of-eight. Those who had been wounded received their first part, after the rate mentioned before, for the loss of their limbs: then they weighed all the plate uncoined, reckoning ten pieces-of-eight to a pound; the jewels were prized indifferently, either too high or too low, by reason of their ignorance: this done, every one was put to his oath again, that he had not smuggled anything from the common stock. Hence they proceeded to the dividend of the shares of such as were dead in battle, or otherwise: these shares were given to their friends, to be kept entire for them, and to be delivered in due time to their nearest relations, or their apparent lawful heirs.

The whole dividend being finished, they set sail for Tortuga. Here they arrived a month after, to the great joy of most of the island; for as to the common pirates, in three weeks they had scarce any money left, having spent it all in things of little value, or lost it at play. Here had arrived, not long before them, two French ships, with wine and brandy, and suchlike commodities; whereby these liquors, at the arrival of the pirates, were indifferent cheap. But this lasted not long, for soon after they were enhanced extremely, a gallon of brandy being sold for four pieces-of-eight. The governor of the island bought of the pirates the whole cargo of the ship laden with cocoa, giving for that rich commodity scarce the twentieth part of its worth. Thus they made shift to lose and spend the riches they had got, in much less time than they were obtained. The taverns and stews, according to the custom of pirates, got the greatest part; so that, soon after, they were forced to seek more by the same unlawful means they had got the former.

THE FIGHT BETWEEN THE DORRILL AND THE MOCA[15]

These truly representeth a scheem of what misfortune has befell us as we were going through the streights of Malacca, in the persuance to our pretended voyage, vizt., Wednesday the 7th July, 5 o'clock morning we espied a ship to windward; as soon as was well light perceived her to bare down upon us. Wee thought at first she had been a Dutchman bound for Atcheen or Bengall, when perceived she had no Gallerys, did then suppose her to be what after, to our dreadful sorrow, found her. Wee gott our ship in the best posture of defence that suddain emergent necessity would permitt. Wee kept good looking out, expecting to see an Island called Pullo Verello [Pulo Barahla, but as then saw it not.

About 8 of the clock the ship came up fairely within shott. Saw in room of our Gallerys there was large sally ports, in each of which was a large gunn, seemed to be brass. Her tafferill was likewise taken downe. Wee having done what possibly could to prepare ourselves, fearing might be suddenly sett on, ordered our people to their respective stations for action. Wee now hoisted our colours. The Captain commanded to naile our Ensigne to the staff in sight of the enimie, which was immediately done. As they perceived wee hoisted our colours they hoisted theirs, with the Union Jack, and let fly a broad red Pendant at their maintopmast head.

The Pirate being now in little more than half Pistoll shott from us, wee could discerne abundance of men who went aft to the Quarter Deck, which as wee suppose was to consult. They stood as we stood, but wee spoke neither to other. Att noone it fell calme, so that [wee] were affraid should by the sea have been hove on one another. Att 1 a clock sprang up a gale. The Pirate kept as wee kept. Att 3 a clock the villain backt her sailes and they went from us. Wee kept close halled, having a contrary wind for Mallacca. When the Pirate was about 7 miles distant tackt and stood after us. Att 6 that evening saw the lookt for island, and the Pirate came up with us on our starboard side within shott. Wee see he kept a man at each topmast head, looking out till it was darke, then he halled a little from us, but kept us company all night.

At 8 in the morning he drew near us, but wee had time to mount our other four guns that were in hold, and now wee were in the best posture of defence could desire. He drawing near us and

---

15 From The Indian Antiquary, Vol. 49.

seeing that if [wee] would, [wee] could not gett from him, he far outsailing us by or large [in one direction or another], the Captain resolved to see what the rogue would doe, soe ordered to hand [furl] all our small sailes and furled our mainesaile. He, seeing this, did the like, and as [he] drew near us beat a drum and sounded trumpets, and then hailed us four times before we answered him.

At last it was thought fitt to know what he would say, soe the Boatswaine spoke to him as was ordered, which was that wee came from London. Then he enquired whether peace or war with France. Our answer, there was an universall peace through Europe, att which they paused and then said, "That's well." He further enquired if had touched at Attcheen. Wee said a boat came off to us, but [wee] came not near itt by several leagues. Further he enquired our Captain's name and whither wee were bound. Wee answered to Mallacca. They too and [would have] had the Captain gone aboard to drink a glass of wine. Wee said that would see one another at Mallacca. Then he called to lye by and he would come aboard us. Our answer was as before, saying it was late. He said, true, it was for China, and enquired whether should touch at the Water Islands [Pulo Ondan, off Malacca]. Wee said should. Then said he, So shall wee. After he had asked us all these questions wee desired to know from whence he was. He said from London, their Captain name Collyford, the ship named the Resolution, bound for China. This Collyford had been Gunners Mate at Bombay, and after run away with the Ketch.

Thus past the 8th July. Friday the 9th do., he being some distance from us, About ½ an hour after 10 came up with us. Then it grew calme. Wee could discerne a fellow on the Quarter Deck wearing a sword. As he drew near, this Hellish Imp cried, Strike you doggs, which [wee] perceived was not by a general consent for he was called away. Our Boatswaine in a fury run upon the poop, unknown to the Captain, and answered that wee would strike to noe such doggs as he, telling him the rogue Every and his accomplices were all hanged. The Captain was angry that he spake without order, then ordered to haile him and askt what was his reason to dogg us. One stept forward on the forecastle, beckoned with his hand and said, Gentlemen, wee want not your ship nor men, but money. Wee told them had none for them but bid them come up alongside and take it as could gett it. Then a parcell of bloodhound rogues clasht their cutlashes and said they would have itt or our hearts blood, saying, "What doe you not know us to be the Moca?" Our answer was Yes, Yes. Thereon they gave a great shout and so they all went out of sight and wee to our quarters. They were going

127

to hoist colours but the ensigne halliards broke, which our people perceiving gave a great shout, so they lett them alone.

As soon as they could bring their chase gunns to bear, fired upon us and soe kept on our quarter. Our gunns would not bear in a small space, but as soon as did hap, gave them better than [the pirates] did like. His second shott carried away our spritt saile yard. About half on hour after or more he came up alongside and soe wee powered in upon him and continued, some time broadsides and sometimes three or four gunns as opportunity presented and could bring them to doe best service. He was going to lay us athwart the hawse, but by God's providence Captain Hide frustrated his intent by pouring a broadside into him, which made him give back and goe asterne, where he lay and paused without fireing, then in a small space fired one gunn. The shott come in at our round house window without damage to any person, after which he filled and bore away, and when was about ¼ mile off fired a gunn to leeward, which wee answered by another to windward. About an hour after he tackt and came up with us againe. Wee made noe saile, but lay by to receive him, but he kept aloof off. The distance att most in all our fireing was never more than two ships length; the time of our engagement was from ½ an hour after 11 till about 3 afternoon.

When [wee] came to see what damage [wee] had sustained, found our Cheife Mate, Mr. Smith, wounded in the legg, close by the knee, with a splinter or piece of chaine, which cannot well be told, our Barber had two of his fingers shott off as was spunging one of our gunns, the Gunner's boy had his legg shott off in the waste, John Amos, Quartermaster, had his leg shott off [while] at the helme, the Boatswaine's boy (a lad of 13 years old) was shott in the thigh, which went through and splintered his bone, the Armorer Jos. Osborne in the round house wounded by a splinter just in the temple, the Captain's boy on the Quarter Deck a small shott raised his scull through his cap and was the first person wounded and att the first onsett. Wm. Reynolds's boy had the brim of his hatt ½ shott off and his forefinger splintered very sorely. John Blake, turner, the flesh of his legg and calfe a great part shott away.

Our ships damage is the Mizentopmast shott close by the cap and it was a miracle stood soe long and did not fall in the rogues sight. Our rigging shott that had but one running rope left clear, our mainshrouds three on one side, two on the other cutt in two. Our mainyard ten feet from the mast by a shott cutt 8 inches deep, our foretopmast backstays shott away, a great shott in the roundhouse, one on the Quarter Deck and two of the roundhouse shott came on the said deck, severall in the stearidge betwixt decks and in the forecastle, two in the bread room which caused us to make much water and damaged the greatest part of our bread. They dismounted one of our gunns in the roundhouse, two in the stearidge, two in the waste, one in the forecastle, with abundance more damage which may seem tedious to rehearse.

Their small shott were most Tinn and Tuthenage [tutenaga, spelter]. They fired pieces of glass-bottles, do. teapots, chains, stones and what not, which were found on our decks. We could observe abundance of great shott to have passed through the rogues foresaile, and our hope is have done that to him which [will] make him shunn having to do with any Europe ship againe. Att night wee perceived kept close their lights. Wee did the like and lay by. In the morning they were as far off as [wee] could discerne upon deck. Wee sent up to see how they stood, which was right with us. In the night wee knotted our rigging and in the morning made all haist to repare our carriages.

Our men, seeing they stood after us, [wee] could perceive their countinances to be dejected. Wee cheared them what wee could, and, for their encouragement, the Captain and wee of our proper money did give them, to every man and boy, three dollars each, which animated them, and promised to give them as much more if engaged againe, and that if [wee] took the ship, for every prisoner five pounds and besides a gratuity from the Gentlemen Employers. Wee read the King's Proclamation about Every, &c., and the Right Honble. Company's.

About 9 o'clock the 10th July wee perceived the rogue made from us, soe wee gave the Almighty our most condigne thanks for his mercy that delivered us not to the worst of our enimies, for truly he [the pirate] was very strong, having at least an hundred Europeans on board, 34 gunns mounted, besides 10 pattererers and 2 small mortars in the head; his lower tier, some of them, as wee judged, sixteen and eighteen pounders. We lay as near our course as could, and next day saw land on our starboard side which was the Maine [Land]. Kept on our way.

The 12th July dyed the Boatswaine's boy, George Mopp, in the morning. Friday the 16th do. in the evening dyed the Gunner's boy, Thomas Matthews. Sunday the 18th at anchor two leagues from the Pillo Sumbelong [Pulo Sembîlan] Islands dyed the Barber, Andrew Miller. Do. the 31st dyed the Cheife Mate, Mr. John Smith. The other two are yet in a very deplorable condition and wee are ashore here to refresh them.... The Chinese further report ... the Mocco was at the Maldives and creaned [careened]; there they gave an end to the life of their commanding rogue Stout, who they murdered for attempting to run away.

JADDI THE MALAY PIRATE[16]

Long before that action with the English man-of-war which drove me to Singapore, I sailed in a fine fleet of prahus belonging to the Rajah of Johore [Sultân Mahmâd Shâh]. We were all then very rich—ah! such numbers of beautiful wives and such feasting!—but, above all, we had a great many most holy men in our force! When the proper monsoon came, we proceeded to sea to fight the Bugismen [of Celebes] and Chinamen bound from Borneo and the Celebes to Java; for you must remember our Rajah was at war with them. (Jadee always maintained that the proceedings in which he had been engaged partook of a purely warlike, and not of a piratical character.)

Our thirteen prahus had all been fitted out in and about Singapore. I wish you could have seen them, Touhan [Tüan, Sir]. These prahus we see here are nothing to them, such brass guns, such long pendants, such creeses [Malay kris, dagger]! Allah-il-Allah! Our Datoos [datuk, a chief] were indeed great men!

Sailing along the coast as high as Patani, we then crossed over to Borneo, two Illanoon prahus acting as pilots, and reached a place called Sambas [West Borneo]: there we fought the Chinese and Dutchmen, who ill-treat our countrymen, and are trying to drive the Malays out of that country. Gold-dust and slaves in large quantities were here taken, most of the latter being our countrymen of Sumatra and Java, who are captured and sold to the planters and miners of the Dutch settlements.

"Do you mean to say," I asked, "that the Dutch countenance such traffic?"

"The Hollanders," replied Jadee, "have been the bane of the Malay race; no one knows the amount of villainy, the bloody cruelty of their system towards us. They drive us into our prahus to escape their taxes and laws, and then declare us pirates and put us to death. There are natives in our crew, Touhan, of Sumatra and Java, of Bianca [Banka] and Borneo; ask them why they hate the Dutchmen; why they would kill a Dutchman. It is because the Dutchman is a false man, not like the white man [English]. The Hollander stabs in the dark; he is a liar!"

However, from Borneo we sailed to Biliton [island between Banka and Borneo] and Bianca, and there waited for some large junks that were expected. Our cruise had been so far successful, and we feasted away—fighting cocks, smoking opium and eating white

---

rice. At last our scouts told us that a junk was in sight. She came, a lofty-sided one of Fokien [Fuhkien]. We knew these Amoy men would fight like tiger-cats for their sugar and silks; and as the breeze was fresh, we only kept her in sight by keeping close inshore and following her. Not to frighten the Chinamen, we did not hoist sail but made our slaves pull. "Oh!" said Jadee, warming up with the recollection of the event—"oh! it was fine to feel what brave fellows we then were!"

Towards night we made sail and closed upon the junk, and at daylight it fell a stark calm, and we went at our prize like sharks. All our fighting men put on their war-dresses; the Illanoons danced their war-dance, and all our gongs sounded as we opened out to attack her on different sides.

But those Amoy men are pigs! They burnt joss-paper; sounded their gongs, and received us with such showers of stones, hot-water, long pikes, and one or two well-directed shots that we hauled off to try the effect of our guns, sorry though we were to do it, for it was sure to bring the Dutchmen upon us. Bang! bang! we fired at them, and they at us; three hours did we persevere, and whenever we tried to board, the Chinese beat us back every time, for her side was as smooth and as high as a wall, with galleries overhanging.

We had several men killed and hurt; a council was called; a certain charm was performed by one of our holy men, a famous chief, and twenty of our best men devoted themselves to effecting a landing on the junk's deck, when our look-out prahus made the signal that the Dutchmen were coming; and sure enough some Dutch gun-boats came sweeping round a headland. In a moment we were round and pulling like demons for the shores of Biliton, the gun-boats in chase of us, and the Chinese howling with delight. The sea-breeze freshened and brought up a schooner-rigged boat very fast. We had been at work twenty-four hours and were heartily tired; our slaves could work no longer, so we prepared for the Hollanders; they were afraid to close upon us and commenced firing at a distance. This was just what we wanted; we had guns as well as they, and by keeping up the fight until dark, we felt sure of escape. The Dutchmen, however, knew this too, and kept closing gradually upon us; and when they saw our prahus bailing out water and blood, they knew we were suffering and cheered like devils. We were desperate; surrender to Dutchmen we never would; we closed together for mutual support, and determined at last, if all hope of escape ceased, to run our prahus ashore, burn them, and lie hid in the jungle until a future day. But a brave Datoo with his shattered prahus saved us; he proposed to let the Dutchmen board her, creese

131

[stab with a kris] all that did so, and then trust to Allah for his escape.

It was done immediately; we all pulled a short distance away and left the brave Datoo's prahu like a wreck abandoned. How the Dutchmen yelled and fired into her! The slaves and cowards jumped out of the prahu, but our braves kept quiet; at last, as we expected, one gun-boat dashed alongside of their prize and boarded her in a crowd. Then was the time to see how the Malay man could fight; the creese was worth twenty swords, and the Dutchmen went down like sheep. We fired to cover our countrymen, who, as soon as their work was done, jumped overboard and swam to us; but the brave Datoo, with many more died as brave Malays should do, running a-muck against a host of enemies.

The gun-boats were quite scared by this punishment, and we lost no time in getting away as rapidly as possible; but the accursed schooner, by keeping more in the offing, held the wind and preserved her position, signaling all the while for the gun-boats to follow her. We did not want to fight any more; it was evidently an unlucky day. On the opposite side of the channel to that we were on, the coral reefs and shoals would prevent the Hollanders following us: it was determined at all risks to get there in spite of the schooner. With the first of the land-wind in the evening we set sail before it and steered across for Bianca. The schooner placed herself in our way like a clever sailor, so as to turn us back; but we were determined to push on, take her fire, and run all risks.

It was a sight to see us meeting one another; but we were desperate: we had killed plenty of Dutchmen; it was their turn now. I was in the second prahu, and well it was so, for when the headmost one got close to the schooner, the Dutchman fired all his guns into her, and knocked her at once into a wrecked condition. We gave one cheer, fired our guns and then pushed on for our lives. "Ah! sir, it was a dark night indeed for us. Three prahus in all were sunk and the whole force dispersed."

To add to our misfortunes a strong gale sprang up. We were obliged to carry canvas; our prahu leaked from shot-holes; the sea continually broke into her; we dared not run into the coral reefs on such a night, and bore up for the Straits of Malacca. The wounded writhed and shrieked in their agony, and we had to pump, we fighting men, and bale like black fellows [Caffre or negro slaves]! By two in the morning we were all worn out. I felt indifferent whether I was drowned or not, and many threw down their buckets and sat down to die. The wind increased and, at last, as if to put us out of our misery, just such a squall as this came down upon us. I saw it was folly contending against our fate, and followed the general

132

example. "God is great!" we exclaimed, but the Rajah of Johore came and reproved us. "Work until daylight," he said, "and I will ensure your safety." We pointed at the black storm which was approaching. "Is that what you fear?" he replied, and going below he produced just such a wooden spoon and did what you have seen me do, and I tell you, my captain, as I would if the "Company Sahib" stood before me, that the storm was nothing, and that we had a dead calm one hour afterwards and were saved. God is great and Mahomet is his prophet!—but there is no charm like the Johore one for killing the wind!

THE TERRIBLE LADRONES[17]

Richard Glasspoole

On the 17th of September, 1809, the Honorable Company's ship Marquis of Ely anchored under the Island of Sam Chow, in China, about twelve English miles from Macao, where I was ordered to proceed in one of our cutters to procure a pilot, and also to land the purser with the packet. I left the ship at 5 P.M. with seven men under my command, well armed. It blew a fresh gale from the N. E. We arrived at Macao at 9 P.M., where I delivered the packet to Mr. Roberts, and sent the men with the boat's sails to sleep under the Company's Factory, and left the boat in charge of one of the Compradore's men; during the night the gale increased. At half-past three in the morning I went to the beach, and found the boat on shore half-filled with water, in consequence of the man having left her. I called the people, and baled her out; found she was considerably damaged, and very leaky. At half-past 5 A.M., the ebb-tide making, we left Macao with vegetables for the ship.

One of the Compradore's men who spoke English went with us for the purpose of piloting the ship to Lintin, as the Mandarines, in consequence of a late disturbance at Macao, would not grant permission for regular pilots. I had every reason to expect the ship in the roads, as she was preparing to get under weigh when we left her; but on our rounding Cabaretta-Point, we saw her five or six miles to leeward, under weigh, standing on the starboard tack: it was then blowing fresh at N. E. Bore up, and stood towards her; when about a cable's length to windward of her, she tacked; we hauled our wind and stood after her. A hard squall then coming on, with a strong tide and heavy swell against us, we drifted fast to leeward, and the weather being hazy, we soon lost sight of the ship. Struck our masts, and endeavored to pull; finding our efforts useless, set a reefed foresail and mizzen, and stood towards a country-ship at anchor under the land to leeward of Cabaretta-Point. When within a quarter of a mile of her she weighed and made sail, leaving us in a very critical situation, having no anchor, and drifting bodily on the rocks to leeward. Struck the masts: after four or five hours hard pulling, succeeded in clearing them.

At this time not a ship in sight; the weather clearing up, we saw a ship to leeward, hull down, shipped our masts, and made sail

---

[17] From The Ladrone Pirates.

towards her; she proved to be the Honourable Company's ship Glatton. We made signals to her with our handkerchiefs at the mast-head, she unfortunately took no notice of them, but tacked and stood from us. Our situation was now truly distressing, night closing fast, with a threatening appearance, blowing fresh, with hard rain and a heavy sea; our boat very leaky, without a compass, anchor or provisions, and drifting fast on a lee-shore, surrounded with dangerous rocks, and inhabited by the most barbarous pirates. I close-reefed my sails, and kept tack and tack 'till daylight, when we were happy to find we had drifted very little to leeward of our situation in the evening. The night was very dark, with constant hard squalls and heavy rain.

Tuesday, the 19th, no ships in sight. About ten o'clock in the morning it fell calm, with very hard rain and a heavy swell;—struck our masts and pulled, not being able to see the land, steered by the swell. When the weather broke up, found we had drifted several miles to leeward. During the calm a fresh breeze springing up, made sail, and endeavored to reach the weather-shore, and anchor with six muskets we had lashed together for that purpose. Finding the boat made no way against the swell and tide, bore up for a bay to leeward, and anchored about one A.M. close under the land in five or six fathoms water, blowing fresh, with hard rain.

Wednesday, the 20th, at daylight, supposing the flood-tide making, weighed and stood over to the weather-land, but found we were drifting fast to leeward. About ten o'clock perceived two Chinese boats steering for us. Bore up, and stood towards them, and made signals to induce them to come within hail; on nearing them, they bore up, and passed to leeward of the islands. The Chinese we had in the boat advised me to follow them, and he would take us to Macao by the leeward passage. I expressed my fears of being taken by the Ladrones. Our ammunition being wet, and the muskets rendered useless, we had nothing to defend ourselves with but cutlasses, and in too distressed a situation to make much resistance with them, having been constantly wet, and eaten nothing but a few green oranges for three days.

As our present situation was a hopeless one, and the man assured me there was no fear of encountering any Ladrones, I complied with his request, and stood in to leeward of the islands, where we found the water much smoother, and apparently a direct passage to Macao. We continued pulling and sailing all day. At six o'clock in the evening I discovered three large boats at anchor in a bay to leeward. On seeing us they weighed and made sail towards us. The Chinese said they were Ladrones, and that if they captured us they would most certainly put us all to death! Finding they gained fast on us, struck the masts, and pulled head to wind for five or six hours. The tide turning against us, anchored close under the land to avoid being seen. Soon after we saw the boats pass us to leeward.

Thursday, the 21st, at daylight, the flood making, weighed and pulled along shore in great spirits, expecting to be at Macao in two or three hours, as by the Chinese account it was not above six or seven miles distant. After pulling a mile or two perceived several people on shore, standing close to the beach; they were armed with pikes and lances. I ordered the interpreter to hail them, and ask the most direct passage to Macao. They said if we came on shore they would inform us; not liking their hostile appearance, I did not think proper to comply with the request. Saw a large fleet of boats at anchor close under the opposite shore. Our interpreter said they were fishing-boats, and that by going there we should not only get provisions, but a pilot also to take us to Macao.

I bore up, and on nearing them perceived there were some large vessels, very full of men, and mounted with several guns. I hesitated to approach nearer; but the Chinese assuring me they were Mandarine junks[18] and salt-boats, we stood close to one of them, and asked the way to Macao. They gave no answer, but made some signs to us to go in shore. We passed on, and a large rowboat pulled after us; she soon came alongside, when about twenty savage-looking villains, who were stowed at the bottom of the boat, leaped on board us. They were armed with a short sword in each hand, one of which they laid on our necks, and the other pointed to our breasts, keeping their eyes fixed on their officer, waiting his signal to cut or desist. Seeing we were incapable of making any resistance, he sheathed his sword, and the others immediately followed his example. They then dragged us into their boat, and carried us on board one of their junks, with the most savage demonstrations of joy, and as we supposed, to torture and put us to a cruel death. When on board the junk, they searched all our pockets, took the handkerchiefs from our necks, and brought heavy chains to chain us to the guns.

At this time a boat came, and took me, with one of my men and the interpreter, on board the chief's vessel. I was then taken before the chief. He was seated on deck, in a large chair, dressed in purple silk, with a black turban on. He appeared to be about thirty years of age, a stout commanding-looking man. He took me by the coat, and drew me close to him; then questioned the interpreter very strictly, asking who we were, and what was our business in that

---

[18] Junk is the Canton pronunciation of chuen, ship.

part of the country. I told him to say we were Englishmen in distress, having been four days at sea without provisions. This he would not credit, but said we were bad men, and that he would put us all to death; and then ordered some men to put the interpreter to the torture until he confessed the truth.

Upon this occasion, a Ladrone, who had been once to England and spoke a few words of English, came to the chief, and told him we were really Englishmen, and that we had plenty of money, adding, that the buttons on my coat were gold. The chief then ordered us some coarse brown rice, of which we made a tolerable meal, having eat nothing for nearly four days, except a few green oranges. During our repast, a number of Ladrones crowded round us, examining our clothes and hair, and giving us every possible annoyance. Several of them brought swords, and laid them on our necks, making signs that they would soon take us on shore, and cut us in pieces, which I am sorry to say was the fate of some hundreds during my captivity.

I was now summoned before the chief, who had been conversing with the interpreter; he said I must write to my captain, and tell him, if he did not send a hundred thousand dollars for our ransom, in ten days he would put us all to death. In vain did I assure him it was useless writing unless he would agree to take a much smaller sum; saying we were all poor men, and the most we could possibly raise would not exceed two thousand dollars. Finding that he was much exasperated at my expostulations, I embraced the offer of writing to inform my commander of our unfortunate situation, though there appeared not the least probability of relieving us. They said the letter should be conveyed to Macao in a fishing-boat, which would bring an answer in the morning. A small boat accordingly came alongside, and took the letter.

About six o'clock in the evening they gave us some rice and a little salt fish, which we ate, and they made signs for us to lay down on the deck to sleep; but such numbers of Ladrones were constantly coming from different vessels to see us, and examine our clothes and hair, they would not allow us a moment's quiet. They were particularly anxious for the buttons of my coat, which were new, and as they supposed gold. I took it off, and laid it on the deck to avoid being disturbed by them; it was taken away in the night, and I saw it on the next day stripped of its buttons.

About nine o'clock a boat came and hailed the chief's vessel; he immediately hoisted his mainsail, and the fleet weighed apparently in great confusion. They worked to windward all night and part of the next day, and anchored about one o'clock in a bay under the island of Lantow, where the head admiral of Ladrones

137

was lying at anchor, with about two hundred vessels and a Portuguese brig they had captured a few days before, and murdered the captain and part of the crew.

Saturday, the 23d, early in the morning, a fishing-boat came to the fleet to inquire if they had captured an European boat; being answered in the affirmative, they came to the vessel I was in. One of them spoke a few words of English, and told me he had a Ladrone-pass, and was sent by Captain Kay in search of us; I was rather surprised to find he had no letter. He appeared to be well acquainted with the chief, and remained in his cabin smoking opium, and playing cards all the day.[19]

In the evening I was summoned with the interpreter before the chief. He questioned us in a much milder tone, saying, he now believed we were Englishmen, a people he wished to be friendly with; and that if our captain would lend him seventy thousand dollars 'till he returned from his cruise up the river, he would repay him, and send us all to Macao. I assured him it was useless writing on those terms, and unless our ransom was speedily settled, the English fleet would sail, and render our enlargement altogether ineffectual. He remained determined, and said if it were not sent, he would keep us, and make us fight, or put us to death. I accordingly wrote, and gave my letter to the man belonging to the boat before mentioned. He said he could not return with an answer in less than five days.

The chief now gave me the letter I wrote when first taken. I have never been able to ascertain his reasons for detaining it, but suppose he dare not negotiate for our ransom without orders from the head admiral, who I understood was sorry at our being captured. He said the English ships would join the mandarines and attack them.[20] He told the chief that captured us, to dispose of us as he pleased.

---

[19] The pirates had many other intimate acquaintances on shore, like Doctor Chow of Macao.
[20] The pirates were always afraid of this. We find the following statement concerning the Chinese pirates, taken from the records in the East-India House, and printed in Appendix C. to the Report relative to the trade with the East-Indies and China, in the sessions 1820 and 1821 (reprinted 1829), p. 387.
"In the year 1808, 1809, and 1810, the Canton river was so infested with pirates, who were also in such force, that the Chinese government made an attempt to subdue them, but failed. The pirates totally destroyed the Chinese force; ravaged the river in every direction; threatened to attack the city of Canton, and destroyed many towns and villages on the banks of the

Monday, the 24th, it blew a strong gale, with constant hard rain; we suffered much from the cold and wet, being obliged to remain on deck with no covering but an old mat, which was frequently taken from us in the night by the Ladrones who were on watch. During the night the Portuguese who were left in the brig murdered the Ladrones that were on board of her, cut the cables, and fortunately escaped through the darkness of the night. I have since been informed they ran her on shore near Macao.

Tuesday, the 25th, at daylight in the morning, the fleet, amounting to about five hundred sail of different sizes, weighed, to proceed on their intended cruise up the rivers, to levy contributions on the towns and villages. It is impossible to describe what were my feelings at this critical time, having received no answers to my letters, and the fleet under-way to sail,—hundreds of miles up a country never visited by Europeans, there to remain probably for many months, which would render all opportunities of negotiating for our enlargement totally ineffectual; as the only method of communication is by boats, that have a pass from the Ladrones, and they dare not venture above twenty miles from Macao, being obliged to come and go in the night, to avoid the Mandarines; and if these boats should be detected in having any intercourse with the Ladrones, they are immediately put to death, and all their relations, though they had not joined in the crime,[21] share in the punishment, in order that not a single person of their families should be left to imitate their crimes or revenge their death. This severity renders communication both dangerous and expensive; no boat would venture out for less than a hundred Spanish dollars.

Wednesday, the 26th, at daylight, we passed in sight of our ships at anchor under the island of Chun Po. The chief then called me, pointed to the ships, and told the interpreter to tell us to look at them, for we should never see them again. About noon we entered a river to the westward of the Bogue, three or four miles from the entrance. We passed a large town situated on the side of a beautiful hill, which is tributary to the Ladrones; the inhabitants saluted them with songs as they passed.

The fleet now divided into two squadrons (the red and the black)[22] and sailed up different branches of the river. At midnight

---

river; and killed or carried off, to serve as Ladrones, several thousands of inhabitants.

[21] That the whole family must suffer for the crime of one individual, seems to be the most cruel and foolish law of the whole Chinese criminal code.

[22] We know by the "History of the Chinese Pirates," that these "wasps of the ocean," to speak with Yuen tsze yung lun, were originally divided into six squadrons.

the division we were in anchored close to an immense hill, on the top of which a number of fires were burning, which at daylight I perceived proceeded from a Chinese camp. At the back of the hill was a most beautiful town, surrounded by water, and embellished with groves of orange trees. The chop-house (custom-house)[23] and a few cottages were immediately plundered, and burned down; most of the inhabitants, however, escaped to the camp.

The Ladrones now prepared to attack the town with a formidable force, collected in rowboats from the different vessels. They sent a messenger to the town, demanding a tribute of ten thousand dollars annually, saying, if these terms were not complied with, they would land, destroy the town, and murder all the inhabitants; which they would certainly have done, had the town laid in a more advantageous situation for their purpose; but being placed out of the reach of their shot, they allowed them to come to terms. The inhabitants agreed to pay six thousand dollars, which they were to collect by the time of our return down the river. This finesse had the desired effect, for during our absence they mounted a few guns on a hill, which commanded the passage, and gave us in lieu of the dollars a warm salute on our return.

October the 1st, the fleet weighed in the night, dropped by the tide up the river, and anchored very quietly before a town surrounded by a thick wood. Early in the morning the Ladrones assembled in rowboats and landed; then gave a shout, and rushed into the town, sword in hand. The inhabitants fled to the adjacent hills, in numbers apparently superior to the Ladrones. We may easily imagine to ourselves the horror with which these miserable people must be seized, on being obliged to leave their homes, and everything dear to them. It was a most melancholy sight to see women in tears, clasping their infants in their arms, and imploring mercy for them from those brutal robbers! The old and the sick, who were unable to fly, or to make resistance, were either made prisoners or most inhumanly butchered! The boats continued passing and repassing from the junks to the shore, in quick succession, laden with booty, and the men besmeared with blood! Two hundred and fifty women, and several children, were made prisoners, and sent on board different vessels. They were unable to escape with the men, owing to that abominable practice of cramping

---

[23] In the barbarous Chinese-English spoken at Canton, all things are indiscriminately called chop. You hear of a chop-house, chop-boat, tea-chop, Chaou-chaou-chop, etc. To give a bill or agreement on making a bargain is in Chinese called chă tan; chă in the pronunciation of Canton is chop, which is then applied to any writing whatever.

their feet: several of them were not able to move without assistance, in fact, they might all be said to totter, rather than walk. Twenty of these poor women were sent on board the vessel I was in; they were hauled on board by the hair, and treated in a most savage manner.

When the chief came on board, he questioned them respecting the circumstances of their friends, and demanded ransoms accordingly, from six thousand to six hundred dollars each. He ordered them a berth on deck, at the after part of the vessel, where they had nothing to shelter them from the weather, which at this time was very variable,—the days excessively hot, and the nights cold, with heavy rains. The town being plundered of every thing valuable, it was set on fire, and reduced to ashes by the morning. The fleet remained here three days, negotiating for the ransom of the prisoners, and plundering the fish-tanks and gardens. During all this time, the Chinese never ventured from the hills, though there were frequently not more than a hundred Ladrones on shore at a time, and I am sure the people on the hills exceeded ten times that number.[24]

October 5th, the fleet proceeded up another branch of the river, stopping at several small villages to receive tribute, which was generally paid in dollars, sugar and rice, with a few large pigs roasted whole, as presents for their joss (the idol they worship)[25]. Every person on being ransomed, is obliged to present him with a pig, or some fowls, which the priest offers him with prayers; it remains before him a few hours, and is then divided amongst the crew. Nothing particular occurred 'till the 10th, except frequent skirmishes on shore between small parties of Ladrones and Chinese soldiers. They frequently obliged my men to go on shore, and fight with the muskets we had when taken, which did great execution, the Chinese principally using bows and arrows. They have match-locks, but use them very unskillfully.

On the 10th, we formed a junction with the black squadron, and proceeded many miles up a wide and beautiful river, passing several ruins of villages that had been destroyed by the black squadron. On the 17th, the fleet anchored abreast four mud batteries, which defended a town, so entirely surrounded with wood that it was impossible to form any idea of its size. The weather was

---

[24] The following is the Character of the Chinese of Canton, as given in ancient Chinese books: "People of Canton are silly, light, weak in body, and weak in mind, without any ability to fight on land."

[25] Joss is a Chinese corruption of the Portuguese Dios, God. The Joss, or idol, of which Mr. Glasspoole speaks is the San po shin, which is spoken of in the work of Yuen tsze.

very hazy, with hard squalls of rain. The Ladrones remained perfectly quiet for two days. On the third day the forts commenced a brisk fire for several hours: the Ladrones did not return a single shot, but weighed in the night and dropped down the river.

The reasons they gave for not attacking the town, or returning the fire, were that Joss had not promised them success. They are very superstitious, and consult their idol on all occasions. If his omens are good, they will undertake the most daring enterprizes.

The fleet now anchored opposite the ruins of the town where the women had been made prisoners. Here we remained five or six days, during which time about a hundred of the women were ransomed; the remainder were offered for sale amongst the Ladrones, for forty dollars each. The woman is considered the lawful wife of the purchaser, who would be put to death if he discarded her. Several of them leaped overboard and drowned themselves, rather than submit to such infamous degradation.

The fleet then weighed and made sail down the river, to receive the ransom from the town before mentioned. As we passed the hill, they fired several shots at us, but without effect. The Ladrones were much exasperated, and determined to revenge themselves; they dropped out of reach of their shot, and anchored. Every junk sent about a hundred men each on shore, to cut paddy, and destroy their orange-groves, which was most effectually performed for several miles down the river. During our stay here, they received information of nine boats lying up a creek, laden with paddy; boats were immediately dispatched after them.

Next morning these boats were brought to the fleet; ten or twelve men were taken in them. As these had made no resistance, the chief said he would allow them to become Ladrones, if they agreed to take the usual oaths before Joss. Three or four of them refused to comply, for which they were punished in the following cruel manner: their hands were tied behind their back, a rope from the mast-head rove through their arms, and hoisted three or four feet from the deck, and five or six men flogged them with three rattans twisted together 'till they were apparently dead; then hoisted them up to the mast-head, and left them hanging nearly an hour, then lowered them down, and repeated the punishment, 'till they died or complied with the oath.

October the 20th, in the night, an express-boat came with the information that a large mandarine fleet was proceeding up the river to attack us. The chief immediately weighed, with fifty of the largest vessels, and sailed down the river to meet them. About one in the morning they commenced a heavy fire till daylight, when an express was sent for the remainder of the fleet to join them: about

142

an hour after a counter-order to anchor came, the mandarine fleet having run. Two or three hours afterwards the chief returned with three captured vessels in tow, having sunk two, and eighty-three sail made their escape. The admiral of the mandarines blew his vessel up, by throwing a lighted match into the magazine as the Ladrones were boarding her; she ran on shore, and they succeeded in getting twenty of her guns.

In this action very few prisoners were taken: the men belonging to the captured vessels drowned themselves, as they were sure of suffering a lingering and cruel death if taken after making resistance. The admiral left the fleet in charge of his brother, the second in command, and proceeded with his own vessel towards Lantow. The fleet remained in this river, cutting paddy, and getting the necessary supplies.

On the 28th of October, I received a letter from Captain Kay, brought by a fisherman, who had told him he would get us all back for three thousand dollars. He advised me to offer three thousand, and if not accepted, extend it to four; but not farther, as it was bad policy to offer much at first: at the same time assuring me we should be liberated, let the ransom be what it would. I offered the chief the three thousand, which he disdainfully refused, saying he was not to be played with; and unless they sent ten thousand dollars, and two large guns, with several casks of gunpowder, he would soon put us all to death. I wrote to Captain Kay, and informed him of the chief's determination, requesting if an opportunity offered, to send us a shift of clothes, for which it may be easily imagined we were much distressed, having been seven weeks without a shift; although constantly exposed to the weather, and of course frequently wet.

On the first of November, the fleet sailed up a narrow river, and anchored at night within two miles of a town called Little Whampoa. In front of it was a small fort, and several mandarine vessels lying in the harbor. The chief sent the interpreter to me, saying I must order my men to make cartridges and clean their muskets, ready to go on shore in the morning. I assured the interpreter I should give the men no such orders, that they must please themselves. Soon after the chief came on board, threatening to put us all to a cruel death if we refused to obey his orders. For my own part I remained determined, and advised the men not to comply, as I thought by making ourselves useful we should be accounted too valuable.

A few hours afterwards he sent to me again, saying, that if myself and the quartermaster would assist them at the great guns, that if also the rest of the men went on shore and succeeded in taking the place, he would then take the money offered for our ransom, and give them twenty dollars for every Chinaman's head they cut off. To these proposals we cheerfully acceded, in hopes of facilitating our deliverance.

Early in the morning the forces intended for landing were assembled in rowboats, amounting in the whole to three or four thousand men. The largest vessels weighed, and hauled in shore, to cover the landing of the forces, and attack the fort and mandarine vessels. About nine o'clock the action commenced, and continued with great spirit for nearly an hour, when the walls of the fort gave way, and the men retreated in the greatest confusion.

The mandarine vessels still continued firing, having blocked up the entrance of the harbor to prevent the Ladrone boats entering. At this the Ladrones were much exasperated, and about three hundred of them swam on shore, with a short sword lashed close under each arm; they then ran along the banks of the river 'till they came abreast of the vessels, and then swam off again and boarded them. The Chinese thus attacked, leaped overboard, and endeavored to reach the opposite shore; the Ladrones followed, and cut the greater number of them to pieces in the water. They next towed the vessels out of the harbor, and attacked the town with increased fury. The inhabitants fought about a quarter of an hour, and then retreated to an adjacent hill, from which they were soon driven with great slaughter.

After this the Ladrones returned, and plundered the town, every boat leaving it when laden. The Chinese on the hills perceiving most of the boats were off, rallied, and retook the town, after killing near two hundred Ladrones. One of my men was unfortunately lost in this dreadful massacre! The Ladrones landed a second time, drove the Chinese out of the town, then reduced it to ashes, and put all their prisoners to death, without regarding either age or sex!

I must not omit to mention a most horrid (though ludicrous) circumstance which happened at this place. The Ladrones were paid by their chief ten dollars for every Chinaman's head they produced. One of my men turning the corner of a street was met by a Ladrone running furiously after a Chinese; he had a drawn sword in his hand, and two Chinaman's heads which he had cut off, tied by their tails, and slung round his neck. I was witness myself to some of them producing five or six to obtain payment!

On the 4th of November an order arrived from the admiral for the fleet to proceed immediately to Lantow, where he was lying with only two vessels, and three Portuguese ships and a brig constantly annoying him; several sail of mandarine vessels were daily expected. The fleet weighed and proceeded towards Lantow. On passing the island of Lintin, three ships and a brig gave chase to us.

The Ladrones prepared to board; but night closing we lost sight of them: I am convinced they altered their course and stood from us. These vessels were in the pay of the Chinese government, and style themselves the Invincible Squadron, cruising in the river Tigris to annihilate the Ladrones!

On the fifth, in the morning, the red squadron anchored in a bay under Lantow; the black squadron stood to the eastward. In this bay they hauled several of their vessels on shore to bream their bottoms and repair them.

In the afternoon of the 8th of November, four ships, a brig and a schooner came off the mouth of the bay. At first the pirates were much alarmed, supposing them to be English vessels come to rescue us. Some of them threatened to hang us to the mast-head for them to fire at; and with much difficulty we persuaded them that they were Portuguese. The Ladrones had only seven junks in a fit state for action; these they hauled outside, and moored them head and stern across the bay; and manned all the boats belonging to the repairing vessels ready for boarding.

The Portuguese observing these maneuvers hove to, and communicated by boats. Soon afterwards they made sail, each ship firing her broadside as she passed, but without effect, the shot falling far short. The Ladrones did not return a single shot, but waved their colors, and threw up rockets, to induce them to come further in, which they might easily have done, the outside junks lying in four fathoms water which I sounded myself: though the Portuguese in their letters to Macao lamented there was not sufficient water for them to engage closer, but that they would certainly prevent their escaping before the mandarine fleet arrived!

On the 20th of November, early in the morning, I perceived an immense fleet of mandarine vessels standing for the bay. On nearing us, they formed a line, and stood close in; each vessel as she discharged her guns tacked to join the rear and reload. They kept up a constant fire for about two hours, when one of their largest vessels was blown up by a firebrand thrown from a Ladrone junk; after which they kept at a more respectful distance, but continued firing without intermission 'till the 21st at night, when it fell calm.

The Ladrones towed out seven large vessels, with about two hundred rowboats to board them; but a breeze springing up, they made sail and escaped. The Ladrones returned into the bay, and anchored. The Portuguese and mandarines followed, and continued a heavy cannonading during that night and the next day. The vessel I was in had her foremast shot away, which they supplied very expeditiously by taking a mainmast from a smaller vessel.

On the 23d, in the evening, it again fell calm; the Ladrones towed out fifteen junks in two divisions, with the intention of surrounding them, which was nearly effected, having come up with and boarded one, when a breeze suddenly sprung up. The captured vessel mounted twenty-two guns. Most of her crew leaped overboard; sixty or seventy were taken immediately, cut to pieces and thrown into the river. Early in the morning the Ladrones returned into the bay, and anchored in the same situation as before. The Portuguese and mandarines followed, keeping up a constant fire. The Ladrones never returned a single shot, but always kept in readiness to board, and the Portuguese were careful never to allow them an opportunity.

On the 28th, at night, they sent in eight fire-vessels, which if properly constructed must have done great execution, having every advantage they could wish for to effect their purpose; a strong breeze and tide directly into the bay, and the vessels lying so close together that it was impossible to miss them. On their first appearance the Ladrones gave a general shout, supposing them to be mandarine vessels on fire, but were very soon convinced of their mistake. They came very regularly into the center of the fleet, two and two, burning furiously; one of them came alongside of the vessel I was in, but they succeeded in booming her off. She appeared to be a vessel of about thirty tons; her hold was filled with straw and wood, and there were a few small boxes of combustibles on her deck, which exploded alongside of us without doing any damage. The Ladrones, however, towed them all on shore, extinguished the fire, and broke them up for fire-wood. The Portuguese claim the credit of constructing these destructive machines, and actually sent a dispatch to the Governor of Macao, saying they had destroyed at least one-third of the Ladrones' fleet, and hoped soon to effect their purpose by totally annihilating them!

On the 29th of November, the Ladrones being all ready for sea, they weighed and stood boldly out, bidding defiance to the invincible squadron and imperial fleet, consisting of ninety-three war-junks, six Portuguese ships, a brig, and a schooner. Immediately the Ladrones weighed, they made all sail. The Ladrones chased them two or three hours, keeping up a constant fire; finding they did not come up with them, they hauled their wind and stood to the eastward.

Thus terminated the boasted blockade, which lasted nine days, during which time the Ladrones completed all their repairs. In this action not a single Ladrone vessel was destroyed, and their loss about thirty or forty men. An American was also killed, one of three that remained out of eight taken in a schooner. I had two very narrow escapes: the first, a twelve-pounder shot fell within three or four feet of me; another took a piece out of a small brass-swivel on which I was standing. The chief's wife frequently sprinkled me with garlic-water, which they consider an effectual charm against shot. The fleet continued under sail all night, steering towards the eastward. In the morning they anchored in a large bay surrounded by lofty and barren mountains.

On the 2nd of December I received a letter from Lieutenant Maughn, commander of the Honorable Company's cruiser Antelope, saying that he had the ransom on board, and had been three days cruising after us, and wished me to settle with the chief on the securest method of delivering it. The chief agreed to send us in a small gunboat, 'till we came within sight of the Antelope; then the Compradore's boat was to bring the ransom and receive us.

I was so agitated at receiving this joyful news, that it was with considerable difficulty I could scrawl about two or three lines to inform Lieutenant Maughn of the arrangements I had made. We were all so deeply affected by the gratifying tidings, that we seldom closed our eyes, but continued watching day and night for the boat. On the 6th she returned with Lieutenant Maughn's answer, saying he would respect any single boat; but would not allow the fleet to approach him. The chief then, according to his first proposal, ordered a gunboat to take us, and with no small degree of pleasure we left the Ladrone fleet about four o'clock in the morning.

At one P.M. saw the Antelope under all sail, standing toward us. The Ladrone boat immediately anchored, and dispatched the Compradore's boat for the ransom, saying, that if she approached nearer, they would return to the fleet; and they were just weighing when she shortened sail, and anchored about two miles from us. The boat did not reach her 'till late in the afternoon, owing to the tide's being strong against her. She received the ransom and left the Antelope just before dark. A mandarine boat that had been lying concealed under the land, and watching their maneuvers, gave chase to her, and was within a few fathoms of taking her, when she saw a light, which the Ladrones answered, and the Mandarine hauled off.

Our situation was now a most critical one; the ransom was in the hands of the Ladrones, and the Compradore dare not return with us for fear of a second attack from the mandarine boat. The Ladrones would not remain 'till morning, so we were obliged to return with them to the fleet.

In the morning the chief inspected the ransom, which consisted of the following articles: two bales of superfine scarlet cloth; two chests of opium; two casks of gunpowder; and a telescope; the rest in dollars. He objected to the telescope not being

147

new; and said he should detain one of us 'till another was sent, or a hundred dollars in lieu of it. The Compradore however agreed with him for the hundred dollars.

Every thing being at length settled, the chief ordered two gunboats to convey us near the Antelope; we saw her just before dusk, when the Ladrone boats left us. We had the inexpressible pleasure of arriving on board the Antelope at 7 P.M., where we were most cordially received, and heartily congratulated on our safe and happy deliverance from a miserable captivity, which we had endured for eleven weeks and three days.

A few Remarks on the Origin, Progress, Manners, and Customs of the Ladrones

The Ladrones are a disaffected race of Chinese, that revolted against the oppressions of the mandarins. They first commenced their depredations on the Western coast (Cochin-China), by attacking small trading vessels in rowboats, carrying from thirty to forty men each. They continued this system of piracy several years; at length their successes, and the oppressive state of the Chinese, had the effect of rapidly increasing their numbers. Hundreds of fishermen and others flocked to their standard; and as their number increased they consequently became more desperate. They blockaded all the principal rivers, and captured several large junks, mounting from ten to fifteen guns each.

With these junks they formed a very formidable fleet, and no small vessels could trade on the coast with safety. They plundered several small villages, and exercised such wanton barbarity as struck horror into the breasts of the Chinese. To check these enormities the government equipped a fleet of forty imperial war-junks, mounting from eighteen to twenty guns each. On the very first rencontre, twenty-eight of the imperial junks struck to the pirates; the rest saved themselves by a precipitate retreat.

These junks, fully equipped for war, were a great acquisition to them. Their numbers augmented so rapidly, that at the period of my captivity they were supposed to amount to near seventy thousand men, eight hundred large vessels, and nearly a thousand small ones, including rowboats. They were divided into five squadrons, distinguished by different colored flags: each squadron commanded by an admiral, or chief; but all under the orders of A-juo-Chay (Ching yïh saou), their premier chief, a most daring and enterprising man, who went so far as to declare his intention of displacing the present Tartar family from the throne of China, and to restore the ancient Chinese dynasty.

148

This extraordinary character would have certainly shaken the foundation of the government, had he not been thwarted by the jealousy of the second in command, who declared his independence, and soon after surrendered to the mandarines with five hundred vessels, on promise of a pardon. Most of the inferior chiefs followed his example. A-juo-Chay (Ching yïh saou) held out a few months longer, and at length surrendered with sixteen thousand men, on condition of a general pardon, and himself to be made a mandarine of distinction.

The Ladrones have no settled residence on shore, but live constantly in their vessels. The after-part is appropriated to the captain and his wives; he generally has five or six. With respect to conjugal rights they are religiously strict; no person is allowed to have a woman on board, unless married to her according to their laws. Every man is allowed a small berth, about four feet square, where he stows with his wife and family.

From the number of souls crowded in so small a space, it must naturally be supposed they are horridly dirty, which is evidently the case, and their vessels swarm with all kinds of vermin. Rats in particular, which they encourage to breed, and eat them as great delicacies; in fact, there are very few creatures they will not eat. During our captivity we lived three weeks on caterpillars boiled with rice. They are much addicted to gambling, and spend all their leisure hours at cards and smoking opium.

THE FEMALE CAPTIVE[26]

Lucretia Parker

The event which is here related is the capture by the Pirates of the English sloop Eliza Ann, bound from St. Johns to Antigua, and the massacre of the whole crew (ten in number) with the exception of one female passenger, whose life, by the interposition of Divine Providence, was miraculously preserved. The particulars are copied from a letter written by the unfortunate Miss Parker (the female passenger above alluded to) to her brother in New York.

St. Johns, April 3, 1825.

Dear Brother,

You have undoubtedly heard of my adverse fortune, and the shocking incident that has attended me since I had the pleasure of seeing you in November last. Anticipating your impatience to be made acquainted with a more circumstantial detail of my extraordinary adventures, I shall not on account of the interest which I know you must feel in my welfare, hesitate to oblige you; yet, I must declare to you that it is that consideration alone that prompts me to do it, as even the recollection of the scenes which I have witnessed you must be sensible must ever be attended with pain: and that I cannot reflect on what I have endured, and the scenes of horror that I have been witness to, without the severest shock. I shall now, brother, proceed to furnish you with a detail of my misfortunes as they occurred, without exaggeration, and if it should be your wish to communicate them to the public, through the medium of a public print, or in any other way, you are at liberty to do it, and I shall consider myself amply rewarded if in a single instance it proves beneficial in removing a doubt in the minds of such, who, although they dare not deny the existence of a Supreme Being, yet disbelieve that he ever in any way revealed Himself to his creatures. Let Philosophy (as it is termed) smile with pity or contempt on my weakness or credulity, yet the superintendence of a

---

[26] From an Old Pamphlet, published in 1825.

particular Providence, interfering by second causes, is so apparent to me, and was so conspicuously displayed in the course of my afflictions, that I shall not banish it from my mind from the beginning to the end of my narration.

On the 28th February I took passage on board the sloop Eliza Ann, captain Charles Smith, for Antigua, in compliance with the earnest request of brother Thomas and family, who had advised me that they had concluded to make that island the place of their permanent residence, having a few months previous purchased there a valuable Plantation. We set sail with a favorable wind, and with every appearance of a short and pleasant voyage, and met with no incident to destroy or diminish those flattering prospects, until about noon of the 14th day from that of our departure, when a small schooner was discovered standing toward us, with her deck full of men, and as she approached us from her suspicious appearance there was not a doubt in the minds of any on board, but that she was a Pirate. When within a few yards of us, they gave a shout and our decks were instantly crowded with the motley crew of desperadoes, armed with weapons of almost every description that can be mentioned, and with which they commenced their barbarous work by unmercifully beating and maiming all on board except myself. As a retreat was impossible, and finding myself surrounded by wretches, whose yells, oaths, and imprecations, made them more resemble demons than human-beings, I fell on my knees, and from one who appeared to have the command, I begged for mercy, and for permission to retire to the cabin, that I might not be either the subject or a witness of the murderous scene that I had but little doubt was about to ensue. The privilege was not refused me. The monster in human shape (for such was then his appearance) conducted me by the hand himself to the companionway, and pointing to the cabin said to me, "Descend and remain there and you will be perfectly safe, for although Pirates, we are not barbarians to destroy the lives of innocent females!" Saying this he closed the companion doors and left me alone, to reflect on my helpless and deplorable situation. It is indeed impossible for me, brother, to paint to your imagination what were my feelings at this moment; being the only female on board, my terror it cannot be expected was much less than that of the poor devoted mariners! I resigned my life to the Being who had lent it,

151

and did not fail to improve the opportunity (which I thought it not improbable might be my last), to call on Him for that protection, which my situation so much at this moment required—and never shall I be persuaded but that my prayers were heard.

While I remained in this situation, by the sound of the clashing of swords, attended by shrieks and dismal groans, I could easily imagine what was going on on deck, and anticipated nothing better than the total destruction by the Pirates of the lives of all on board. After I had remained about one hour and a half alone in the cabin, and all had become silent on deck, the cabin doors were suddenly thrown open, and eight or ten of the Piratical crew entered, preceded by him whom I had suspected to be their leader, and from whom I had received assurances that I should not be injured. By him I was again addressed and requested to banish all fears of personal injury—that they sought only for the money which they suspected to be secreted somewhere on board the vessel, and which they were determined to have, although unable to extort a disclosure of the place of its concealment by threats and violence from the crew. The Pirates now commenced a thorough search throughout the cabin, the trunks and chests belonging to the captain and mate were broken open, and rifled of their most valuable contents—nor did my baggage and stores meet with any better fate, indeed this was a loss which at this moment caused me but little uneasiness. I felt that my life was in too much jeopardy to lament in any degree the loss of my worldly goods, surrounded as I was by a gang of the most ferocious looking villains that my eyes ever before beheld, of different complexions, and each with a drawn weapon in his hand, some of them fresh crimsoned with the blood (as I then supposed) of my murdered countrymen and whose horrid imprecations and oaths were enough to appal the bravest heart!

Their search for money proving unsuccessful (with the exception of a few dollars which they found in the captain's chest) they returned to the deck, and setting sail on the sloop, steered her for the place of their rendezvous, a small island or key not far distant I imagine from the island of Cuba, where we arrived the day after our capture. The island was nearly barren, producing nothing but a few scattered mangroves and shrubs, interspersed with the miserable huts of these outlaws of civilization, among whom power formed the only law, and every species of iniquity was here carried to an extent of which no person who had not witnessed a similar degree of pollution, could form the most distant idea.

As soon as the sloop was brought to an anchor, the hatches were thrown off and the unfortunate crew ordered on deck—a command which to my surprise was instantly obeyed, as I had harboured strong suspicions that they had been all murdered by the Pirates the day previous. The poor devoted victims, although alive, exhibited shocking proofs of the barbarity with which they had been treated by the unmerciful Pirates; their bodies exhibiting deep wounds and bruises too horrible for me to attempt to describe! Yet, however great had been their sufferings, their lives had been spared only to endure still greater torments. Being strongly pinioned they were forced into a small leaky boat and rowed on shore, which we having reached and a division of the plunder having been made by the Pirates, a scene of the most bloody and wanton barbarity ensued, the bare recollection of which still chills my blood. Having first divested them of every article of clothing but their shirts and trousers, with swords, knives, axes, etc., they fell on the unfortunate crew of the Eliza Ann with the ferocity of cannibals. In vain did they beg for mercy and intreat of their murderers to spare their lives. In vain did poor Capt. S. attempt to touch their feelings and to move them to pity by representing to them the situation of his innocent family; that he had a wife and three small children at home wholly dependent on him for support. But, alas, the poor man intreated in vain. His appeal was to monsters possessing hearts callous to the feelings of humanity. Having received a heavy blow from one with an ax, he snapped the cords with which he was bound, and attempted an escape by flight, but was met by another of the ruffians, who plunged a knife or dirk to his heart. I stood near him at this moment and was covered with his blood. On receiving the fatal wound he gave a single groan and fell lifeless at my feet. Nor were the remainder of the crew more fortunate. The mate while on his knees imploring mercy, and promising to accede to anything that the vile assassins should require of him, on condition of his life being spared, received a blow from a club, which instantaneously put a period to his existence! Dear brother, need I attempt to paint to your imagination my feelings at

153

this awful moment? Will it not suffice for me to say that I have described to you a scene of horror which I was compelled to witness! and with the expectation too of being the next victim selected by these ferocious monsters, whose thirst for blood appeared to be insatiable. There appeared now but one alternative left me, which was to offer up a prayer to Heaven for the protection of that Being who has power to stay the assassin's hand, and "who is able to do exceeding abundantly above what we can ask or think,"—sincerely in the language of scripture I can say, "I found trouble and sorrow, then called I upon the name of the Lord."

I remained on my knees until the inhuman wretches had completed their murderous work, and left none but myself to lament the fate of those who but twenty-four hours before, were animated with the pleasing prospects of a quick passage, and a speedy return to the bosoms of their families! The wretch by whom I had been thrice promised protection, and who seemed to reign chief among them, again approached me with hands crimsoned with the blood of my murdered countrymen, and, with a savage smile, once more repeated his assurances that if I would but become reconciled to my situation, I had nothing to fear. There was indeed something truly terrific in the appearance of this man, or rather monster as he ought to be termed. He was of a swarthy complexion, near six feet in height, his eyes were large, black and penetrating; his expression was remarkable, and when silent, his looks were sufficient to declare his meaning. He wore around his waist a leathern belt, to which was suspended a sword, a brace of pistols and a dirk. He was as I was afterward informed the acknowledged chief among the Pirates, all appeared to stand in awe of him, and no one dared to disobey his commands. Such, dear brother, was the character who had promised me protection if I would become reconciled to my situation, in other words, subservient to his will. But, whatever might have been his intentions, although now in his power, without a visible friend to protect me, yet such full reliance did I place in the Supreme Being, who sees and knows all things, and who has promised his protection to the faithful in the hour of tribulation, that I felt myself in a less degree of danger than you or any one would probably imagine.

As the day drew near to a close, I was conducted to a

small temporary hut or cabin, where I was informed I might repose peaceably for the night, which I did without being disturbed by any one. This was another opportunity that I did not suffer to pass unimproved to pour out my soul to that Being, who had already given me reasons to believe that he did not say to the house of Jacob, seek you me in vain. Oh! that all sincere Christians would in every difficulty make Him their refuge; He is a hopeful stay.

Early in the morning ensuing I was visited by the wretch alone whom I had viewed as chief of the murderous band. As he entered and cast his eyes upon me, his countenance relaxed from its usual ferocity to a feigned smile. Without speaking a word, he seated himself on a bench that the cabin contained, and drawing a table toward him, leaned upon it resting his cheek upon his hand. His eyes for some moments were fixed in stedfast gaze upon the ground, while his whole soul appeared to be devoured by the most diabolical thoughts. In a few moments he arose from his seat and hastily traversed the hut, apparently in extreme agitation, and not unfrequently fixing his eyes stedfastly upon me. But, that Providence, which while it protects the innocent, never suffers the wicked to go unpunished, interposed to save me and to deliver me from the hands of this remorseless villain, at the very instant when in all probability he intended to have destroyed my happiness forever.

On a sudden the Pirate's bugle was sounded, which (as I was afterward informed) was the usual signal of a sail in sight. The ruffian monster thereupon without uttering a word left my apartment, and hastened with all speed to the place of their general rendezvous on such occasions. Flattered by the pleasing hope that Providence might be about to complete her work of mercy, and was conducting to the dreary island some friendly aid, to rescue me from my perilous situation, I mustered courage to ascend to the roof of my hovel, to discover if possible the cause of the alarm, and what might be the issue.

A short distance from the island I espied a sail which appeared to be lying to, and a few miles therefrom to the windward, another, which appeared to be bearing down under a press of sail for the former—in a moment the whole gang of Pirates, with the exception of four, were in their boats, and with their oars, etc., were making every possible exertion to reach the vessel nearest to their island;

155

but by the time they had effected their object the more distant vessel (which proved to be a British sloop of war disguised) had approached them within fair gunshot, and probably knowing or suspecting their characters, opened their ports and commenced a destructive fire upon them. The Pirates were now, as nearly as I could judge with the naked eye, thrown into great confusion. Every possible exertion appeared to have been made by them to reach the island, and escape from their pursuers. Some jumped from their boats and attempted to gain the shore by swimming, but these were shot in the water, and the remainder who remained in their boats were very soon after overtaken and captured by two well manned boats dispatched from the sloop of war for that purpose; and, soon had I the satisfaction to see them all on board of the sloop, and in the power of those from whom I was fully satisfied that they would meet with the punishment due to their crimes.

In describing the characters of this Piratical band of robbers, I have, dear brother, represented them as wretches of the most frightful and ferocious appearance—blood-thirsty monsters, who, in acts of barbarity ought only to be ranked with cannibals, who delight to feast on human flesh. Rendered desperate by their crimes and aware that they should find no mercy if so unfortunate as to fall into the hands of those to whom they show no mercy, to prevent a possibility of detection, and the just execution of the laws wantonly destroy the lives of every one, however innocent, who may be so unfortunate as to fall into their power—such, indeed, brother, is the true character of the band of Pirates (to the number of 30 or 40) by whom it was my misfortune to be captured, with the exception of a single one, who possessed a countenance less savage, and had the appearance of possessing a heart less callous to the feelings of humanity. Fortunately for me, as Divine Providence ordered, this person was one of the four who remained on the island, and on whom the command involved after the unexpected disaster which had deprived them forever of so great a portion of their comrades. From this man (after the capture of the murderous tyrant to whose commands he had been compelled to yield) I received the kindest treatment, and assurances that I should be restored to liberty and to my friends when an opportunity should present, or when it could be consistently done with the safety of their lives and liberty.

This unhappy man (for such he declared himself to be) took an opportunity to indulge me with a partial relation of a few of the most extraordinary incidents of his life. He declared himself an Englishman by birth, but his real name and place of nativity was he said a secret he would never disclose! "although I must (said he) acknowledge myself by profession a Pirate, yet I can boast of respectable parentage, and the time once was when I myself sustained an unimpeachable character. Loss of property, through the treachery of those whom I considered friends, and in whom I had placed implicit confidence, was what first led me to and induced me to prefer this mode of life, to any of a less criminal nature—but, although I voluntarily became the associate of a band of wretches the most wicked and unprincipled perhaps on earth, yet I solemnly declare that I have not in any one instance personally deprived an innocent fellow creature of life. It was an act of barbarity at which my heart ever recoiled, and against which I always protested. With the property I always insisted we ought to be satisfied, without the destruction of the lives of such who were probably the fathers of families, and who had never offended us. But our gang was as you may suppose chiefly composed of and governed by men without principle, who appeared to delight in the shedding of blood, and whose only excuse has been that by acting with too much humanity in sparing life, they might thereby be exposed and themselves arraigned to answer for their crimes at an earthly tribunal. You can have no conception, madam (continued he), of the immense property that has been piratically captured, and of the number of lives that have been destroyed by this gang alone, and all without the loss of a single one on our part until yesterday, when by an unexpected circumstance our number has been reduced as you see from thirty-five to four! This island has not been our constant abiding place, but the bodies of such as have suffered here have always been conveyed a considerable distance from the shore, and thrown into the sea, where they were probably devoured by the sharks, as not a single one has ever been known afterward to drift on our shores. The property captured has not been long retained on this island, but shipped to a neighboring port, where we have an agent to dispose of it.

"Of the great number of vessels captured by us (continued he) you are the first and only female that has been so unfortunate as to fall into our hands—and from the moment that I first saw you in our power (well knowing the brutal disposition of him whom we acknowledged our chief) I trembled for your safety, and viewed you as one deprived perhaps of the protection of a husband or brother, to become the victim of an unpitying wretch, whose pretended regard for your sex, and his repeated promises of protection, were hypocritical—a mere mask to lull your fears until he could effect your ruin. His hellish designs, agreeable to his own declarations, would have been carried into effect the very morning that he last visited you, had not an all-wise Providence interfered to save you—and so sensible am I that the unexpected circumstance of his capture, as well as that of the most of our gang, as desperate and unprincipled as himself, must have been by order of Him, from whose all-seeing eye no evil transaction can be hidden, that were I so disposed I should be deterred from doing you any injury through fear of meeting with a similar fate. Nor do my three remaining companions differ with me in opinion, and we all now most solemnly pledge ourselves, that so long as you remain in our power, you shall have nothing to complain of but the deprivation of the society of those whose company no doubt would be more agreeable to you; and as soon as it can be done consistently with our own safety, you shall be conveyed to a place from which you may obtain a passage to your friends. We have now become too few in number to hazard a repetition of our Piratical robberies, and not only this, but some of our captured companions to save their own lives, may prove treacherous enough to betray us; we are therefore making preparation to leave this island for a place of more safety, when you, madam, shall be conveyed and set at liberty as I have promised you."

Dear brother, if you before doubted, is not the declaration of this man (which I have recorded as correctly as my recollection will admit of) sufficient to satisfy you that I owe my life and safety to the interposition of a Divine Providence! Oh, yes! surely it is—and I feel my insufficiency to thank and praise my Heavenly Protector as I ought, for his loving kindness in preserving me from the evil designs of wicked men, and for finally restoring me to liberty and to my friends!

I cannot praise Him as I would, But He is merciful and good.

From this moment every preparation was made by the Pirates to remove from the island. The small quantity of stores and goods which remained on hand (principally of the Ann Eliza's cargo) was either buried on the island, or conveyed away in their boats in the night to some place unknown to me. The last thing done was to demolish their temporary dwellings, which was done so effectually as not to suffer a vestige of any thing to remain that could have led to a discovery that the island had ever been inhabited by such a set of beings. Eleven days from that of the capture of the Ann Eliza (the Pirates having previously put on board several bags of dollars, which from the appearance of the former, I judged had been concealed in the earth) I was ordered to embark with them, but for what place I then knew not.

About midnight I was landed on the rocky shores of an island which they informed me was Cuba, they furnished me with a few hard biscuit and a bottle of water, and directed me to proceed early in the morning in a northeast direction, to a house about a mile distant, where I was told I would be well treated and be furnished with a guide that would conduct me to Mantansies. With these directions they left me, and I never saw them more.

At daybreak I set out in search of the house to which I had been directed by the Pirates, and which I had the good fortune to reach in safety in about an hour and a half. It was a humble tenement thatched with canes, without any flooring but the ground, and was tenanted by a man and his wife only, from whom I met with a welcome reception, and by whom I was treated with much hospitality. Although Spaniards, the man could speak and understand enough English to converse with me, and to learn by what means I had been brought so unexpectedly alone and unprotected to his house. Though it was the same to which I had been directed by the Pirates, yet he declared that so far from being in any way connected with them in their Piratical robberies, or enjoying any portion of their ill-gotten gain, no one could hold them in greater abhorrence. Whether he was sincere in these declarations or not, is well known to Him whom the lying tongue cannot deceive—it is but justice to them to say that by both the man and his wife I was treated with kindness, and it was

159

with apparent emotions of pity that they listened to the tale of my sufferings. By their earnest request I remained with them until the morning ensuing, when I set out on foot for Mantansies, accompanied by the Spaniard who had kindly offered to conduct me to that place, which we reached about seven in the evening of the same day.

At Mantansies I found many Americans and Europeans, by whom I was kindly treated, and who proffered their services to restore me to my friends, but as there were no vessels bound direct from thence to Antigua or St. Johns, I was persuaded to take passage for Jamaica, where it was the opinion of my friends I might obtain a passage more speedily for one or the other place, and where I safely arrived after a pleasant passage of four days.

The most remarkable and unexpected circumstance of my extraordinary adventures, I have yet, dear brother, to relate. Soon after my arrival at Jamaica, the Authority having been made acquainted with the circumstance of my recent capture by the Pirates, and the extraordinary circumstance which produced my liberation, requested that I might be conducted to the Prison, to see if I could among a number of Pirates recently committed, recognize any of those by whom I had been captured. I was accordingly attended by two or three gentlemen, and two young ladies (who had politely offered to accompany me) to the prison apartment, on entering which, I not only instantly recognized among a number therein confined, the identical savage monster of whom I have had so much occasion to speak (the Pirates' Chief) but the most of those who had composed his gang, and who were captured with him!

The sudden and unexpected introduction into their apartment of one, whom they had probably in their minds numbered with the victims of their wanton barbarity, produced unquestionably on their minds not an inconsiderable degree of horror as well as surprise! and, considering their condemnation now certain, they no doubt heaped curses upon their more fortunate companions, for sparing the life and setting at liberty one whom an all-wise Providence had conducted to and placed in a situation to bear witness to their unprecedented barbarity.

Government having through me obtained the necessary proof of the guilt of these merciless wretches,

160

after a fair and impartial trial they were all condemned to suffer the punishment due to their crimes, and seven ordered for immediate execution, one of whom was the barbarian their chief. After the conviction and condemnation of this wretch, in hopes of eluding the course of justice, he made (as I was informed) an attempt upon his own life, by inflicting upon himself deep wounds with a knife which he had concealed for that purpose; but in this he was disappointed, the wounds not proving so fatal as he probably anticipated.

I never saw this hardened villain or any of his equally criminal companions after their condemnation, although strongly urged to witness their execution, and am therefore indebted to one who daily visited them, for the information of their behavior from that period until that of their execution; which, as regarded the former, I was informed was extremely impenitent—that while proceeding to the place of ignominy and death, he talked with shocking unconcern, hinting that by being instrumental in the destruction of so many lives, he had become too hardened and familiar with death to feel much intimidated at its approach! He was attended to the place of execution by a Roman Catholic Priest, who it was said labored to convince him of the atrociousness of his crimes, but he seemed deaf to all admonition or exhortation, and appeared insensible to the hope of happiness or fear of torment in a future state—and so far from exhibiting a single symptom of penitence, declared that he knew of but one thing for which he had cause to reproach himself, which was in sparing my life and not ordering me to be butchered as the others had been! How awful was the end of the life of this miserable criminal! He looked not with harmony, regard, or a single penitent feeling toward one human being in the last agonies of an ignominious death.

After remaining nine days at Jamaica, I was so fortunate as to obtain a passage with Capt. Ellsmore, direct for St. Johns—the thoughts of once more returning home and of so soon joining my anxious friends, when I could have an opportunity to communicate to my aged parents, to a beloved sister and a large circle of acquaintances, the sad tale of the misfortunes which had attended me since I bid them adieu, would have been productive of the most pleasing sensations, had they not been interrupted by the melancholy reflection that I was the bearer of tidings of the

161

most heart-rending nature, to the bereaved families of those unfortunate husbands and parents who had in my presence fallen victims to Piratical barbarity. Thankful should I have been had the distressing duty fell to the lot of some one of less sensibility—but, unerring Providence had ordered otherwise. We arrived safe at our port of destination after a somewhat boisterous passage of 18 days. I found my friends all well, but the effects produced on their minds by the relation of the distressing incidents and adverse fortune that had attended me since my departure, I shall not attempt to describe—and much less can you expect, brother, that I should attempt a description of the feelings of the afflicted widow and fatherless child, who first received from me the melancholy tidings that they were so!

Thus, brother, have I furnished you with as minute a detail of the sad misfortunes that have attended me, in my intended passage to Antigua, in February and March last, as circumstances will admit of—and here permit me once more to repeat the enquiry—is it not sufficient to satisfy you and every reasonable person, that I owe my life and liberty to the interposition of a Divine Providence?—so fully persuaded am I of this, dear brother, and of my great obligations to that Supreme Being who turned not away my prayer nor his mercy from me, that I am determined to engage with my whole heart to serve Him the residue of my days on earth, by the aid of his heavenly grace—and invite all who profess to fear Him (should a single doubt remain on their minds) to come and hear what he hath done for me!

I am, dear brother, affectionately yours,

Lucretia Parker

162

THE PASSING OF MOGUL MACKENZIE

The Last of the North Atlantic Pirates[27]

Arthur Hunt Chute

In the farther end of the Bay of Fundy, about a mile off from the Nova Scotian coast, is the Isle of Haut. It is a strange rocky island that rises several hundred feet sheer out of the sea, without any bay or inlets. A landing can only be effected there in the calmest weather; and on account of the tremendous ebb of the Fundy tides, which rise and fall sixty feet every twelve hours, the venturesome explorer cannot long keep his boat moored against the precipitous cliffs.

Because of this inaccessibility little is known of the solitary island. Within its rampart walls of rock they say there is a green valley, and in its center is a fathomless lake, where the Micmac Indians used to bury their dead, and hence its dread appellation of the "Island of the Dead." Beyond these bare facts nothing more is certain about the secret valley and the haunted lake. Many wild and fabulous descriptions are current, but they are merely the weavings of fancy.

Sometimes on a stormy night the unhappy navigators of the North Channel miss the coast lights in the fog, and out from the Isle of Haut a gentle undertow flirts with their bewildered craft. Then little by little they are gathered into a mighty current against which all striving is in vain, and in the white foam among the iron cliffs their ship is pounded into splinters. The quarry which she gathers in so softly at first and so fiercely at last, however, is soon snatched away from the siren shore. The ebb-tide bears every sign of wreckage far out into the deeps of the Atlantic, and not a trace remains of the ill-starred vessel or her crew. But one of the boats in the fishing fleet never comes home, and from lonely huts on the coast reproachful eyes are cast upon the "Island of the Dead."

On the long winter nights, when the "boys" gather about the fire in Old Steele's General Stores at Hall's Harbor, their hard gray life becomes bright for a spell. When a keg of hard cider is flowing freely the grim fishermen forget their taciturnity, the ice is melted from their speech, and the floodgates of their souls pour forth. But

---

27 From Blackwood's Magazine.

ever in the background of their talk, unforgotten, like a haunting shadow, is the "Island of the Dead." Of their weirdest and most blood-curdling yarns it is always the center; and when at last, with uncertain steps, they leave the empty keg and the dying fire to turn homeward through the drifting snow, fearful and furtive glances are cast to where the island looms up like a ghostly sentinel from the sea. Across its high promontory the Northern Lights scintillate and blaze, and out of its moving brightness the terrified fishermen behold the war-canoes of dead Indians freighted with their redskin braves; the forms of cœur de bois and desperate Frenchmen swinging down the sky-line in a ghastly snake-dance; the shapes and spars of ships long since forgotten from the "Missing List"; and always, most dread-inspiring of them all, the distress signals from the sinking ship of Mogul Mackenzie and his pirate crew.

Captain Mogul Mackenzie was the last of the pirates to scourge the North Atlantic seaboard. He came from that school of freebooters that was let loose by the American Civil War. With a letter of marque from the Confederate States, he sailed the seas to prey on Yankee shipping. He and his fellow-privateers were so thorough in their work of destruction, that the Mercantile Marine of the United States was ruined for a generation to come. When the war was over the defeated South called off her few remaining bloodhounds on the sea. But Mackenzie, who was still at large, had drunk too deeply of the wine of a wild, free life. He did not return to lay down his arms, but began on a course of shameless piracy. He lived only a few months under the black flag, until he went down on the Isle of Haut. The events of that brief and thrilling period are unfortunately obscure, with only a ray of light here and there. But the story of his passing is the most weird of all the strange yarns that are spun about the "Island of the Dead."

In May, 1865, a gruesome discovery was made off the coast of Maine, which sent a chill of fear through all the seaport towns of New England. A whaler bound for New Bedford was coming up Cape Cod one night long after dark. There was no fog, and the lights of approaching vessels could easily be discerned. The man on the lookout felt no uneasiness at his post, when, without any warning of bells or lights, the sharp bow of a brigantine suddenly loomed up, hardly a ship's length in front.

"What the blazes are you trying to do?" roared the mate from the bridge, enraged at this unheard-of violation of the right of way. But no voice answered his challenge, and the brigantine went swinging by, with all her sails set to a spanking breeze. She bore directly across the bow of the whaler, which just grazed her stern in passing.

"There's something rotten on board there," said the mate.

"Ay," said the captain, who had come on the bridge, "there's something rotten there right enough. Swing your helm to port, and get after the devils," he ordered.

"Ay, ay, sir!" came the ready response, and nothing loth the helmsman changed his course to follow the eccentric craft. She was evidently bound on some secret mission, for not otherwise would she thus tear through the darkness before the wind without the flicker of a light.

The whaler was the swifter of the two ships, and she could soon have overhauled the other; but fearing some treachery, the captain refrained from running her down until daylight. All night long she seemed to be veering her course, attempting to escape from her pursuer. In the morning, off the coast of Maine, she turned her nose directly out to sea. Then a boat was lowered from the whaler, and rowed out to intercept the oncoming vessel. When they were directly in her course, they lay on their oars and waited. The brigantine did not veer again, but came steadily on, and soon the whalemen were alongside, and made themselves fast to a dinghy which she had in tow. A few minutes of apprehensive waiting followed, and as nothing happened, one of the boldest swung himself up over the tow-rope on to the deck. He was followed by the others, and they advanced cautiously with drawn knives and pistols.

Not a soul was to be seen, and the men, who were brave enough before a charging whale, trembled with fear. The wheel and the lookout were alike deserted, and no sign of life could be discovered anywhere below. In the galley were the embers of a dead fire, and the table in the captain's cabin was spread out ready for a meal which had never been eaten. On deck everything was spick and span, and not the slightest evidence of a storm or any other disturbance could be found. The theory of a derelict was impossible. Apparently all had been well on board, and they had been sailing with good weather, when, without any warning, her crew had been suddenly snatched away by some dread power.

The sailors with one accord agreed that it was the work of a sea-serpent. But the mate had no place for the ordinary superstitions of the sea, and he still scoured the hold, expecting at any minute to encounter a dead body or some other evil evidence of foul play. Nothing more, however, was found, and the mate at length had to end his search with the unsatisfactory conclusion that the St. Clare, a brigantine registered from Hartpool, with cargo of lime, had been abandoned on the high seas for no apparent reason. Her skipper had taken with him the ship's papers, and had not left a single clue behind.

A crew was told off to stand by the St. Clare to bring her into port, and the others climbed into the long-boat to row back to the whaler.

"Just see if there is a name on that there dinghy, before we go," said the mate.

An exclamation of horror broke from one of the men as he read on the bow of the dinghy the name, Kanawha.

The faces of all went white with a dire alarm as the facts of the mystery suddenly flashed before them. The Kanawha was the ship in which Captain Mogul Mackenzie had made himself notorious as a privateersman. Every one had heard her awe-inspiring name, and every Yankee seafaring man prayed that he might never meet her on the seas. After the Alabama was sunk, and the Talahassee was withdrawn, the Kanawha still remained to threaten the shipping of the North. For a long time her whereabouts had been unknown, and then she was discovered by a Federal gunboat, which gave chase and fired upon her. Without returning fire, she raced in for shelter amongst the dangerous islands off Cape Sable, and was lost in the fog. Rumor had it that she ran on the rocks off that perilous coast, and sank with all on board. As time went by, and there was no more sign of the corsair, the rumor was accepted as proven. Men began to spin yarns in the forecastle about Mogul Mackenzie, with an interest that was tinged with its former fear. Skippers were beginning to feel at ease again on the grim waters, when suddenly, like a bolt from the blue, came the awful news of the discovery of the St. Clare.

Gunboats put off to scour the coast-line; and again with fear and trembling the look-out began to eye suspiciously every new sail coming up on the horizon.

One afternoon, toward the end of May, a schooner came tearing into Portland harbor, with all her canvas, crowded on, and flying distress signals. Her skipper said that off the island of Campabello he had seen a long gray sailing-ship with auxiliary power sweeping down upon him. As the wind was blowing strong inshore, he had taken to his heels and made for Portland. He was chased all the way, and his pursuer did not drop him until he was just off the harbor bar.

Many doubted his story, however, saying that no one would dare to chase a peaceful craft so near to a great port in broad daylight. And, again, it was urged that an auxiliary vessel could easily have overhauled the schooner between Campabello and Portland. The fact that the captain of the schooner was as often drunk as sober, and that when he was under the influence of drink he was given to seeing visions, was pointed to as conclusive proof that his yarn was a lie. After the New Bedford whaler came into port

166

with the abandoned St. Clare, it was known beyond doubt that the Kanawha was still a real menace. But nobody cared to admit that Mogul Mackenzie was as bold as the schooner's report would imply, and hence countless arguments were put forward to allay such fears.

But a few days later the fact that the pirates were still haunting their coast was absolutely corroborated. A coastal packet from Boston arrived at Yarmouth with the news that she had not only sighted Kanawha in the distance, but they had crossed each other's paths so near that the name could be discerned beyond question with a spyglass. She was heading up the Bay of Fundy, and did not pause or pay any heed to the other ship.

This news brought with it consternation, and every town and village along the Fundy was a-hum with stories and theories about the pirate ship. The interest, instead of being abated, was augmented as the days went by with no further report. In the public-houses and along the quays it was almost the only topic of conversation. The excitement became almost feverish when it was known that several captains, outward bound, had taken with them a supply of rifles and ammunition. The prospect of a fight seemed imminent.

About a week after the adventure of the Boston packet Her Majesty's ship Buzzard appeared off Yarmouth harbor. The news of the Kanawha had come to the Admiral at Halifax, and he had dispatched the warship to cruise about the troubled coast.

"That'll be the end of old Mogul Mackenzie, now that he's got an English ship on his trail," averred a Canadian as he sat drinking in the "Yarmouth Light" with a group of seafaring men of various nationalities. "It takes the British jack-tar to put the kibosh on this pirate game. One of them is worth a shipload of Yankees at the business."

"Well, don't you crow too loud now," replied a Boston skipper. "I reckon that that Nova Scotian booze-artist, who ran into Portland the other day scared of his shadow, would not do you fellows much credit."

"Yes; but what about your gunboats that have had the job of fixing the Kanawha for the last three years, and haven't done it yet?" The feelings between Canada and the United States were none too good just after the Civil War, and the Canadian was bound not to lose this opportunity for horse-play. "You're a fine crowd of sea-dogs, you are, you fellows from the Boston Tea-Party. Three years after one little half-drowned rat, and haven't got him yet. Wouldn't Sir Francis Drake or Lord Nelson be proud of the record that you long-legged, slab-sided Yankees have made on the sea!"

"Shut your mouth! you blue-nosed, down-East herring-choker!" roared the Yankee skipper. "I reckon we've given you traitors that tried to stab us in the back a good enough licking; and if any more of your dirty dogs ever come nosing about down south of Mason and Dixon's Line, I bet they'll soon find out what our record is."

"Well, you fools can waste your tongue and wind," said a third man, raising his glass, "but for me here's good luck to the Buzzard."

"So say we all of us," chimed in the others, and the Yankee and the Canadian drank together to the success of the British ship, forgetting their petty jealousies before a common foe.

Everywhere the news of the arrival of the British warship was hailed with delight. All seemed to agree that her presence assured the speedy extermination of the pirate crew. But after several days of futile cruising about the coast, her commander, to escape from a coming storm, had to put into St. Mary's Bay, with the object of his search still eluding his vigilance. He only arrived in time to hear the last chapter of the Kanawha's tale of horrors.

The night before, Dominic Lefountain, a farmer living alone at Meteighan, a little village on the French shore, had been awakened from his sleep by the moaning and wailing of a human voice. For days the imminent peril of an assault from the pirates had filled the people of the French coast with forebodings. And now, awakened thus in the dead of night, the lonely Frenchman was wellnigh paralyzed with terror. With his flesh creeping, and his eyes wide, he groped for his rifle, and waited in the darkness, while ever and anon came those unearthly cries from the beach. Nearly an hour passed before he could gather himself together sufficiently to investigate the cause of the alarm. At last, when the piteous wailing had grown weak and intermittent, the instinct of humanity mastered his fears, and he went forth to give a possible succor to the one in need.

On the beach, lying prostrate, with the water lapping about his feet, he found a man in the last stage of exhaustion. The blood was flowing from his mouth, and as Dominic turned him over to stanch its flow, he found that his tongue had been cut out, and hence the unearthly wailing which had roused him from his sleep. The beach was deserted by this time, and it was too dark to see far out into the bay.

Dominic carried the unfortunate man to his house, and nursed him there for many weeks. He survived his frightful experiences, and lived on for twenty years, a pathetic and helpless figure, supported by the big-hearted farmers and fishermen of the French shore. Evidently he had known too much for his enemies, and they had sealed his mouth forever. He became known as the "Mysterious Man of Meteighan," and his deplorable condition was

168

always pointed to as a mute witness of the last villainy of Mogul Mackenzie.

On the night following the episode of the "Mysterious Man of Meteighan," a wild and untoward storm swept down the North Atlantic and over the seaboard far and near. In the Bay of Fundy that night the elements met in their grandest extremes. Tide-rips and mountain waves opposed each other with titanic force. All along the bleak and rock-ribbed coast the boiling waters lay churned into foam. Over the breakwaters the giant combers crashed and soared far up into the troubled sky; while out under the black clouds of the night the whirlpools and the tempests met. Was ever a night like this before? Those on shore thanked God; and those with fathers on the sea gazed out upon a darkness where no star of hope could shine.

Now and again through the Stygian gloom a torrent of sheet-lightning rolled down across the heavens, bringing in its wake a moment of terrible light. It was in one of these brief moments of illumination that the wan watchers at Hall's Harbor discerned a long gray ship being swept like a specter before the winds towards the Isle of Haut. Until the flash of lightning the doomed seamen appeared to have been unconscious of their fast approaching fate; and then, as if suddenly awakened, they sent a long thin trail of light, to wind itself far up into the darkness. Again and again the rockets shot upward from her bow, while above the noises of the tempest came the roar of a gun.

The people on the shore looked at each other with blanched faces, speechless, helpless. A lifetime by that shore had taught them the utter puniness of the sons of men. Others would have tried to do something with what they thought was their strong arm. But the fishermen knew too well that the Fundy's arm was stronger. In silence they waited with bated breath while the awful moments passed. Imperturbable they stood there, with their feet in the white foam and their faces in the salt spray, and gazed at the curtain of the night, behind which a tragedy was passing, as dark and dire as any in the annals of the sea.

Another flash of lightning, and there, dashing upon the iron rocks, was a great ship, with all her sails set, and a cloud of lurid smoke trailing from her funnel. She was gray-colored, with auxiliary power, and as her lines dawned upon those who saw her in the moment of light, they burst out with one accord, "It's the Kanawha! It's the Kanawha!" As if an answer to their sudden cry another gun roared, and another shower of rockets shot up into the sky; and then all was lost again in the darkness and the voices of the tempest.

Next morning the winds had gone out with the tide, and when

in the afternoon the calm waters had risen, a boat put off from Hall's Harbor and rowed to the Isle of Haut. For several hours the rocky shores were searched for some traces of the wreck, but not a spar or splinter could be found. All about the bright waters laughed, with naught but the sunbeams on their bosom, and not a shadow remained from last night's sorrow on the sea.

So Mogul Mackenzie, who had lived a life of stress, passed out on the wings of storm. In his end, as always, he baffled pursuit, and was sought but could not be found. His sailings on the sea were in secret, and his last port in death was a mystery. But, as has been already related, when the Northern Lights come down across the haunted island, the distress signals of his pirate crew are still seen shooting up into the night.

THE LAST OF THE SEA-ROVERS

The Riff Coast Pirates[28]

W. B. Lord

O nay, O nay, then said our King,
O nay, this must not be,
To yield to such a rover
Myself will not agree;
He hath deceived the Frenchman,
Likewise the King of Spain,
And how can he be true to me,
That hath been false to twain?

OLD SEA SONG OF THE YEAR 1620.

Probably by this time the greater part of the piratical craft along the Riff coast has been destroyed, and the long-promised Moorish gunboat stationed there to protect foreign shipping.[29] These steps have doubtless been hastened by the fact that the pirates, unfortunately for themselves, attacked a vessel some little time ago belonging to the Sultan of Morocco. For years past the Governments of several European Powers have sought to put friendly pressure upon the Sultan of Morocco to effectually stop the depredations of the Riffian coast pirates. No strong measures, however, were really taken until the above episode occurred. It is said that in early days the Moors were some time in accustoming themselves to the perils of the deep. At first they marvelled greatly at "those that go down to the sea in ships, and have their business in great waters," but they did not hasten to follow their example. One eminent ruler of ancient times, in that region, when asked what the sea was like, replied, "The sea is a huge beast which silly folk ride like worms on logs." But it afterwards became clear that the Moors had a strong fancy for the "worms" and "logs" too. They gave up marvelling at those who went to sea, and went on it themselves in search of plunder. The risk, the uncertainty, the danger, the sense of superior skill and ingenuity, that attract the adventurous spirit, and the passion for sport, are stated by some writers to have brought

---

[28] From the Nautical Magazine.
[29] About twenty years ago.

171

such a state of things into existence. One fact seems to be pretty certain, that when these depredations were first made, they took the form of reprisals upon the Spaniards. No sooner was Granada fallen, than thousands of desperate Moors left the land, disdaining to live under a Spanish yoke. Settling along a portion of the northern coast of Africa, they immediately proceeded to first attack all Spanish vessels that could be found. Their quickness and knowledge of the coasts gave them the opportunity of reprisals for which they longed. Probably this got monotonous in course of time, for in their wild sea courses they took to harrying the vessels belonging to other nations, and so laid the foundation for a race of pirates, which has continued down to quite recently. As nowadays, the Moors cruised in boats from the commencement of their marauding expeditions. Each man pulled an oar, and knew how to fight as well as row. Drawing little water, a small squadron of these craft could be pushed up almost any creek, or lie hidden behind a rock, till the enemy came in sight. Then oars out, and a quick stroke for a few minutes. Next they were alongside their unsuspecting prey, and pouring in a first volley. Ultimately the prize was usually taken, the crew put in irons, and the pirates returned home with their capture, no doubt being received with acclamation upon their arrival.

As far back as the sixteenth century the Spanish forts at Alhucemas—not to mention other places—were established for the purpose of repressing piracy in its vicinity. Considerable interest is attached to several of the piracies committed during the past few years, as they culminated in strong representations being made to the Sultan of Morocco by the various Governments under whose flag the respective vessels sailed. Some of them went so far as to send warships to cruise along the Riffian coast. This step apparently had some moral effect upon the pirates, for from that time onwards attacks upon foreign vessels practically ceased. Something more than this, however, was needed, for no one could say how soon the marauding expeditions might be renewed upon a larger scale than ever, so as to make up for lost opportunities. On August 14, 1897, the Italian three-masted schooner Fiducia was off the coast of Morocco, in the Mediterranean, homeward bound from Pensacola to Marseilles. Here she got becalmed, and while in that condition two boats approached her from the shore. At first the crew of the Fiducia thought they were native fishing boats. When, however, the latter got within a hundred yards or so of the helpless vessel, the suspicions of the crew were aroused. The captain warned the Moors not to approach any nearer; a volley of bullets was returned by way of reply, followed by a regular fusillade as the boats advanced. There

172

were only three revolvers on board the schooner, and with these the crew prepared to defend themselves. Soon, however, their supply of ammunition became exhausted, and the pirates boarded the schooner without further opposition. The vessel was at once ransacked, even the clothes of the crew being taken. The ship's own boat was lowered, and into this the marauders put their booty, and took it ashore, also carrying the captain and one of the crew with them. About an hour later another boat, containing about twenty pirates, came off and fired on the ship. The crew, seeing that they could offer no effective resistance, hid themselves away in the hold. The other pirates had left very little for the new arrivals to take, and this seemed to annoy them so much that they gave vent to their ill-feelings in several ways, not the least wanton being the pollution of the ship's fresh water. They also smashed the vessel's compass, and tore up the charts. For the next two days the crew existed on a few biscuits, which the pirates had left behind. The following day the British steamship Oanfa, of London, hove in sight. The crew of the schooner hoisted a shirt as a signal, which was fortunately seen, and a boat sent off in response thereto. Assistance was promptly rendered, and the Fiducia put in a position to resume her voyage. This was done until spoken by the Italian cruiser Ercole, which assisted the schooner to her destination.

In October, 1896, the French barque Prosper Corue was lying becalmed off Alhucemas, a place fortified by the Spaniards to keep the pirates in check, when several boats full of armed Moors seized the vessel and made the crew prisoners. They then completely pillaged the ship, removing almost everything of any use or value. While the miscreants were thus busily engaged a Spanish merchant steamship, named the Sevilla, happened to come along, and was in time to capture one boat and rescue several of the prisoners. The Sevilla then made towards the barque, but the pirates opened fire on the steamer, killing and wounding some of the crew. The Spaniard was compelled to retire, leaving the captain of the barque in the hands of the Moors. Subsequently the barque was picked up in an abandoned condition by the British steamship Oswin, and towed into Almeria. An arrangement was afterwards made with the pirates to release the captains of the Fiducia and the Portuguese barque Rosita Faro—a much earlier capture—and some members of both crews, in exchange for the Riffians captured by the Spanish steamer Sevilla and a ransom of 3,000 dollars. It was only after prolonged negotiations and a large sum of money that a French warship succeeded in obtaining the freedom of the captain of the Prosper Corue and a few other Frenchmen. For some reason or other, the pirates seemed very much disinclined to part with these

173

prisoners. Only a short time before the attack on the French barque took place, a notice was issued by the British Board of Trade, in which the attention of ship-owners and masters of vessels was called to the dangers attending navigation off the coast of Morocco. The document then proceeded to detail the case of the British schooner Mayer, of Gibraltar, which was boarded about 10 miles from the Riff coast by twenty Moors armed with rifles and daggers. As usual, the pirates ransacked the vessel, destroyed the ensign and ship's papers, brutally assaulted the men on board, and then made off in their boat. Scarcely had the foregoing notice been generally circulated than another case of a similar character happened in connection with the Italian schooner Scatuola. Again, there is the Spanish cutter Jacob. She was running along the Moorish coast one fine summer's evening a few years since, when a boat full of pirates suddenly came alongside, and speedily upset the quietness which had previously reigned on board the Jacob. Five of the crew managed to escape in the cutter's boat and were picked up some days later by a passing vessel. Those who remained on board the cutter fared very badly. After the vessel had been pillaged, the rigging and sails destroyed, the men were all securely bound and left to their fate. Fortunately the weather continued fine, and the Jacob drifted towards the Spanish coast, where she was seen and assistance promptly rendered.

The captain of another Spanish vessel had quite a "thrilling" adventure among these pirates in May, 1892. He left Gibraltar in command of the barque San Antonio for Alhucemas, and when about six miles from Peñon de la Gomera a boat manned by thirteen Moors was observed to be approaching the vessel. When near enough they opened fire, and ordered the captain to lower his sails, which was done, as the Spaniards were, practically speaking, without arms. The Moors then boarded the San Antonio and took her in tow. When close to the land the captain was rowed ashore, and the pirates spent part of the night in unloading the cargo. Next morning the San Antonio was seen drifting out to sea, and the captain, who was afraid of being put to death, suggested that he should go on board and bring her back to the anchorage. Probably thinking that some of their comrades were on the barque, but unable to set the necessary canvas to return, only two Moors were sent off with the captain, and these remained in the boat when the vessel was reached. Upon gaining the deck of the barque the captain was surprised to find himself alone. Without hesitating for a moment he released the crew, who were confined below, hoisted sail and stood out to sea. The Moors who had been left in the boat were speedily cut adrift, much to their amazement, for it so happened

174

that none of the pirates had stayed on board. No doubt they were eager to find a safe hiding-place for their plunder, and, thinking the barque quite secure till morning, took no further heed of the matter. A few days later the San Antonio arrived at Gibraltar, where full particulars of the outrage were furnished to the authorities. Space will not admit of details being given of the attacks on the Spanish barque Goleta, the Portuguese barque Rosita Faro, the British felucca Joven Enrique, and other vessels. It should be mentioned, however, that several famous British and foreign sailing yachts upon various occasions have had remarkably narrow escapes from being captured by these sea ruffians.

It is sincerely to be hoped that the Sultan of Morocco is carrying out his task in such a manner as will induce the inhabitants of the Riff coast to follow some occupation in future which is more likely to be appreciated by those who have to navigate vessels in the Mediterranean. Previous to stern measures being taken by the Sultan, it was not at all uncommon for his envoys to the native tribes—for the purpose of obtaining the release of captives—to be received with derision. Often, too, they were maltreated to such an extent that they were glad to escape with their lives. Some of the neighboring tribes continually endeavored to purchase captives for the pleasure of killing them, but it is satisfactory to learn that no sales are recorded, as the anticipated ransom was always largely in excess of the sums offered by the bloodthirsty natives.

www.ingramcontent.com/pod-product-compliance
Lightning Source LLC
Chambersburg PA
CBHW011523240626
47154CB00009B/2944